STORIES

FOR SHORT ATTENTION SPANS

by Ann E. Loewen

FriesenPress

Suite 300 - 990 Fort St
Victoria, BC, Canada, V8V 3K2
www.friesenpress.com

Copyright © 2015 by Ann E. Loewen
First Edition — 2015

Cover photography by Wichan Yingyongsmomsawas
Iceberg Watching at Blackhead, NL
www.flickr.com/photos/tuanland

ISBN
978-1-4602-5755-5 (Hardcover)
978-1-4602-5756-2 (Paperback)
978-1-4602-5757-9 (eBook)

1. Fiction, Short Stories (single author)

Distributed to the trade by The Ingram Book Company

To Hannah and Ayda,
who tell me their stories
and
who listen to mine.

To see a World in a Grain of Sand
And a Heaven in a Wild Flower:
Hold Infinity in the palm of your hand
And Eternity in an hour.

Auguries of Innocence
William Blake

I tell everyone a different story
That way nothing's ever boring
Even when they turn and say you lied.

the walking (and constantly)
Jane Siberry

TABLE OF CONTENTS

TO THE READER:

Time is our most valued currency. We spend it, save it, bank it, sometimes waste it, we always want more of it. The inclusion of word counts and reading times for each of these stories is, admittedly, tongue in cheek, as is the title. Writing's ultimate achievement is to have the reader lose themselves in the storytelling, to forget about time and the world as they otherwise know it.

Several stories in this collection have characters and events that are linked, and are readily identified by names and plot details. Although these stories may find themselves in a novel someday, for now each is crafted to stand alone and at the same time be enriched by its companion narratives. Like threads of conversation in our lives, they come and go at intervals.

Thanks are due to writing instructors and mentors Liz Steinson, Rachel Krushner and David Adams Richards, writer-participants and instructors at the Canadian Mennonite University Writing School, proofreaders David and Lynn Loewen.

Two of the stories in this collection, 'Hearts' and 'On Love & Life', have been previously published in *Other Voices* literary journal. 'On Love & Life' won the *Other Voices* 2011 Short Fiction Contest.

The stories in this collection are fictional, with one exception. *Cavalier* is a composite of several of my horses, their characters and their lives. I think they're okay with that.

A.E.L.

TABLE OF STORY LENGTHS

Title	Approx. word count	Reading time*
Cats & Dogs	1480	5 – 6 min
Ghetto	1780	6 - 7 min
Hearts	1820	6 – 7 min
Pure	2830	9 - 10 min
On Love & Life	3190	10 – 12 min
Mr. Wrong at the Window	4060	13 – 16 min
Ruby	5230	17 – 21 min
Cavalier	5660	19 – 23 min
Grateful Migration	5670	19 – 23 min
Snow	6020	20 – 24 min
Critical	6070	20 – 24 min
Last Resort	6400	21 – 25 min
Drive	6950	23 – 28 min
Forty	7290	24 – 29 min
Silence & Settled Dust	7470	25 – 30 min
Try Not to Care So Much	8170	27 – 33 min
Flood	8810	29 – 35 min

*Based on average reading speed of 250 – 300 words/minute;
individual reading speeds may vary

CATS & DOGS

The Cats

There's too many cats. Don't say you haven't noticed, they're everywhere. Right here, this city alone, there's fifty or a hundred thousand strays. They just said it on the news. I look out back and I see a different one every time. They drive my dog crazy, so I let him chase them whenever I can. The woman next door, Beasley I think her name is, she's a cat woman. Not the kind that's swarmed her house with them and gone all strange. Just she favours them and she doesn't like it when I open the back door and say "Go get it" to Buster in a way that gets him all wound up. He's deaf, my Buster, always has been. It's in his breeding and it's how come he ended up in a shelter. But something gets through to him and he takes off. When Beasley sees me doing that she doesn't hold back, she cuts loose on me like I do Buster on the cats and tries to shame me. You leave the cats alone you bully, she hollers. They're after the birds in my feeder I yell back whether or not it's true. I tell you these women around here they have no problem letting you know what they think. And everybody better listen up or else.

Now the cats, you got to hand it to them, they stay under the radar. If there was fifty thousand of anything else roaming about, causing a ruckus — rats, dogs, rubbies — you know there'd be hellfire all over the call-in lines and raining down on the politicians to get something done. And they would do it, too. Let alone a hundred thousand. But the cats, they're so smooth, they know how to keep just this side of serious trouble. I know some women like that, too. They get on your nerves and still nobody says or does nothing. There's some want to protect them, even. Like they need it, they're practically running the place.

Slackers are people too

My son made a toboggan slide of life and he doesn't seem to mind the ride. Faster the better. Down he goes, whoops there goes the job, whoa that was your wife leaving, hey that used to be your house but you've been kicked out 'cause you didn't pay the mortgage. He's living in a park downtown, coupla three months now, him and a bunch of his type. They're in some kind of a camp and he's doing all right, far as he's concerned. Gone feral, like the cats. Maybe spreading himself around like them. You can't neuter them all but sometimes it seems like a good idea.

He had a problem at school and he never could read proper. There's ways around that, just look at me. Couldn't make out much myself when they sent reports home from school, but the wife read them to me and explained it all and always went to the meetings. I just told him to stay out of trouble. I never got no visits from the cops and he never tried to pull anything on me but I think he knew better.

Whenever he drops in these days he goes on about how independent he is, then he asks can he use my computer. Then he complains it's too slow. Same thing every week. He says he's doing something called blogging, somebody might pay him for it. That the computer helps him with his writing but there's an

STORIES FOR SHORT ATTENTION SPANS

even better program if I feel like buying it. My son, the writer, can you believe it. I say he's a slacker and that's all there is to it.

This world not the next

There was a gift our parish gave the priest once, back home on the island, that didn't go over so well with the wife. A scanner, it was. Something what could listen in on all the radios the Mounties and the bootleggers used, before cell phones. Everyone our end of the Burin Peninsula had one. Sort of a pastime. Once somebody caught a disabled girl being treated rough, 'cause they tuned in to the baby monitor in her room. Anyway, the parish bought one for the new priest, Christmas gift I think, and the wife didn't think that was right. She wasn't like the rest of us, see, she was from up here on the mainland. She wouldn't go to church for a while, though you had to know her to know what kind of a big deal that was. Eventually she got back at it, sort of put it behind her, so I went to church again too. She was like that, she could find a way to hold two thoughts in her head the same as you might hold two stones you find on the beach in your one hand.

Can't see much point going to church without her, now. She had such a voice for singing and praying, like she really meant it. There's a church just down the road here but it's too empty, without her, without hardly anyone.

Lots of things are different, here on the mainland. Don't know if I'll ever get used to it. For one, back there you couldn't be homeless, like my son is now. They wouldn't let you. It wasn't against the law or anything, I don't think so anyway. Besides, the Mounties were too busy to care. They were always out on the bay, in the fog, chasing the bootleggers bringing in liquor from the French islands. It was more like you'd be invited into someone's house if you were roaming about with no place to stay. Then if you didn't come over, some joe'd start building a roof over your head 'cause he saw you settin' there and he had a bit of board out back he's not using and he's on the pogey anyway so might as well build you a place. And that would be that.

He said, he said

He said he's going to write about me. No, that's not right. He said he's going to blog about me. I said what for. He said he writes about understanding and that I'm from out east and a widower, and in this country west don't understand east and the living don't understand the dead and men don't understand women and rich don't understand poor and cats and dogs can't even get along. I don't know if he said the cats and dogs part but he went on like that. I said: I repeat, what do you want to write about me for. He said, I want to write about things that are important to me without using the words I and me. I said nothing surprises me anymore and I stomp my foot hard. Shawn, that's my son, he hates it when I do that. Makes him all jumpy. But that's how I call Buster, seeing as he's deaf. When Buster comes over and I starts giving him a scratch, Shawn says I have a pet cat now. I bet it's one of them strays I say. Yes, came right into my tent and lay on me purring. Probably full of rabies and distemper so when you're foaming at the mouth don't come running to me, I say. Then he has one of his ideas, Shawn does. Hey dad what if I introduce him to Buster maybe they could be friends. I stop scratching Buster and I look Shawn full in the eye. I wouldn't bet on it and don't forget I still got my single-shot, I say. After that he leaves. I don't mean to make him mad he just gets that way. He'll be back.

Boy in the basement

He's moved into the basement, seeing as the cops come in the night and broke up the camp. He says it's his room anyway so why not. Hasn't lived there since he was eighteen and far as I was concerned he couldn't leave soon enough back then but the wife took it hard. I wanted to make his room into a den or something but she never came 'round to the idea.

I asks myself, could I have saved us all kinds of trouble and stayed where I was at, back on the island. Now that there's offshore oil and all. But Shawn, he never would have been a hand to work on a rig. He's happy poking away at the keyboard. Maybe he won't be such a mooch after all. He already gave me his cheque 'cause the bank don't want nothing to do with him. Have to see can we make it through the year without a murder.

He brought the cat, 'course he did. Saw him talking over the fence to Beasley already. I told him better not let that thing upstairs. We can't be held responsible for our actions, Buster and me.

GHETTO

> "Let us go then, you and I,
> When the evening is spread out against the sky
> Like a patient etherized upon a table..."
> *The Love Song of J. Alfred Prufrock*, T. S. Eliot

You love to walk about in the city. Especially in our own neighbourhood, you never tire of it. We call it the ghetto but that is just wordplay, a nickname, its charm increased by being called what it's not. Around here you can stroll anywhere, day or night, because it's safe. Of course, everyone knows of a break-in, and the depanneur over on the corner was held up just last year. Remember when we first moved here, how everyone still avoided that high-rise where there'd been a murder? Still, nothing like the wastelands of other urban centers, the public housing failures and acres of abandoned industrial zones. Where disease and dispossession sprout like the weeds that grow according to the cracks in the neglected concrete. Here, even graffiti enlightens and entertains: we were grateful that *LANDLORD MUST DIE(t)* wasn't painted over for years.

You often point out an especially beautiful greystone or dignified apartment building, the deep grain of a wooden door, the precision of beveled glass and carefully wrought ironwork.

We still know some students and seniors who call this neighbourhood, and these old buildings, home. But more and more they are confined to newer, less comely structures. Over the years adventurous retrofitters and those decamped from the humdrum of outlying areas, who see themselves as partial to the thrum and vicarious activity of urban life over the sedation of suburbia, have arrived and made the old new.

I like to walk, too, especially when the asphalt shines after a late-day rain, the traffic is calm and the air is cool but not chilly, when it implies a softer quality that means spring. Snow has just melted to reveal battered sidewalks, damaged by the tiny strength of phase changes — ice to water, water to ice — all through the long winter. Salt has nibbled into the curbs and snowplows have bitten off bigger chunks of cement, so be careful you don't trip. With the snow receded, an entire season's waste is suddenly exposed. Sodden posters and dog droppings along with the dregs of hurried indulgences are all underfoot. Disintegrating coffee cups, mashed cigarette butts and torn wrappers form a soluble pastiche of life as the neighbourhood dissolves into another place that will eventually be called summer. No one is so attached to the area that they go about picking up garbage, and nobody bothers complaining to the city about the condition of the pavement. Everyone simply takes heed to avoid the hazards.

When we walk together I notice how your gait has a slight lilt, and I remember you told me once about a car accident that left one leg a bit shortened. I'm glad I said yes when you asked, on a night like this. We see each other all the time, at school and in passing, but walking for pleasure and without purpose is a kind of intimacy we only share once in a while. To the north, the mountain absorbs much of the city's buzz that would otherwise blunt the sensitive edge of our hearing. We can talk as we wander, without needing to raise our voices. Come, then, let's go. Now that it's dark, and windows are lit from within. They tempt the curious eye to wander inside, to wonder how that life is lived.

669, rue Milton — Stark fluorescence bears witness to the corners and clutter of his sprawl. He lives here alone, his only contact with neighbours via hear-through walls. We all know him, though actually we don't. He walks the ghetto alone, muttering oaths or blessings or ritual musings — I admit I've avoided getting close enough to tell. His lower lip and jaw project forcefully, overhung by a bulging, rounded forehead: a man-in-the-moon face. Lank cords of thin grey hair cling to the sides of his head. He always dresses the same: a black suit jacket several sizes too small so that his wrists dangle from the cuffs, crumpled black trousers dragging their hems. His gloveless hands are cracked and red in the winter.

There are times when we have seen him rummaging slowly, intent on gleaning the best additions to his collection, a block ahead of the garbage truck as it barges its way up the street. He doesn't seem to be looking for food, in fact we have often noticed him buying groceries at the store. A glance through his window conveys the results of his foraging: the entire apartment is populated by a garbled array of treasured junk. There on the kitchen table is a broken lamp that has a partly-burned shade with a schooner print on it, along with a collection of small flags in an iridescent vase and numerous small bowls and ashtrays. On a small end table is what might be an ancient adding machine. A velvet painting of a galloping horse by night, a generic moonlit ocean print and two antique car calendars all hang above the sagging couch.

And a doll. Tonight she leans stiffly against the couch and wears a red velvet dress with satin bow and pretend-patent shoes. She stands about three foot six and keeps her arms outstretched and partly flexed. Her glassy-wide eyes feign innocence above her pout.

He never bothers anyone; he doesn't panhandle or disrupt the neighbourhood in any way. We leave him to his pursuits, he leaves us to our disquiet.

455, rue Durocher — An amber hardwood floor has been laid since we last passed by and looked in here. There is an antique wingback chair in the corner, comfortably upholstered and inviting with its matching footstool. A long gun is hung above the bricked-in fireplace across the room. It points upwards and is flanked by ornate candelabras on the mantle. In the window a fish tank gleams. It holds small ripples of gold and blue and silver that swim about and forever see only their own reflection as we gaze in at them.

The walkway gets cleared in the winter, and small struggling petunias appeared in the tiered landscaping last summer, so someone must live here. But we have never seen anyone coming or going, so we must imagine the occupants. Childless, we assume, for there is no evidence of the trappings and the disorder typical of family life. Professionals, we also presume, and perhaps they live at more than one address.

Another time, during the ghetto's heyday, looking out from this same street-level window one would have seen a three story-high dragon, a whimsical mural in peeling paint on the brick wall opposite. It was a classically styled, fairy-tale beast, entirely green with sawtooth backbone and fiery tongue, forever reaching for his demure and fair maiden-lady prey. Back then, a student friend of ours lived here. He would gaze out his window at the dragon with incredulous eyes, red from studying and despair, while his family lit candles and prayed that he would pass his next set of exams.

No such intensity lives here now. The space is calm, stilly suspended, barely breathing. When the time and market prices are right, they will probably sell.

450, avenue du Parc — We linger at the window of the patisserie, choosing without obligation the best-looking treat. The profiteroles nestle in a small pyramid, situated between a strict alignment of Napoleons and the more softly indulgent tiramisu. An assembly of marzipan, tiny fruits made of pastel sweetness, are arranged beside a tray of glazed peach tarts. You point to the crullers, your favourite, and I choose the flaky perfection of *pain au chocolat*. Beyond the window-front temptations, the day's remaining loaves and baguettes stand at attention in their wicker baskets. They expect to be replaced before the coming day manages to break.

We must come back here some time, one of us is sure to say. We see ourselves seated in the elegant little chairs on the patio, making memorable observations about the world as it walks by. The sun warms us and we savour the moment. We discuss this idea easily, indulgently, because we know it will never happen. We have said it and not done it for so long, the promise is altogether as empty as the prospect of a pastry from a bakery already closed for the day.

410, rue Prince Arthur — An older building, with the aura of having been well-maintained as opposed to recently-redone. Stained glass adorns the upper portions of its windows and scrolled stonework frames the doorway. Looking up, I see the second-floor window still reveals the open lid of a baby grand piano, and shelves as high as the moulding around the ceiling are still filled with books. The adjacent room, as always, has the drapes drawn; the light inside fills the window with an ivory glow. Lovely old building, you muse.

I wonder who lives here now. Perhaps it is still the one I thought so much about, once upon a time. But I haven't seen that face, even in passing, for ages. I am quiet, and keep to myself all traces of significance; no one else ever knew anyway. I don't bother to go out of my way to pass by here anymore, maybe I don't remember for sure which window to check. Maybe it wasn't so important, that longing, that encounter, that revelation I didn't want. The one that shattered any reason for me to hope. I think it happened exactly here, but I could be wrong.

*   *   *

We wait for the light to change in our favour. We are neither early nor late, there is no need to chase the clock by running across a busy road. Beside us is a line of cars waiting to make a left turn, their signals blinking in an asynchronous chorus. The drivers are assembled in a convergence of purpose, then they will disperse and never think of this exact moment again.

We drift, we look, we talk. The last bits of early April cloud have skidded away, and now we can see the moon, a curl of silver. It's over there, by the cross, about to disappear behind the mountain. Do you want to go back now? Night is settling. You put your arm through mine and we turn towards home. A living room light is switched off, and we are a distorted reflection in the bay window to our right. Inside, a silhouette takes a drag from a cigarette, and seems to be looking at us.

HEARTS

J Boulanger

From: Alexandra Mourondros<alexmourondros@rha.hsc-mb.ca>
To: Jeanne Boulanger <labellemaman@gmail.com>
Sent: 15 March 2008
Subject: J'ai besoin de parler

Jeanne

First, pardon the absence of a salutation. I am working to mend
my ways, those of my former pen and paper, letter-writing days
and not be such a Luddite as to forgo the conveniences of this
medium. You know you are so dear to me, and my not saying
so is no indication of any diminution of our long-enduring
fondness. But one does not address anyone as "Dear" in emails,
I have learned, having made that mistake professionally and
afterwards feeling foolish (and with, shall we say, colleagues of
diversity, it is even more embarrassing). If I am to avoid such
blunders, I realize I must be consistent and not use archaic

greetings anywhere, save perhaps in those rare instances of a handwritten thank-you note or card of sympathy, if indeed that is still done.

Now I must get right to the point or I will meander endlessly after being so long out of touch, and not tell you what I really need to: I have had my heart go completely astray. You, of all people, know what it is for me to say so. When we did our medical training together so many years ago, and especially our residency, we always upheld the standard we felt we had to represent. We were one of them and yet distinct from the old boys' club, differing but not offending because respect was so hard to come by. And we were right there with the men in agreeing that the use of the heart as metaphor, in meaning and significance, in society at large and culture at all levels — high, low, pop, avant-garde — was completely misappropriated and only science could set the standard right. I do still feel some truth in that position, by the way, but less strongly now. Having come through what I have, I see, and feel, differently.

This winter I decided, finally, that it was time. Time to try again, to see if there was any possibility, anyone, anywhere, out there for me. Demographics are not in my favour, I recently read in the paper. So the odds are against me, I know. Still, I have observed other women of a certain age resurrecting their earlier selves, and achieving very satisfactory results. Why not me?

Why not indeed — but how to go about it? I cannot just dress up and go to bars and social events with the express purpose in mind. That would be so unnatural as to surely land me with the wrong person, like the last time. I meet many men professionally, to be sure, but they are mostly cardiologists or their ilk, and if I recognize anything about myself it is the need to balance that left-brained dominion with rather less structure, more spontaneity, intuition, emotion. Which is to say I need a man who is more like a woman. No wonder I stay single.

13

A pop-up ad, of all things, directed me to a website that "matches" people with prospective suitors (!) electronically, based on some sort of a psychological and personality profile. I thought it rather like a dumbed-down Myers Briggs — you remember back when that little man administered it to all of us at the Heart Institute? I suspect he was shocked at the results.

Did you know that's what people do now? I certainly didn't. The charge was nominal, cheaper than psychotherapy, which had gone about as far as my aforementioned left brain would allow. If nothing else, it would be interesting and possibly revealing, especially for someone like me who understands so little in this area relative to my usual level of comprehension. Being thus detached was also comforting to me. That is one thing to be said for all this communication via electronics — so many identifiers, whether handwriting, signature, real name, return address — can be concealed.

And so the "matches", such as they are, come along. Predictably, some are instantly off-putting, some are in need of a ministering mother, others are clearly looking for a fling, at least to start things off. Many are seemingly, genuinely (if all they say about themselves is true, always bearing that in mind) fine people who will surely find the right woman. She just isn't me. A few have sent their queries; just by the nature of the first questions I can tell we are not suited. So, as graciously as possible under the circumstances, I decline to engage further.

Then there was one who was different. A full week passed between his first foray, and my even noticing it, coming as it did when I was away at the American Heart Association conference (how I wished you could have attended this year! I would so liked to have had, and now feel I can say without flinching, a heart-to-heart with you there). But that delay seemed not to dissuade him. And something told me this one was worth pursuing. Then our correspondence, daily, incrementally, forged a connection I never would have thought possible. Wonderful, I hear you saying, and I can even see you smiling as you read this. But Jeanne, I felt like I was under siege and I can't really say why except that I was overcome by uncertainty and a powerful clutch of emotion that was entirely unanticipated.

And I feel so hopelessly shallow telling you all of this, as you bear the loss of your Henri nearly two years now. The separate paths of our loneliness draw us together but send us apart, too. You grieve for what you had, I for what never was, not now, perhaps not ever. I hesitate to burden you with this account, but as I said, you are the one person who will understand the significance of what I have experienced. For I have felt my heart, Jeanne, not as a physiologic entity, but as a metaphysical one. The times he sent emails that spoke kindly, flatteringly, even, I especially felt it. Not in my head, or my psyche or soul, wherever they are, but right there, intrathoracic, retrosternal. That is to say, anatomically correct in location, if not function. The tears that came while reading his emails, they were like none I have experienced before either. Not that there have been many, you know how I am. Now I feel the very center of what I thought was my self to have been turned upside down. Bouleversé, you would say, and I do not know how to set it right again. I do not know if I even want to. I do know it's a good thing I gave up doing procedures in the cath lab a year ago. They would be investigating me for some neuromuscular degenerative disease, either that or substance abuse, the way I am so distracted and my hands sometimes shake.

Do you remember the time of our menopause? The way we went through it together, as though we were still synchronized, like girls living in residence. We suffered, or so we thought, and felt it a time of crisis even. But we could do the literature searches, evaluate the evidence, draw conclusions, and make our best decision. We could look risk squarely in the eye, make an objective assessment of its magnitude versus measurable benefits, and arrive at an informed decision. Of course we doubted the cardioprotective role of estrogen even before the HERS and Women's Health Initiative studies were published, but the quality of life improvement was undeniable. You probably don't even remember now, but you asked me at the time if I experienced loss of libido, for you were greatly troubled by that symptom. I made as if I hadn't noticed. That was a lie, my friend, to avoid any discussion that would approach the truth. I was no more unaware of my libido, though unused, than I am unaware of having a left hand even if I am right-handed.

And now it has been two full weeks since this man, my "match", last communicated. I do not know what to make of it, although the tone of his letters had become rather more perfunctory. And what exactly does it mean, when someone, when a man, concludes with the words "Talk to you soon"? You don't have to answer that question, by the way. I just felt it needed to be asked. But that was his last sign-off. We never have spoken. He didn't offer, I didn't ask. He did direct me to his professional website, early on, I suppose as a gesture of legitimacy and a way of establishing trust. So I could call his workplace. But then what? Beg? Flirt? Accuse? Inquire politely, as in: "Excuse me, this is Alexandra, surely you recall...."

As I said earlier, the odds are against me. I know that. I accept that. I will not lower myself to behaviour straight out of some clichéd chorus or romantic comedy. I will strive not to cry so often (somehow, driving while listening to music seems to be especially provocative — probably not very safe, either). I'm sure I will, eventually, be able to sleep soundly through the night, and eat normally again. But it does seem that this aspect of life, once acknowledged, cannot be denied again.

Please, do not worry about me. I am distressed, to a degree, but not depressed, an important distinction. I think this shakeup is long overdue. You are probably thinking, as I am, that I will be better for it. It helps so much just writing this down, framing a bewildering experience into coherent sentences, knowing that you know. We must talk, and soon. I wish, as I have so many times before, that we lived closer together. I am up to my ears with field data as our submission deadline is April 1, so I must send this from work. I don't know how much access IT has to my Inbox, and I don't know what they'd say about it. Actually, I know exactly what IT would say about it — they'd have a field day — so I will be very careful to Delete Forever once this has been sent.

I sign off with deepest affection, for it feels too heartless (there I go again!) to do otherwise. All my love,

A.

PS Did you hear about the lead presentation at the AHA conference I attended? Strong correlation between negative outcomes after cardiac events and increased depression scores in men. Who would have thought? But I understand so much more, now.

PPS I learned something new on the computer yesterday. If you press Control, then Z, the last thing done gets deleted. Repeat, and events are undone in reverse chronological order. Would that there could be such a function in our lives.

PURE

Feeling unaccountably good today. Sulphurous autumn leaves against oceanic blue sky may have something to do with it. Unaccountable, because last night I had that dream again and I cried myself awake. Which should make for a day, a morning at least, of misery. Always the same question: why still frightened? It's over, he's gone. Years now.

I remember how the children had the most awful dreams after we fled; so many nights I heard their voices, small and stricken, down the hall. It wasn't until they got older that they could tell me about the harrowing places they'd been in their sleep. No escape from the hurt, the loss, the fear. We all remember the possibility of death.

I'm going to beat the face off of you! Hear me? It's all you fault we're here in this mess. He doesn't even take off his Sorels when he comes through the door and strides across the living room floor. When I see his fist I realize that supper isn't going to be enough, a clean house isn't going to be enough, nothing's ever going to be enough.

Will they go on forever, these memories and dreams? Is a marriage like that ever really over? Eleven years and finally I allow myself to try again, to be willing to reframe my assumptions, to trust a man. His name was Luke. I liked his name, and our three months of dining, dating, discovery. A doctor and a lawyer may have seemed incongruous but we didn't think so, at first. Then we broke up, an event so banal it wouldn't deserve to be noticed except that I am jarred into replay. Once again I can't stop the past from pushing up through the floorboards of my subconscious and into the enclosure of my sleep.

Three weeks today since we last spoke. Not that I'm counting.

*   *   *

There's just one thing to do on a day like this: get out and do some work in the garden. Cheaper than therapy and just as effective. As soon as I start I begin to feel better. A lot of things get sorted out between the dirt and the weeds, though my joints can only stand so much. Middle age makes me get stuck when I straighten up, and distinct bursts of protest come from inelastic tendons. Back pelvis knees all complain against the white noise of un-tuned muscles. But these bodily sensations generously stand in for shame and regret, fear and dread, and after a while my thoughts begin to float, eased along by a stream of endorphins from all this exertion.

As I dig I marvel at the earthworms who manage to chunnel their bodies through the compacted earth. How do they do it? I sometimes bend the neck of my spade working in the same hard ground. So much strength in their softness. I don't mind in the least when I encounter them. They are honest and their face-ends are quite sweet if you look closely.

Farther back in the yard I wade through the shroud of fallen leaves all copper and gold; I look forward to the meditative scratch and rhythm of raking, a chant for the coming season of cold. It will be satisfying to assemble a hillock of leaves, to allow bacteria and fungi to ply their entropic way through the cellulose all winter. Higher levels of order will decay and be made elemental again, back to their original chemistry: carbon nitrogen potassium. Next year I will exhume the fragmented and indistinct pieces and use them to soften my riverside clay like shortening cut into flour. Likewise I need to plunge myself into the cool grey soil, I need the life that death breathes back into the world. Like the earthworms who move through this tough soil, digging opens channels that sadness has compressed; it brings oxygen to places my lungs cannot, no matter how often I sigh.

The fist — the bang — the child. It all happens so fast and close. What are these spots, small and red all over the floor? I just cleaned but I guess I didn't do enough. Carry the child away from the scene that shouldn't be seen. Where are you, my other little lamb? Come dear take Mommy's hand we have to go. I don't know where we just have to go.

I do ask for help with the more strenuous yard work, I've gotten better at that. He's coming at one-thirty, someone I hired from that treatment center nearby. Good for people there to get out, earn a bit of money. So I think. How do I know what's good for anyone, what do I know about alternative sentencing. Choices made, right at the time, right in their own mind. As inscrutable to me as my decisions must appear to others.

I look at my watch. I've got just enough time to find the rakes and get organized. And here he is. Right on time.

Oh shit. He's gorgeous.

Why. Why why why. It isn't even a question. Although it's natural to wonder, even at my age. Would I, could I, ever fall again. Hardly anyone asks, I'd mostly stopped asking myself until I met Luke, and in moments like this. Especially when he's that little bit taller than me, even with my work boots on. Flexor and extensor muscles of the arms, dorsal tendons on the hands — I try not to notice. How can a brush cut and T-shirt and jeans possibly look so good? Don't look.

And it's only a conversation about yard work that we're having, a homeowner who wants the task done just so. A moment of eye contact is all that's needed.

"My yard ends here, so can you rake the leaves this way."

"Okay. You got something I can put them in?"

"I have a tarp. You can rake them onto it then haul them over to the end of the lot. That work for you?"

"Sure. Lotta leaves."

"Umm-hmm. Let me know if you need a drink of water or anything."

"Yeah. Nice place though, with the river and all the trees."

"Yes. We like it here."

If my life was a novel this would be part of an evolution, a series of consequences, a proof based on a stratagem leading to a summation. Even a short story would probably manage to fit in a crisis of wavering values, proceeding to some form of surrender. But not here. Not with an abundance of chestnut and auburn leaves that so obviously need to be gathered. And never mind how efficiently he pulls the fan rake and corrals the frisky bits of spent leaf life. He strips off the leaves that stick to the tines and then rakes some more, as absorbed as one can be on a saturated day such as this, in no way attracted to the next nearest human being. Is not now and never shall be so why don't you just get your share of the work done, I say to myself.

Anyone would like to think themselves irresistible. For a while I thought that was how Luke felt about me. A captivating beauty, one who overwhelms resistance and deserves to be the object of affection. Adoration, even. I enjoyed the fantasy in which I lowered all my barriers and allowed myself to be fully embraced. But then I panicked. What if I ended up enmeshed, unable to tear away again? Being an object of obsession is like drowning or strangling. Buried alive. I already know that. Would Luke go on to confine me within the strict boundaries of relentless attention? I couldn't wait to find out, I needed distance. Which in the early vulnerable stages of pursuit is as good as saying it's over. What I want, what I need, what I can and should versus what I cannot and shouldn't ever have. After all these years I still don't know.

We finish the raking, but before he goes I offer lemonade and fresh bread and payment in cash. He accepts all three. Am I too obviously generous? I pay for my weaknesses in so many ways. He sits in the one remaining lawn chair and seems to enjoy looking at the flawless sky, now sketched with high-flung mare's tails. He notices that a good many leaves still cling to the little mountain ash; they are just beginning to change to rufous and are always the last to fall. He gestures towards it with a crust of bread.

"I'll drop by and clean up after that one in a couple weeks. If you can trust an ex-con with the yard tools."

"Well, you never really know who's an ex-con."

He smiles and gets up. Our task is complete. There is no further action or interpretation needed to complete our story. Now he is gone and I can start.

I go through the back door and into the kitchen. I begin with the croutons I made earlier today from a heel of bread, ostensibly to use up leftovers and meant for my salad. They are perfection in taste and texture, and temporarily replace my grief over my deficiencies. I open the fridge and cupboards and take out whatever I see. Quantities of cheese, big bag nacho chips, a tin can of peaches followed by an unknown number of cookies, breakfast cereal by the handful. I stand and fill my mouth to achieve salvation. The sensation momentarily soothes my emptiness. This is not eating, this is stuffing. Eating is seated mannerly measured companioned nurturing nourishing. I am doing gluttony greed guilt.

Afterwards I go for a walk to prove I am not worthless, I even affirm my virtue by picking up garbage along the way. The breeze has increased and makes a shimmer of sound through the waxy cottonwood leaves that still cling and ripple. Soon they too will descend thirty feet to their gutter graves. But for today they hold on and make one last show of glory in the translucent horizontal spotlight of the setting sun.

Three weeks since we broke up. He didn't want to say so but I knew it was over, even in a long-distance call. He was gentle, polite, truthful but not brutally so. We're both mid-career and over-employed, we live in different cities, which made it easy to explain to ourselves why we couldn't go on. So different from how my marriage ended, and yet I feel a bit like I did then. The sad self-loathing that makes one want to go out and stand in harm's way. There must be something wrong with me. Is what I automatically think before I can make my opposing voice heard. And I thought I had cried all tears for all time back then, but lately it would seem not. Today I didn't cry except from my awakening nightmare. Which doesn't count, because it's not the same as the conscious transport into tears. It won't be so bad this time round, I tell myself. It can't possibly be.

I increase my pace, I breathe deeply and attach my thoughts to beautiful things. That cloud's periphery gone pink, some marigolds not yet extinguished by frost and next to them purple ornamental cabbage. The certain crunch of leaves underfoot. How I love autumn: the colours, the mercurial changes in weather and light, the Canada geese everywhere and in endless conversation whether flying or floating.

I thought I was so much closer to the mark with Luke, is all.

*   *   *

It feels like a movie night. Having been so active all day, now I need rest and a heating pad applied to the most strident body part. Lately I have been doing a sort of film study, alternating Westerns with Clint Eastwoods. Luke described himself as a Clint Eastwood type on one of our first dates, or maybe it was in an early email, and that he liked Westerns. I had to admit I'd never watched any of those movies. And although he was understated about it, I noticed how he identified with the cowboy image.

The man at the local movie store thinks I'm on thin ice when I ask him for another recommendation. He knows the type of movie I usually pick, obscure dramas that are low on action and big on dialogue and don't stay in circulation very long. There's a certain skeptical slant to his entire upper face when he asks how I liked his last suggestion, a *Lone Ranger* remake. I keep my comments brief and irony-free because I don't want him to take offense and stop advising. In particular he knows approximately the level of violence I tolerate, and can be charmingly protective that way.

It's surprising how many insights I glean when I watch these films. In the Westerns, for example, I see drover coats — I think that's what they're called — everywhere. The good guys wear them, and so do the bad, as well as the guys who do bad things but who are actually good. No wonder my ex was so happy when he got one for himself. Wearing it defines the role, but not the character. You still get to pick your persona. And I have to admit, as I did back then, how good it looks on a man.

And you, Mr. Eastwood, are you of any help. Even if we didn't go out for very long, I can appreciate that both you and Luke are communication minimalists. Did I fall for an archetype or a cliché and in the end does it matter. I fell.

In every dream we are married again. It is all my fault.

The movie ends and stiffly I climb the stairs to my room. In spite of, because of, the bad dreams — I don't know which — the bed is still my refuge. Many elements of comfort are aligned here: flannel sheets, duvet, warm pyjamas. A shawl for the shoulders. Bedside lamp with amber shade, piles of books, softening creams, inevitable journal, all within arm's reach. Pens, bookmarks, many pillows. I know my back will hurt even more if

I sit and read too long but it's such a pleasure to be absorbed into this safe warm place. To delay the moment when the underworld begins its machinations.

From my bed sometimes I can see the moon, a silver face suddenly in the south window. I have this fantasy of lying here enjoying it and I am not alone. What if this space could also be one of pleasure. How I long for that to be my chain of associations: life warmth protection awakening arousal response reflection sleep. Expansion and contraction both. It makes me understand the desire to die in one's own bed, a shelter carved out over many years. When I started out as a physician I couldn't understood why anyone would want to die at home, without access to all that medicine has to offer. Now I find myself wanting that very deliverance when the time comes, and being just as unreasonable about it as some of the patients I have known.

One of the reasons I sometimes can't fall asleep is because I start to think about how much being asleep is like being dead. How a day, like a life, must at some point end whether we are ready or not. If I were to die with this central need — to love and be loved — unfulfilled, would it make me more or less tethered to this world at the time of departure? If we do indeed float like helium for a while before exiting, I wonder if I could look down and see the things that might have been but weren't. I would like that, to be able to say farewell to my longings as I was about to be ultimately redeemed or voided, whichever option it turns out to be. My children, now grown and gone, will either take on the ghosts of our shared past or release them along with me. When I get to see them these days, they seem so much happier than I was at their age. That will have to be consolation enough.

I can take my spirit apart after so many years of introspection, reassemble it without the desire part and then I see myself as one with the elements. Made of a single atomic particle that repeats itself over and over again, like a crystal. No longer conflicted or trying to accommodate the incongruent, my own self being the least likely to fit any known paradigm. Perhaps there is no other piece to my puzzle.

While I'm lying here not falling asleep it helps to go through the periodic table. I had to memorize the first four lines of it in high school and it has stayed with me. One of those beautifully useless sequences captured by the mind that eventually gets put to good use. I often get lost in around the transition elements — vanadium scandium titanium — they're all there but I get the order mixed up so I start over. By the third or fourth attempt I'm gone and the memory has served its purpose.

ON LOVE & LIFE

A Match Wanting to be Made

We are currently representing an exceptional match, above average in many respects including height, intelligence, income, and energy level. This accomplished individual is tendering a single status and wishes to be transitioned to coupledom. In accordance with current screening and search standards, we are equally accepting of applicants whose language, personality, behaviour and thought patterns predominate in either of the two hemispheres. We would appreciate, however, your explicit disclosure as to either right or left dominance in the cover letter in order to expedite processing of applications. Applications not accompanied by recent photograph (authenticated and dated by Nextus technology) will be discarded.

To whom it may concern:

I am deeply, remorselessly, unsentimental. Passionate, provocative, perceptive, warm, romantic (more likely Romantic), sensual, all these, but not a sentimental bone in my body. I'll take unhappy endings, misconstrued meanings, novels without punctuation or compromise over heart-warming any day.

"Give me emotion, not sentiment. I want the inside, not the outside." Igor Stravinsky, conductor and composer. Yes.

As you consider my application for this position, I bring to your attention an honest assessment of my qualifications and limits. No hearts, watercolours, or pastels, nor rhyming verse unless at least a century old and worthy of surviving. Chocolate is acceptable, though, as a colour, a restorative and an edible, all three. Flowers, anytime.

I favour the delivery deadpan, live, error prone and awkward. Skip the stage makeup, the rehearsals and the filters. Serve it straight up, grant permission to cry and rant, ban circuitous conversation and small talk. You may forgo niceties, though manners are appreciated and respect *de rigueur*, or I'll be out of here before you can say Sweeny Among the Nightingales. T.S. Eliot. He had social phobia, did you know that? I understand. I know it to be in both my own, and my esteemed father's, carry-on baggage. Which does get less burdensome over the years, by the way, as we learn to travel lighter.

Surprised? Don't be. There's more to me than meets the mind's eye.

Because trying is what leads to learning a smidgen more about what is going on. Maybe this next one will teach me to let loose the knot, the one that we cling to at the end of the rope swing. I need only to open my hands and I will be set free.

So expect me to be honest but not brutal, loyal but not blind, clear but not see-through. If I saw and felt less, I would perhaps live longer and more peacefully. But not necessarily better.

Yours truly, sincerely, utterly and honestly because that's the way I am and know no other,

A.

*   *   *

Dear Applicant:

Many thanks for your introductory letter and supporting materials. We are always happy to review the profiles of those who express interest, and will most certainly give your application due consideration.

As you may be aware from perusing our vision statement, we are open to considering applicants from all backgrounds and many persuasions, as well as both hemispheres. Despite superficial indicators to the contrary, we strive to be forward-looking and lateral thinking as we proceed with these encounters. An application such as yours piques our curiosity as much as, shall we say, a more conventional left-hemispheric one.

As we advise all our candidates, please be aware that we have more applicants than available positions. Demographic trends, economics, social norms, communication advances and changing values have all contributed to the current disproportion. Hence the need to make a standardized application process mandatory. We trust you will understand the necessity for this degree of objectivity and regulation of capacity, and that rejections are inevitable and not to be taken personally. Having said that, your application deviates from the mean in several significant, and intriguing, ways. We are unaccustomed to such a combination of candour and coyness in a cover letter, and we look forward to more.

We are, of course, a values-driven entity (again, please refer to our vision statement). We trust by now you have completed the Mutual Awareness Assessment. Additionally, we acknowledge that the spice of life is rendered ever so much more piquant through shared activities. Therefore, please provide us with the following information:

- Interests — please include books read, movies enjoyed, previous and/or planned travel destinations, favourite bands, golf handicap.
- Food preferences — observances, allergies, ethnicities enjoyed.

- Food attitudes — while recognizing this may be a sensitive topic for some, appreciate that it can have a significant impact on outcome.
- Sociability — do you tend more towards introversion or extroversion? How does that influence your conduct at dinner and cocktail parties, etc.?
- Educational achievements — especially clubs, sororities, awards.
- Your age (this was apparently omitted in your initial demographic information).

Finally, in order to be able to establish a framework for both suitability and sustainability, we would ask for a brief outline of past experience(s). Intimate detail is not necessary at this point.

Again, our heartfelt thanks for your introduction. We eagerly anticipate more.

Regards,

B.

PS Do you ever wear makeup?

*　　*　　*

B:

How to begin? If a question marks the start, from the first word it foreshadows not only the intonation and punctuation, but a certain probing and persistence. To answer a question with a question implies evasiveness, yet it can also quietly turn one towards the answer. As the poet P.B. Shelly tells us, "The great instrument of moral good is the imagination, and poetry administers to the effect by acting on the cause".

What, then, is your favourite poem? Do you have a favourite poet? Do you read their works aloud, during the insomniac hours, crying well before the last line and stricken by those truths that make the unknown known, and life even more unbearably beautiful because of it? I do. I do because I have to.

Because socializing can make me feel all the more alone. What extroverts don't know is that the inner world of an introvert can be far more worthwhile than what's actually going on around us. Particularly when the latter consists of superficial chit-chat, conversational one-upmanship or the insights of the intoxicated.

My usual stance is to listen politely and attentively, offering supportive interjections to affirm that the speaker is being heard. I am able to do this regardless of topic, save for those I find truly offensive. In those cases I will either assume a more active role and change the subject, or, I confess, lie and invoke another obligation in order to extract myself. If pressed for my opinion, I will indeed express it. I have found, however, that on such diverse subjects as literacy, water management, cross-border shopping, and, as it invariably comes up, golf, many people are not pleased to have their closely held truths critiqued, and the conversation ends abruptly. It would seem there is a great aversion to objective knowledge, and that the use of logic is considered a gaffe in social settings, to be taken entirely personally when the conclusion is contrary to one's own.

A.

PS "A lovely lady, garmented in light
        From her own beauty."
Shelly, again.

*   *   *

A:

If I said I wanted a captive beauty at its fleeting best, to hold it close so as not to lose it, you would understand, wouldn't you? Wanting to be lit by the incandescence of another's radiant symmetry is an ageless desire. The breadth of one's powers can be estimated, in part, by our ability to influence and activate not just the present, but the malleable part of the future. I am accustomed to assuming the active, not prone to passive acceptance of my circumstances if they are in any way deficient. Hence the current approach which may seem brash and unfeeling to some. I assure you it is neither. Most in my circle are, as far as I can observe, deliciously paired. Some, I believe, by exactly this process. Hence my palpable interest in your responses to my opening questions, as well of course to any additional information you feel comfortable disclosing.

You will appreciate that these dealings are private and would only be referred to indirectly, if at all, in the presence of others.

Regards,

B.

PS Does that mean your preference is for the light-diffusing varieties of makeup? I have indeed found those to be quite fetching.

*   *   *

B:

There is no call for pressure. The timeliness of our lives is measured by the ages. If we are only dancing here for a short while, it may be because we are destined to be recast in another vestment, a different bodily apparatus, a higher way of thinking and feeling. The conventional teachings of birth, life, death and afterlife do not always guide us well in our daily decisions. Instead they may only spread a false sense of urgency and facilitate poor decision-making.

I defer to a many-angled perspective, one that rotates in three or more dimensions, that is capable of dilating with time, or of collapsing to impenetrable smallness if cooled to absolute zero, as we were taught in chemistry class.

A.

*   *   *

A:

Interesting that you should make reference to chemistry, and express a familiarity with the concepts of physics. Had there been a more direct route, shall we say, to manna through those disciplines, we might have followed them. As it stands, they are a pleasant memory of a glimpse into both the biggest and smallest versions of our selves, an interesting intellectual exercise that unfortunately does not land one on the far side of the ledger.

In discussing chemical and physical processes, the prospect of immutability with time is, of course, only relatively achievable. However, it is certainly not unrealistic that with the careful application of protectants, relative freedom from stress, and regular interventions, you would be able to retain your fairness a good while. We would be most supportive of that goal.

Recalling your question (as you no doubt recall all of ours) about a favourite poet, something did come to mind in this context. We can't place it, apart from its appearance in the latter years of public school. It went something like

"The grave's a fine and private place,

But none, I think, do there embrace."

Of course no one wants to dwell on any of that, but the *get on with it* messaging does bear remembering and reiterating. As you will recall all that we ask of you, in the interest of greatest timeliness.

Yours,

B.

PS You will pardon our regression into first-person singular in our immediately-preceding communication. We briefly lost our head.

*   *   *

B:
"But at my back I always hear
   Time's wingéd chariot hurrying near."
Indeed.

It is all about chemistry, is it not? The laws of attraction and repulsion, predicting the precision and regularity of atomic and molecular structure at one end of the continuum, the irrationality and waywardness of human behaviour at the other. If only there could be a universal algorithm of allure or affinity in order to clarify decision-making and prioritization, to mitigate against ambivalence and under-confidence.

Just to clarify, I would not in fact engage in any sort of anti-aging activity. I accept the consequences of oxidative decay, in myself and in others, and I would expect tolerance in that regard as I gradually succumb. I will take reasonable precautions against the worst of its ravages. But the truth is, whatever one has in the moment, is gone in the next, if only because it is no longer the same. So much for holding on — best to seize the moment, then see what the next one brings. So sayeth Andrew Marvell himself, anyway.
   A.

*   *   *

Dear A:
You will, of course, interpret the salutation as a formality and not an endearment. There is still place for the traditions of correspondence, by way of establishing respect and boundaries. Note also the use of the colon, in contrast to the current more common, universal use of the comma. The implied distance in the punctuation establishes an appropriate degree of contact at this stage.

A stage which we may say is still in the starting blocks. We had hoped for rather more concrete answers to our queries. However, respecting that the paths to responsiveness may vary widely, we will allow them to remain open, to be answered at your convenience. We will mention, though, that by now we have received full accounts from some of the other candidates. We strive to understand our applicants' values, just as we have made the effort to explicitly delineate our own.

We had, as mentioned, assumed right-dominant. And yet you express strong views in favour of the use of logic, as well as more than a passing familiarity with the so-called hard sciences. This is contrary to the usual tendency to cerebral hemispheric dominance. Have we missed some cues as to correct labelling? Would you care to declare your predominance now? Handedness will, of course, be taken into consideration. Please specify.

We again note no mention of past. We do emphasize that we respect privacy as a fundamental value. However some minimal disclosure is an absolute necessity to avoid presumption or misunderstanding. We trust you will not find this request onerous or intrusive.

We remain intrigued and look forward to more revealing exchanges. Perhaps you would be more comfortable with an open-ended line of inquiry. Therefore, in addition to the previously-posed questions, for which we anticipate answers forthwith, we would ask the following: What is your greatest joy, your greatest regret? How important is it to you that an adult be fiscally independent, and not in need of financial support? How do you share decision-making within a relationship?

Yours truly, and with anticipation,

B.

PS Perhaps we overlooked it — did you tell us how old you are?

*   *   *

B:

It is possible that I suffer from an excess of sincerity. And that I cause others around me to suffer because of it. How much does a person want, need? Honesty need not be a breaking point, but it does tend in that direction. So many mitigations can be in place — flattery, coyness, white lies, false memory — as to render the concept of truth redundant.

Alas, that would not be me. It would be so much simpler, of course. And why not flattery? Is that not what this tradition is all about?

You have mentioned values several times. I wonder, at what point do values become vulnerabilities? I survey the lists of questions and wonder how much I should betray. Never mind who I am to you — who am I to myself?

However, having embarked on this course of action, there is an obligation to play by the rules. I will do my best to answer all previously-posed questions:

Food is a gift to all the senses, education a lifelong slope to be scaled, this beautiful Earth a treasure to be discovered in both solitary and companionable adventure.

I have one consideration with regards to golf: the dream of galloping a horse across a golf course of an early summer morning. Sacrilege, to be sure, but it is only a fantasy. Other than that, the thought of chasing a little white ball over an entirely man-made landscape dressed in unflattering clothes, consummated by a mediocre clubhouse meal, holds no appeal.

My greatest regret is also my greatest joy: that this flight through all the tangents and troubles of life has been a solo one. Taking risks with intuition and experience as my only consultants, making decisions entirely through internal cost/benefit analysis: do I want to change this formula? Perhaps, perhaps not. Decision-making is ultimately an utterly personal action, and despite conversation and consultation the buck stops with one's own frontal lobes, assuming the process is a reasoned one. I don't know if that will ever change for me. Do you think it will for you?

I feel the same way about financial independence as I do about emotional independence: I do not expect support, nor do I expect to have to support another.

A.

*   *   *

Dear A:

Your particular combination of reserve and forthrightness is both charming and confounding. It would seem a shame not to progress to an in-person encounter. Your photograph alone, despite the apparent lack of cosmetic enhancement, heralds certain delights. However, the obliqueness and opaqueness of responses thus far is trying to the patience. Particularly when there are a good many others in waiting, whose images show them to be nearly equally deserving.

We are certain that, just as we have all had expected of us in other realms, the satisfactory attainment of certain deliverables is not excessively onerous in this most important aspect of life. Even in this rare but apparent scenario of non-hemispheric dominance, we might very well feel justified in our expectation of more concrete responses.

You have mentioned nothing with regards to your age, or your last relationship (although, typically, there was an oblique reference to some previous liaison in your cover letter). Is there something you are hiding?

Regards,

B.

*   *   *

To B:

And so what if there is no past relationship? What if there is no past? Could the present alone be sufficient? It is as much a part of the reality, or its perception, as the other tenses put together. However one's life went before, is not as it is now. If I do not fit into the orderly passage of past into present, it may be that I was old before I knew it, and am younger now than my years.

Have you ever watched a baby or a toddler, and taken the time to observe its confidence and innate knowledge? It is a different state of consciousness, not one that we can comprehend from our own past because it is just beyond the reach of reliable memory. Through meditation and creativity, I strive to remain connected to that age.

There is a similarly un-tethered state, which happens to be the dream phase of sleep. Whatever aspect of our homeostasis or self-balance is disturbed during the day, our dream-state seeks to realign according to our truest impulses within our hidden selves. What do you dream about?

A.

*   *   *

Dear A:

Truly, we would prefer not to enter into discussions about dreams, for they are largely silliness. The other night we had a dream that had Albert Einstein in it, and even he didn't make sense.

We will consider your entire file over the coming days. We would be most appreciative of additional information IF it materially supports responses to questions already posed. However, the provision of circuitous, ambiguous, paradoxical or otherwise unhelpful intelligence is discouraged and will not serve to build your profile in any meaningful way.

B.

*   *   *

B:

Is it possible that although we started this journey with the proverbial first step, at the same time it was taken with the wrong foot? The dispersal of both ambivalence and self-determination does not usually happen as a result of passage along an assembly line, yet it may have happened here. As Robert Louis Stevenson said, "If you are going to make a book end badly, it must end badly from the beginning."

C'est fini, alors. Adieu.

A.

MR. WRONG AT THE WINDOW

What if I've got it all wrong? Ever thought about that? The game plan, the sling in the slingshot, the soldering in the circuit board — maybe I have it all screwed up and I don't even know it. What if I'm going through my day, misreading the same set of directions, praying to the same false god, oblivious. I think I'm getting somewhere but it's just a screen that's scrolling past as I pound on a treadmill. Could be. How would I know? If I'm fifty-five that means it's more than half over and I'm not getting too many more kicks at the can. In fact, I may have just about used them all up, be out of circulation soon.

Don't think like that. In fact, how about just don't think. Once I get going in those circles they wear down into ruts and trenches in no time flat.

All right, so I quit, it's true. A year ago today was the last day of my working life as I knew it. Hallelujah. I jumped, I wasn't pushed, and it seemed like the right thing to do at the time. It was all polite enough, even though the buggers from head office were as corrupt as a city contractor and I finally got to say so the day I left. Money's still okay, I can get by for now. I don't think my fingers are up to churning out a CV, so I'll just stay in this holding pattern a while. Going nowhere but the view's incredible. Used to be I'd either land on my feet or else I'd be back on them pretty quick any time I was out of a job. Now I'm more like a turtle flipped over on the hot asphalt, shell busted, soft parts showing and wrinkly legs flailing. Go ahead, anyone, take a stab. Or just run me over and be done with it.

I wasn't going to think like that.

But when I do, that's when I start to wonder if everyone else knows something I don't. Because I paid for that introduction service to help me meet someone, like Marie-Ange wanted. I should just call and demand I get my money's worth. How do I explain it all ends, though, when I take my hat off and they see the thing. Happened again yesterday on one of those coffee dates. If a living creature hit my forehead at sixty miles an hour and stuck, it couldn't have done a better job. *C'est un don du bon Dieu*, Marie-Ange would say. A gift from God. No one but her would think that about it. She saw good where no one else could. But these women I go out with, they give me a look like I'm putrefying before their eyes. Maybe I am. Maybe the thing decays faster than the rest of me. I saw a show on Discovery channel about aging and they talked about that. All I know is that it's big and red and getting more visible every year as my scalp emerges from my hairline. These women I go out with, they can't notice that I'm tall, that I make an effort and wear a suit for them. I know my manners and I show them respect. I keep my hands really nice, when you work in sales you have to and it's a habit now. Nope, nothing else matters. Not once they see the thing. They're looking for Mr. Right, and he's not me.

I — meaning of course, Marie-Ange — asked around at the hospital where she worked about getting rid of it once, way back. The plastic surgeon seemed really sorry when we got in to see him. But he said it couldn't be fixed without a big scar and a bald spot. So we left it alone. Marie-Ange didn't mind. She's a nurse, after all. Was a nurse. She studied and understood about life and saw what could go wrong with people's bodies all the time.

Made it easier to accept someone like me, stained from day one, I suppose. But it was like her to be earthy about it too. She could even get real sexy about the thing when we made love. It hurts so much to lose that.

So they all go the same way, these dates. Except the one with the doctor. She was so interested she all but had me lie down on the table for an examination and maybe a little surgery. Which would have been okay if I thought she really cared, but it was detached and clinical and zero chemistry. When she found out I was unemployed, between jobs as I say, I thought she was going to ask if she could check my bank balance and credit rating before we ordered. Worse, offer to pay for us both. It didn't happen, but it didn't matter. The message was clear: you can't provide. You're not adequate.

*   *   *

Every April, then, I've got two things to commemorate, to commiserate, to coagulate. The day I quit my job, and the day I lost Marie-Ange. Couldn't for the life of me remember our anniversary, all those years. But those two dates? Branded onto my brain.

I probably even have them, in among all these stacks of newspapers. Maybe right here in the hall with me. April 14, 2006, Marie-Ange's last day on earth, is somewhere about two-thirds down that pile. And April 21, 2010 is probably around the corner, now that the front hall is full. When she was admitted to the General there was too much space in the house. Now it's like I have an addiction in reverse — instead of wanting something badly, I can't stand to lose anything else. Marie-Ange could walk into the living room right now and start flipping through the flyers and check out the sales she'd missed, all five years' worth. The mail is in the dishwasher. Why not? I never use it, so instead of smelling like a dead animal it's what you call useful storage.

Filing, even. Magazines are up in the bedroom, she always liked to have one close by and there's plenty 'cause I never cancelled any of her subscriptions. English, French, she'd read them all.

It's become a bunker, this house. I never used to need protection, but I found out I'm not ready for alone.

Still, if I don't do something about this place even an arsonist's going to think it's not worth torching. I sound like I'm asking for trouble, but it's that kind of neighbourhood. And this could end up that kind of house. You got to hit the right middle ground with your home maintenance here: not bad enough to be mistaken for a crack-house, but not done up with heritage colours or landscaping or fancy stuff on the porch to make it a B & E target either. Routine repairs, minor upgrades, that's it. The step doesn't sag since I fixed it last fall, the tiny bit of grass gets cut in the summer. But the paint on all the trim is peeling like a fourteen-year-old's sunburn. If you look in through the front window you can see the piles of newspapers in so many shades of yellow. The gate hangs crooked and expects a wrestling match every time you go through.

Never would have been like that when Marie-Ange was here. She didn't nag, exactly, but she didn't let you forget. Or she'd struggle with the gate latch just a bit longer than she needed, to make a point.

When you live in a big city like Montreal there are things you have to put up with. Which we did, for all of our thirty-one years together. There was a sugar factory that used to give us a blast of some kind of stench when the wind was from the southwest, but it's been closed a few years now. That added a few undershirts chugging Molsons outside the two-storeys along rue Mirabelle here, probably made all our property values go down a notch. When the wind is right the St. Lawrence sends us its regards with all that southern Ontario sewage coming our way, not to mention contributions from the nation's capital. Must be extra special when it comes out of a politician. We had to live with the sirens yowling past, mostly ambulances on their way to Sacré-Coeur. And then there were the drunks in the back alley on weekends, coming off the bars on St-Denis.

We talked about getting out of the city, buy a bigger place with more of a yard. Out in *les banlieus*, maybe off the island where prices were cheaper. But the time never seemed right for buying, or we never got up the courage to stick our necks out and make a down payment. If we'd ever managed to have a kid that might have changed our outlook, but for just the two of us it kind of suited to live downtown. We liked to go for a walk along Ste-Catherine, among all *les blondes* with hoop earrings dangling off their earlobes and them dangling off some guy's biceps, youngsters done up skin-tight and checking each other out, middle-agers like ourselves, invisible except to each other, the wall-to-wall tourists any Saturday night that wasn't the middle of winter. We could watch the fireworks from the end of our street on festival nights if we didn't feel like walking all the way down to Pont Jacques-Cartier. No big thrill but nice to know they're there, sort of like a spouse after thirty-odd years.

Truth is, we liked the hum, the life, the way we felt at the center of something. The suburbs, they felt like the center of nothing to us. We always made our friends France and Alain think we loved their place when we went out to St-Hyacinth for a barbeque. Interlocking stone? Great! Pond garden? Wish we could have one. *Certainment.* And then we'd go home for a late drink on the Main or a walk along rue Prince Arthur and no more talk of moving for a while.

We found a way to be happy here. Then all the rituals and routines left with her. I doubt I even cleaned the windows last year. Now that it's spring and the sun is getting stronger I can see that they look worse every day. I stare out but I only see a pebbly grey surface, as though all the dust we get pulverized into ends up on them. If I'm a loose end, then a squeegee might be as good as anything to hang on to. I have that expensive one around here somewhere. The one she almost got mad about — imagine a woman getting angry with her man for buying a household cleaning tool. One that he intends to use, no less.

"Why'd you have to get such a fancy one?" she said when I showed it to her. "I can do the job with a newspaper and a bottle of ammonia water."

"Look at this, *ma chère*. It's got a metal handle and a rubber blade on it exactly the same as the professional ones. So I can do it right," I coaxed.

"And how have I been doing it all these years?" All she did was raise her eyebrows and I was reminded that it is a delicate thing, a conversation with a woman.

"You've been doing such a great job, I can't hope to equal it without a superior device."

"And you're going to do it."

"*Bien sûr*. No getting up on ladders for you."

I didn't say "any more" but we both heard it. I have to admit, that last year when she was so sick, I really got off on doing things for her. She'd never allowed me to make her a *tisane* because she liked it just so. It took me a while but eventually I got it right: one teaspoon of leaves in the tea ball, then put it in the teacup *before* the hot water, let it steep exactly four minutes, then stir in half a teaspoon of honey. When she got weaker I would take her books to the library and pick out some new ones. I got good at noticing when she needed a new box of tissue. I even did some of her gardening.

"Over there, *là-bas là*."

She'd point, I'd plant. I hated the dirt under my fingernails — that was something I wasn't used to. I would go at them with a nail file till they bled and they still didn't seem properly clean. One day Marie-Ange saw me at it.

"*Tiens*. You need a manicure. Come over and let me do it." She was still able to shuffle around a bit then.

45

We sat at the kitchen table and she soaked and rubbed my nails and cuticles and trimmed off all the dead stuff and all but painted them. After she was done they looked and felt great. The only bad part was the hard-on I got while she did it. She was so far gone at that point I felt like I was lusting for my grandmother but it'd been over a year and I'm a guy and still I feel so much shame.

In the last month, when she was at home but couldn't get out of bed any more, I was really glad we'd put that window in our bedroom. My friend André did it with me. He's a bit of a slacker, that guy, especially since he got some sort of minor inheritance. Nothing you could live off for long, just enough to make him stop calling his clients back and probably shoot his business in the foot for a while. But it meant he could come over and do the job as soon as I asked him and I never could have done it myself. It was a sliding glass door, actually, but with such friggin' cold winters like we've had it we mostly used it as a window. After it was done Marie-Ange and I would lie in bed and watch the moon, just us and that silver face, and we'd talk until her nerve pills kicked in and she could go to sleep.

We nearly argued over it when we first talked about putting some sort of window in. That was something we almost never did, especially once she got sick.

"I think we should put in a window, or maybe even a patio door. Right there." I pointed to the south wall one chilly Sunday morning when we didn't have any need to unwrap ourselves and get up out of bed. My free arm framed out not just the place but the size I wanted.

"I heard there was another break-in this week," was Marie-Ange's reply. "At the Savards. Someone got in through a window, or maybe it was through their patio door, I can't remember."

"It would let in so much light. And we'd go outside a lot more in the summer. You know we hardly ever sit out there even when it's nice weather," I said.

"Micheline told me she forgot to set the alarm. And I remember now, they pried open a window. That's how they got in."

"You can get good locks on these things now. They're pretty secure."

"Micheline said it wouldn't be so bad except it ruined the casement and now they probably have to replace the whole frame." She seemed to need to talk about this break-in more than my home improvements. I tried my best to reassure her.

"If we put in a patio door we could get one of those bars for across the base. Even if someone broke through the handle they couldn't push the door on its slider."

"It's terrible when the weather-stripping gets damaged in a winter like this. Micheline says the whole house feels chilly now." Marie-Ange shuddered a bit. It really was cold that morning, so I pulled the comforter higher up on her shoulders.

"Andre's free to do it with me, he hasn't got any jobs on the go now."

"Micheline says her contractor isn't returning her calls, he's so busy."

"Maybe she should call André." I was trying to be helpful.

"Micheline has a few leads on another one. It's hard to find someone you can trust."

"Well, we know we can trust André. I don't know if his financial advisor can, but that's his problem."

"Micheline said the worst is that now she's so scared. All the time. She always feels like there's someone in the house, waiting for her."

"I'll have to ask the guys at hockey practice about it next time. No one said anything last week."

"It's a terrible thing, to feel scared," Marie-Ange said.

"Are you scared?"

"Yes."

*   *   *

Maybe I should have paid for that scan. Maybe we should have gone to a private clinic and had it done that way. I would've, she wouldn't. Price was a rip-off, and they would have made us sign up for other things you didn't want or need when you've already got the feeling the balance sheet of life isn't adding up in your favour. I would've expected the guys at head office to come up with a scam like that. Not such a big deal when it's just a used vehicle, but we're talking about the only living body you've got.

Would it have changed anything? Would it have changed everything? Maybe, and maybe not. That resident who looked after her at the General, he said it's not always a help to find out that the ovaries have cancer sooner than later. It's the same conviction, you just get a longer sentence. Those were his words. Sounds pretty harsh, but he was a straight shooter and at a certain point you come to appreciate that. Just give us the goods so we know where we stand.

So we didn't pay and it took three months to get the scan. We sat in the community clinic in the Métro station where the chairs were all dingy and worn like the floors, waiting for the verdict, holding hands as though we were dating and not dying. The only people who go to that kind of clinic are the ones who are like us, and we are like the words in parentheses, I thought once. I remember when I learned to read, the teacher said if a sentence is really long and it has a parenthesis in it, just skip what's inside the parenthesis. You'll still get the meaning because the main idea is all there, outside the parentheses. So the ones who go to the community clinic in the Métro, who don't pay to get their scans and specialist appointments faster, we're the ones you can read around. We aren't the main idea.

Still, if that resident was right, then the lady next to Marie-Ange in the General got just a bit more time to go around the bases before her last inning. She was nice, and rich, and she had the same damn thing as Marie-Ange. She and Marie-Ange would have never been roommates but patients with that 'flu used up all the private rooms so Westmount and Outremount and Saint-Henri and NDG all had to share.

*   *   *

The day before her last I brought her a maple leaf, scalded red with October air even though it was April. I'd found it pressed in a phone book and thought she might like to see fall colours one last time. She held it the whole day. I noticed the veins on the leaf were still straight and strong even in death. But when I held her hand I could see her veins so weak and tortured: IVs, chemicals, chemo, cancer. I knew it wouldn't be long.

The very last day, she told me where to find the mouse traps in case I saw any droppings, and they were exactly where she said. So were the mouse droppings, the little pests. That's why I can't figure out what she said after, and whether she really meant it. If she'd been confused and ranting I wouldn't bother trying to understand. But she was in her right mind up to the end. While she was in the hospital she had made all those lists of what I should and shouldn't do after she was gone, how to organize the memorial, where all the warranties and statements were, how often things needed fixing or changing or replacing.

Maybe it's because she said it in French, is that why it's so hard to get her gist? She only spoke French once we got to that last stop, which wasn't our usual but no bother to me. Sometimes I miss out, though, like I don't get the punch line of a joke or the real meaning of a movie. Maybe it was the gridlock of memories interfering: some of them you'd like to hold on to, ride out for a while and just enjoy, then there are the others that barge into the path and keep inflicting themselves over and over again. Awake, asleep, neither one of us could get away from the traffic. Just let it rest, I would tell her, let it rest.

"*Tu dois laisser ouvert une fenêtre.*" Leave a window open. She said it right after telling me to try and find another woman someday. I didn't want to hear it then, but now that I'm seeing my life through atomized ash I realize there's something to it. Much as I wish it could all be over, looks like I'm going to be around for a while. So I crack the window open, even if the blast that comes in makes me shut it up tight again for a while. I'm trying, Marie-Ange, I'm really trying.

"*T'es devenu un vrai adulte.*" That's it. With the last bit of breath and good sense she had in her, she gives me that intelligence. I thought I'd been a real adult for a long time, but maybe there's another level that we're moved towards, ready or not.

*   *   *

It's been a long time since I've been out for a walk. Can't blame it on snow or the weather now that it's April. I step heavily on the way downhill towards Ste. Catherine, my bad knee worsening along the way — thump, flop, thump, flop.

It's turning into one of those shadowless evenings. The sun brightens up the edges of the clouds but it doesn't shine straight through so it's all soft and almost glowing. There must have been rain, and there must have been a festival, or maybe a demonstration. Both are evaporating, the sidewalk is dry along the edges, the stage is empty and the speakers are putting out eighties rock. The crowd gets less dense as I walk through a closed-off section of the street.

I realize I've forgotten to put my hat on. Meaning everyone who sees me, everyone who spares an instant to glance in my direction, maybe even makes fleeting eye contact, sees the thing. But I don't notice anyone recoil, no one stares, there's no grimace. I absorb this acceptance, I don't take it for granted.

I move among the other wanderers and laggards. No one's in a hurry because there is a kind of togetherness. Suddenly I am struck by the fact that every person here has suffered. We are an accumulation of all our life spans, plus all the lives of everyone's children, which must make up an eternity of suffering. I don't know any other way to describe the feeling except to call it love.

It stays with me as I separate and go home. I push at the gate, I squeak the door. Sliding past the piles of newspapers in the front hall, I am overwhelmed by exhaustion. The stack I sit down on slips to the ground under my weight and I stay on the floor among all the old words and dates.

RUBY

This, as they say, is it. Ruby Greene, this is your life. Does it look like a movie yet? That's what I'm waiting for. Technicolor dream. Don't expect any commercial breaks. No breaks at all, as a matter of fact. Just this big one. And now it's over. What's on my soundtrack? Hotel California, that'd work.

I'm thirty-nine, I still got a great body. Not that it's worth much anymore. I never had kids and that helps, though my mother would say I had the parts for it. We weren't friends, my mom and I, the way I see some of these girls and their moms now. She never harped about grandkids. Only that I had the kind of body looked like it was made for pushing one in a stroller while I had another bun in the oven, was how she'd put it. Right before saying I was such a slut I was gonna be that woman before I was twenty. I guess I'll never know, now. Just as well. Since I started serving time I've seen those moms who only get to be with their kids when it's family visiting hours. How bad they cry when the kids leave. How much worse off they are for having seen them.

So here I am, thirty-nine and on my way back, back inside. And a good figure still. I've got nice long legs, big firm breasts, the way the guys like them, all natural. A wide mouth that turns into a million-dollar smile whenever I need it. Then they just melt. I remember all the lines, all the moves. I could still be at it.

But I didn't want anything to do with that scene. Look where it got me — twenty-five in Furlong Medium Security. I'm supposed to be rehabilitated, or at least rehabilitating, aren't I? Seemed like I was getting somewhere, for a while there.

Not that there weren't opportunities, even here. You'd be surprised, these little hick towns with all their churches and their corny welcome signs. Their so-called service clubs. They've still got room for my kind of skills. You walk around town and check out the sleaze level, and there's always a hotel with a greasy spoon on one side of the lobby and a bar off on the other. The sign outside is way faded, everyone knows the place so there's no need to advertise. You walk in all confidant and ask to speak to the manager. You got to be asking in the right tone of voice, wearing the right outfit. And you say if there are any stags or anything else like that coming up, you're available. And you take it from there.

You might think that's how I met Lenny. And you'd be right, except that he came looking for a job with us. Lenny? That's my husband. Or is he my ex-husband? What do you call your husband when he's dead, especially if you're the one who killed him? My widower? I widowed myself, if it comes to that.

Anyhow, my husband, the now-dead Lenny, managed a bar operating at exactly that sleaze level. So if you look at the little blips in my life — and God knows plenty of people will be looking at them now, all over again — you could imagine I walked in and met him the way I just said. But it wasn't like that. He took over the bar I was working at — the whole syndicate we were under, actually — when I was about ready to leave.

*   *   *

"Good evening, and welcome to this week's episode of Citizen's Arrest. Tonight we have two cases, both identified in the last month, and both in Canadian cities. You'll remember we've had the case of Ruby Markham, alias Ruby Greene, who made her escape from Furlong Medium-Security Federal Prison. She had been serving a twenty-five-year sentence for the second-degree murder of her husband, Lenny Markham. Just to recap, Ruby escaped on April nineteenth, crawling through a basement window to...."

*   *   *

Me and the other girls were fed up. I mean, when you're in a line of work like ours you don't expect much. All part of one long grope that started before I was even in high school. But you've got to draw the line when your life's at stake. That's the point it was getting to. Two of the girls got attacked with knives in the change room. Another was almost strangled in some guy's car. She still couldn't talk right a year later. The foreign girls got it especially rough 'cause everyone knew they couldn't put enough English together to tell anyone what was going on. Maybe they were afraid to get sent back home to wherever. Even the audience around the stage was out of hand. It was like they all thought they could get away with murder.

Along comes Lenny, so cool he could actually pull off wearing a cowboy hat and boots. Not a tooth missing, no jailhouse tattoos only the fancy ones done by an artiste — no siree this guy's making it. He got things back on track again and all us girls of course just head over heels about the guy for saving us.

Imagine how great I felt when he seemed to like me. Me! No one ever liked me. Lots of guys all over me, all right. But not the *me* in me. Lenny was different. Why else would I have married him? Nobody'd asked me to marry them before. And I thought it meant more than just having somebody to sleep with whenever you felt like it. You can shack up with anyone if that's all you're after. But Lenny was all about looks, and together we made the place look more respectable. The manager of the strip joint — well, at least he's married. That's something. Yeah, something. Trouble is, we didn't know what.

*   *   *

"Ms. Markham was convicted of second degree murder, ummm, four-five years ago. Given a twenty-five-year sentence, no parole for twelve, if my memory serves me right. I was on the regular police force in Detroit at the time. For some reason I remember the incident well.

"They'd been drinking, doing some coke too I think. A fight broke out between her and her husband, something about her accusing him of sleeping with another woman. The neighbours called us, complaining about the racket. We'd been there before, y'know — thought we knew what to expect.

"It was a busy night, the usual for us on a Saturday. So it was a while before my partner and I actually got there.

"This time, though, we come in to find her there with a piece of pipe about, oh, so long still in her right hand. And Lenny, her husband, with a great bruise on the temple. She looked kind of roughed-up herself, nothing too bad though. We put two and two together and hustled them both off, Lenny to the hospital and Ruby- er, Ms. Markham straight to the station.

"Well, Lenny, he was okay there at first. I mean, he walked out to the cruiser by himself, cursing and hollering at his wife all the way. He said this time he'd press charges, said he'd been out cold first when she hit him and he'd woke up not long before we arrived.

"But on the way to the hospital he got sleepier and sleepier and by the time we all got there, couldn't wake him. I guess they did everything they could, but no go. They unplugged the machines a few days later.

"Sure, she never had no convictions before the murder. And nice to know she can behave herself on the outside when her time for parole comes up, if it ever does now. But what else you gonna do with people like her, besides lock 'em up again? They all think they're too good for prison. People got to pay for their mistakes. At least, the ones we catch got to pay. Nobody gonna pay for you."

*   *   *

I lived alone in my basement apartment, here in this flat little town all by itself in the middle of the country. Alone, just me and my fear. I was afraid all the time, those first weeks. More afraid than when I went into prison, first. So afraid of losing everything I had. You wake up with it in the morning, and it's like you smell different because of it. I wanted to get rid of the fear and the tension and the smell, I swear I could smell it. I'd put the radio on and sing in the shower and force myself to have breakfast. I never ate breakfast before, not since I was six or something. But I wanted my life to work, for once. How can you start the day on an empty stomach? That's my grandma talking now. The only one who ever made a big deal about me and my breakfast.

I'd wear something special in my hair on days when the fear smell seemed like it was getting to be too much. A hair band, or a barrette or even a ribbon. It was a colour, and I made the colour have a meaning, just to help me get through the day. I'd keep reminding myself about it so I didn't freak out. Purple was the best. It's like you never know what to expect with it. Hot and cold at the same time. I told myself I could do anything if I wore purple. Green was next best, new and growing. Yellow was for laughing. And so on. Sounds silly, now. But you know, it worked.

By the time I went out the door, if the smell was gone I sometimes felt like shouting "Hey, look at me. I'm making it on the outside!" But of course I didn't. I'd just say "duck boots" or something dumb like that over and over again on the way to work or the store or dance class when I felt I had to hold myself together. And hope like hell I'd never never ever get caught.

*　　*　　*

"Working with Ruby as her prison social worker was easy in some ways, hopeless in others. Easy because she was so passive. She never gave you a hard time about anything. But I felt I got nowhere with her.

"She would hardly tell me anything about herself, except that she ran away at fifteen. She did tell me of her grandparents, who seemed to be more stable. But she lost contact with them around the age of twelve, something to do with her dad losing custody and access and they were the paternal grandparents. The only happy times Ruby mentioned were weekends at their house.

"As for the rest of it, nothing. Just that she'd once hoped Lenny'd make everything work out right. If she would have participated more in our groups and activities, she'd have had a chance to get some of that sorted out. I'm sure of it.

"I know a lot goes on inside her. Just look at how she planned her breakout, how far away she got and for how long — that was no spur-of-the-moment run. And I can understand how she'd want someone like Lenny to be her saviour, someone who could turn her life around. Poor judgment, bad luck, no one there to help her out — hard not to feel sorry for her. Sorry and helpless. But when someone's as passive as her, well, they've got to learn to help themselves first."

*   *   *

Like I say, not too many real jobs waiting around for a girl with my credentials. But I kept looking and I ended up pumping gas. Kind of smelly and grungy, but actually not half so bad as a change room at a strip joint, always jammed with cigarette butts and greasy bits of makeup and the sweaty costumes we had to start out wearing. Even the can at the gas station was better, not to mention safer.

And I'm good at what I do. I was good at what I did, is what I have to say now. I liked being the ordinary kind of nice, not sexy nice. To be able to just say hi to the drivers, ask them how much farther they had to go that day or how old their kids were. Everyone in such a hurry to cross that big empty space and driving 'round the clock, but glad for a chance to ease up and chat a bit after being so wired for the road. And I got to know the names of the local folks, the regulars.

I was pretty good PR for the place. I made people think of our station the next time they drove by. The manager knew that too. The manager was a woman, first time I ever worked for one. I could feel her sizing me up the day I met her, but in a different way from all my other bosses, let me tell you.

"You'll have to wear our uniform," she said.

I knew she said it to discourage me. You could tell she didn't think I was cut out for the job. She had a point. I mean, there I was, still in all my mascara and nail polish, some goofy kid thing in my hair, saying sure I'd pumped gas before, when of course I hadn't ever except at the self-serve when Lenny was too wasted to do it. But she took me on anyhow. Maybe it was her business sense, or her sixth sense, I don't know. They say the station's done better since she took over after her husband died. I hope all this publicity about me doesn't hurt her now. Maybe it will help.

So I went at it, bouncing around in that big old red shapeless coverall, the station name on a patch over my right breast, my own name machine embroidered above my left. Only in that get-up I might as well not have had breasts at all. It didn't even try to fit, but somehow I felt safe with it on. It was my armour. People paid attention to me for a change, not my body. It was like I'd discovered a new kind of power.

Every now and then, though, there'd be one of those men. Driving alone, head half out the window and leaning his face on his hand so that the side of it scrunched up. I'd see him staring at me. Only not at me, through me, guessing who I was under the coveralls. He might say something when I brought him his receipt. I'd keep my face just so, no smile for you, buddy, but have a nice day anyway and drive safe. And far. On to the next car, and away he'd go. Waiting just one more second before gunning it out onto the highway.

It was creepy, being stared at like that. Imagine, me, who could wear a G-string in front of thirty or more guys. Now feeling awkward about just one seeing nothing at all. I couldn't figure it out. Maybe it's because it was such a public place, with all the minivans and RVs and farmers around. Maybe it's because an audience can be made into a blur. Maybe it was my armour. I was like Eve, I'd learned to cover up. Hard to go back after that.

That's how I lived there. A good citizen. I didn't even sleep with anyone the whole eight months. Not that I didn't think about it — after four years on the inside you get a bit crazy that way. But I wanted my life to work this time, no messing up. As in forever, maybe. Started to save some money for the first time. Paid my rent on time every month. My biggest worry was someday I was going to have to figure out how to pay income tax. Actually, my biggest worry was getting caught but I couldn't think about that or I'd slip up for sure.

*   *   *

"I'm the one who hired Ruby, yes. She seemed adequate for the job when I interviewed her. We're pretty informal here. Don't bother with resumes or references or anything like that. And I'm certainly not in the habit of checking people's immigration status or criminal record. I suppose I'm going to have to think about that now, though.

"Still, I can't say I'd do anything different if I was in the same situation again. I mean, Ruby did her work, never gave us any trouble, got along with everyone, took a lot of extra shifts when we were short. We're actually all a bit shocked.

"I daresay, though, it might make me a bit more suspicious of people in the future."

*   *   *

People liked me here. Really liked me. I think I know the difference now. Susan the caretaker for the apartment would call me over for tea and we'd talk for hours. Actually, she'd do most of the talking, I had to be so careful what I said I mostly listened. But it was a nice feeling, sitting there together and being friends.

And the people in my dance class, I'm pretty sure they liked me too. I really wanted them to, so I always said positive things to even the dumpiest babes who didn't have a clue what it was like to let the music move you. You can't imagine how great I'd feel twice a week, walking into that class and seeing all those smiles and thinking, hey, they like me. Nothing I'd done before ever felt like that.

Even the guys at work were friendly. There was a lot of teasing and some flirting going down, but nothing heavy-duty. I kept my hair in a braid, simple like, and after I got hired didn't wear any make-up and just kind of made it clear I wasn't interested. I was keeping my record clean, remember? Wasn't that hard, when I think back on it all.

But I could still have fun. And I did, especially when it was crazy-busy and you just had to laugh at the jokes Bob at the till made under his breath about the tourists and the truckers. Or at the end of the shift and we'd have a water fight out back. It was like being a kid again. The kid I never was. I felt like I belonged. I never felt that before.

Thirty-nine and still wanting to be part of the gang. Jeez, Ruby, you got a lot of growing up to do.

*   *   *

"Ruby rented the basement apartment in the building my husband and I manage. She told me she was from the States. I could tell that from her accent. She didn't say a whole lot more about herself, just that she was recently divorced and wanted to make a new start. She was more a listener than a talker. I never asked her too many questions, I figured if she needed to talk she'd tell me when she was ready.

"Oh, you can't imagine how surprised we are to hear all this. Shocked, really. I never would have thought it in a million years. She was very warm and thoughtful, she loved to try baking different things and she would bring us some of whatever she'd made when it worked out. She'd got this cookbook at a garage sale and was trying all the recipes. Sometimes it would be a big flop, and then she'd call me over to see. We'd laugh so hard. But it was strange, too, because it was like she didn't know anything about how to cook, and she was just getting around to teaching herself. Usually by her age a person's either got it figured out, or they've given up on cooking. I never gave it much thought at the time.

"And we certainly trusted her. We let her have the apartment the first month with no deposit or rent, even. She said her support payments hadn't come through yet and she'd work it off by cleaning if we wanted. After that she always paid on time. Just the other weekend we left her the master key and she showed some people an apartment for us. We never had any problems with her at all. And her dance class, that was a big hit here in town — she was a great teacher. At first she filled in for someone who was sick, then everyone loved her so much they gave her a class of her own.

"I have to say it. I'm going to miss her."

*   *   *

It was so cold when I first got here, I didn't think I was going to stay. But I was tired of being on the run, and then all of a sudden it was summer and it was so hot. Like the weather everything fell in place real quick — apartment, job, even a friend. Susan and I would sit on the cement step out back where it was cooler. Those nights I wasn't working the sunset and the evening would go on forever and we'd eat the peas straight off the plants along the wall. They grew up the strings she'd posted for them, Susan said the higher you let them grow the more peas you get. We'd talk while the trains moved back and forth on the siding across the road. Sometimes we had to shut up if they got real loud, but that was okay because Susan was the kind of person you didn't have to be yakking with all the time. She'd planted yellow and orange lilies and all kinds of other flowers around the edge of the property. She said it wasn't really a garden just a little yard but it was all she had to work with so she'd done her best. It's true it was small but it was beautiful. I never knew anyone could care about plants as much as she did.

She'd always ask me what I'd dreamed last night, and then she'd say now I'm going to interpret it. I couldn't remember — or didn't want to remember — anything about my dreams so I got good at making something up. After she'd thought a bit she would do her interpretation, I think that's what she called it, and she was always so pleased with herself. This is what she said some guy called Young told her: dreams are a path to the subconscious. I said I didn't think I had one of those. She laughed and said she pretty much had me figured out.

I guess everyone's got to believe in something. When it was slow at work, Bob at the till would sit me down and tell me about this book he'd been reading on Buddhism. Not much good to preach to me, I told him. I tuned out all that religion stuff way long ago. But still, I think I get it now why people want to believe in reincarnation. It makes all this crap on earth a whole lot easier to take. No matter what kind of shit goes down, you can always say, okay, next time it'll be better. Or, if there's some really really evil dude in your life you can hope they'll come back as a mosquito and get what they deserve.

I know what I want to come back as. A bird. Yeah, sure, everyone wants to be a bird, all that freedom and soaring. But what about eating worms and being taken down by a cat? Ever think of that? So I don't want to be just any bird. I want to be a hummingbird. Then I won't just be Ruby Greene, like I called myself here. I'll be ruby and green. And iridescent. And so fast no one can catch me.

I won't have to deal with ugly bugs and crawlies. I'd just drink nectar from flowers and the sweet stuff in hummingbird feeders. I'll come to the same feeder every summer, and make the little old ladies happy like my grandma used to be. I'll zoom back and forth and everybody will be all excited when they see me. And who would hurt a hummingbird? No one shoots them, they're way too fast for a cat. I'll be so pure and happy and little. I'll know how they make their wings go so fast.

I guess I'd be a male hummingbird. Funny, I never thought about being a guy before. But the male hummingbirds have the bright colours, and they do the dives and swoops so well. I suppose the females could do those too, but I won't have to make decisions once I'm a bird. I'll work on instinct.

That seems like a plan. Instinct instead of decisions. I've had enough decision-making for this lifetime. Seems I can only make the wrong ones.

Someone done good by my arrest, though. They said it was the highest rating that show got all season. They must've found me before the day of the actual arrest. How else could they have had that TV crew ready? They're not just wandering around a town like this, waiting for a story to happen. No way. It was a movie take, for sure, and I was the star. Woo-hoo, baby.

It wasn't the busiest day at work, but it was steady. Just to make it that much worse, to rub it right in my face, and in the face of everyone who'd been so good to me. Everything at the gas station stopped, not just the people and the pumps, but time and Ruby Greene and bright shiny colour and everything. And there was something about the arrest that reminded me of something else, only I couldn't tell just then. Now that it's the next day and time's unstuck and everything's going on again only none of it's the same, I remember what I couldn't yesterday. Do you know how crows can swoop in and do something terrible? Have you ever seen that happen? They're scary when there's a bunch of them — they can take down a big old owl if they want to. The only time I saw my granddad mad at a living creature was the day the crows stole some baby robins straight out of a nest. Grandma was crying over it, granddad waving his arms and shouting he wished he had a goddam gun and nobody noticing him cursing with me there. And the crows got them all. We'd been watching them grow, grandma and me, from the upstairs bedroom window. I held grandma's hand while she cried. The worst part was the mom and dad robin hanging around the next few days, wondering if it was really true that their babies were gone. So anyway, these police cars, black, white, some ghost cars — you can always tell 'cause they have a sneaky look about them — they all swoop down on the gas station like a bunch of crows and that's it, go ahead and roll the cameras, boys and girls.

Somebody somewhere is making themselves rich and famous because they can squeeze so much misery from you. See the ugly criminal and her terrible crime, don't miss an episode 'cause you need to know who to hate next week after a word from our sponsor.

Everyone at the gas station did as they were told that day except Bob at the till. He always made a set of rules for himself, which meant sometimes he didn't get along so well with the manager. "There he goes, being a free-thinker again," she'd say. But he was really dedicated, she had to admit that. There'd been a hold-up at the station just before I started to work there, so usually he would never leave his spot in case anything happened around the till. But on the day of my arrest he walked right out of the building against all the orders being screeched out of megaphones and asked real loud if maybe they were making a mistake.

Oh Bob, you old sweetheart, no one makes that kind of mistake, I'm sure of it. Not whoever's writing my script.

*   *   *

" *...tune in next week when we'll bring you two new cases —both from high-security penitentiaries in California.*

"Until then, remember — the one we're looking for might be right there in your community, so be on the lookout. Good night."

*   *   *

I never used to think the way I do now. Think and cry, two things I never did until I made my break. After the fear smell went away, I started to cry about the smallest things. Sometimes it was because I felt bad, but sometimes I felt good and I cried about that. Strange. And I used to make everything into a blank. That way there was nothing to cry over, nothing to think about. Just blanks. Mom would hit me and say I was useless, so I'd blank her out. Life on the street, blank. Just concentrate on food and bed, anyone's bed, to get through the night. The strip joint, blank. Prison, blank. For sure you don't think or cry there, or you've had it.

Lenny was Lenny and not a blank at first. When I couldn't get what I needed from him, what I thought he would give me, I turned him into another blank. Then he died — no, when I killed him, say it, Ruby — then I killed him, and there was nothing gone from my life. How can you miss someone who is a blank? How do you care for nothing? I can't even say I feel guilty. Maybe I'm glad he's gone. I only wish I hadn't been so stupid as to get rid of him that way and get myself into this mess.

So, back to blanks now. I'm already doing it. This crummy cell, with cold water only from the tap, the one scratchy blanket and the security camera that watches me pee, it's all a blank. The TV show with my picture on it, the one that landed me here, blank. The person who ratted on me, blank. I'm going back in, and my skin's already getting back to that whitish-grey colour you get from living under fluorescent lights, like skim milk.

The last eight months will be harder to erase. They've been like a new box of crayons, with sixty-four colours and a sharpener on the side. Nothing blank about them at all. What can I do with all the good memories?

Break them in half. Every one of them. What you never wanted to happen to your beautiful crayons was for them to get broken. But I have to do it. I'll just keep the ruby and the green and be a hummingbird in my head when blanking-out doesn't work. And if it comes to that, I'll go ahead and see if I can be that hummingbird. I can do it, if I want. After all, it's my life. Right?

CAVALIER

I wonder where my family is. I was all of a sudden away, the day the horseswallower[1] took me from the big wideness and travelled me into this cage. There are many comforts to being in a cage, and we are not complainers so I will not be one now. Underfoot there is great softness, daily the managers come at our hungrytimes and give us bellyfill, sometimes even deliciousness, there is always good water. No dangers exist except the loud maw mouth in the mornings, and one gets used to it eventually. There are companionable enough types in the neighbouring cages, but we cannot make a mingle of ourselves so we never find our natural order of leader, follower, friend or fighter. All the others here are like myself, standing or circling about their cage, and they are no more than a presence because we do not really know each other.

I measured my track about the cage the day I arrived. Door: one pace. Wall with bars: two paces. Wall with daylight but too high to see: three paces. Another wall with bars: two paces. Place for deliciousness and bellyfill: two paces, and then I am back to door. Beside me — though separated by the wall with bars — is a chestnut gelding, and on my other side a black mare. That

---

1   Glossary at end of story.

mare, she takes me to task at times, showing me her teeth and the ugliness of her face with her ears flat back whenever deliciousness and bellyfill come. But she tells a good tale, and some evenings I would have worn through the floor from circling if it wasn't for her.

She takes me to her mountain home with her stories, a place where the dangers were very different from those I knew before I came here. In the mountains, large furred hunters left their scent tales on smoky breezes. One never ignored either of those signals, for both hunters and the great tree fires wanted to be breathstoppers. Even the swiftest in her herd couldn't always outrun them. Those solitary hunters could make a meal of a friend, or especially, of a foal. There were also hunters who came in packs, who were bigger than the yowlers we had in the big wideness. She showed me the jagged markings near her hock from the time they had nearly taken her down. From that she learned to always check in shadow and dell wherever she went, which sometimes made our managers quite impatient with her. And she was never able to search the horizon the way I did. Megara had taught our family to scan for danger while it was still far away. Like me, the black mare had left her family behind to come here. Hers were still in the mountains, mine in the big wideness.

Alone in my cage, waiting for something to happen, I spend much of my time remembering my family. We left the old farm together in a horseswallower and arrived together in the big wideness where I lived with them for a full sun-cycle. For the three hungrytimes of the trip we were tethered and balancing and rebalancing. We were given food enough for only one hungrytime, and no water, so we were pushy and therefore pushed and slapped on our arrival. Tinglefoot and Roughly had a fearsurge coming off the horseswallower, which of course made everything more difficult. Still, we were together, the five of us:

Megara, Roughly, Samsam, Tinglefoot, and me, Sonoro, in the big wideness for that one sun-cycle before I left to live here.

Megara is our leader. I still say that even though I am not with her, because here I do not have a leader and I hope to be led by her again one day. All the others, Tinglefoot, Roughly and Samsam, surely feel the same. True, we have all had the outline of her teeth on our sides, but she did that to make sure we lived. She could always find a way to the shelterbelt when everything became a whiteness and we battled against it for our breath. She was blind in one eye but she could see even without the good one, we all knew that and depended on it. She hated to be challenged, though every now and then Tinglefoot especially would try and would come up on Megara's blind side. She could get so far, and once I saw her teeth marks on Megara's withers. Then she was disciplined, for sure: Megara chased her away from the pond and made her go a whole sun-turn, four hungrytimes, with no water. Megara knew just how much punishment to impose, the exact equation. How to make you realize you had wronged and you should not do it again. She is a good leader — how could we have lived without her? Almost every night during highest-sun time the yowlers would appear at the start of the darkening hour, running about in their little clusters with their heads and tails down as if we can't see them when they do that. These were the hunters we had to fear. They made themselves into a small but fierce team, scruffy and sharp of tooth. We would crowd around confused if they got close but Megara could stare at them straight. Then she would toss her whole self at them and once she pushed a big yowler far away with her hind hoof. I heard it crying all night before it stopped.

Roughly and I are full brothers, two sun-cycles apart, even though I came out splotched and he is a bay. My whiteness makes a big sign of me wherever I go, though Megara taught me to go inside myself, to not notice when I was being noticed. Roughly was different from me in every way: he naturally blended in and easily made himself part of any herd. He would submit to all that our managers asked of us, while I always have to defy as a first impulse. He was only so named because as a yearling he liked to play hard, and his coat was unusually coarse before the full gloss of his black bay set in. In fact he was the gentlest of us all. He became quite graceful and muscular when we had regular managing times at the old farm. He actually enjoyed the various pressures and paces we had to be put through, and I watched him grab for that hard jointed jangly bar with his mouth, anticipating what some of us just endured.

Samsam is a littlebig, which means he looks little on the outside but is ever so big inside. He and Megara did their best to tolerate each other, mostly because he is Megara's son. But more than once I saw Megara corner him and try to give him a hoof pummeling. Lucky for Samsam his littleness gets him out. That and his beautiful bright eyes that never miss anything. There he'd be after having escaped again, all little and big and wise-eyed, with his lovely smooth wide face and strong round body, and I would be glad to have such a wonderful littlebig in the family. Back at the old farm he often had a funny story about his managing times. He could find a spook in a corner that no one else could see and unseat his small straddler into a heap if he suddenly swerved just the right way. Then he would dash about pell-mell as though the spook was about to eat him alive and disrupt another straddler or two in the process. The managers would be cross with him and tie him up and leave him for a while and yet it never lasted. By the next day there would be plaits with ribbons in his mane and a round red crunchy treat in his bowl. For me, he was the best at head-tails because he was the only one who would keep flies off my face with his tail and scratch my belly with his teeth at the same time.

Finally there is Tinglefoot. With her mane all flaxen and full, her stockings that made her legs even more of a joy to watch, her bend and flex as supple as a young tree, allowing her long back and neck to curve through so many windings and turns, the coppery dapple of her coat in high-sun time, she was the most beautiful of us all. We were born in the same warming time when our mothers' winter coats were just beginning to fall free and the finest spears of grass were showing through. She was my half-sister but only through our sire, so we lived like siblings without jealousy for our dams were different. Our forelegs and muzzles were the first we felt in play. Those sharp little newborn hooves and teeth were always ready to plant a painful nudge, and we quickly learned to dodge each other so that we could later be safe from bigger, stronger ones. On the same day we both had to learn to balance three-legged for the manager to handle our hooves and then even longer for the hammerer. We shared a head-holder, and we had our first managing from above one day apart. Tinglefoot liked it even less than I did. She had such freedom in her stride I think it was never meant to be confined by anyone else's orders.

There is a mare here in my new home who makes a memory-flash so strongly of Tinglefoot I almost nicker her name when she is led past. She came out of a horseswallower — eyes bulging and white — not long after I arrived. Since then I have noticed how lovely she is, and how slowly she is adjusting to her new home. She has a glistening red-gold coat and refined ears that curve inwards when attentive. Her hooves were long like mine were when she first arrived, now that they are cared for they make such a bright clop already I know when she is coming before I see her. Only once, when the loud maw mouth was making its way between our cages, she was put in the one beside me. She was very afraid, so I told her to stand along my cage-side for company. There we shared our breath, she squealed softly and then let me feel the lip of her nostril again. She said she also once lived in a wide open place, but different from mine.

"We ran together, all mothers and foals," she said.

"You had no managing?"

"Not the first year. Our mothers were allowed to teach us, then as yearlings we taught each other. After that we were taken away to be managed, but only for running."

"Running?" I liked the novelty of this, even if I wasn't sure it was true.

"Yes, we love running. Or loved it. When we were in the herd it was all we did, and likewise when I was managed," she tossed her head with the memory of all that freedom.

"Do you still do it?" I asked. I wanted her to go on, although I still couldn't quite understand, or believe, her.

"No. When they get tired of us running, they send us to be traded. That is how I ended up here." From her tone I determined she felt she deserved better, though I thought our home quite adequate, if lonely. Still, I wanted no argument with her and continued to inquire politely.

"And your family, where are they?"

"I have no family. They hungried us all together and we never saw our mothers again. Then they took us all away from each other for the running."

"And so who taught you?"

"Taught us? We didn't need to be taught. We already knew how to run, we only really needed to learn how to start and when to stop." Again that tone, disdainful and aloof, not so much towards me as the whole world which was beneath her.

"No, I mean who taught you about the world, and how to be in it," I explained patiently.

"We know how to be in it. We only need to know how to run, which we already knew, and now, how not to run, which is foolishness. And to stay away from the stud."

"But the greenness that causes gutwrap, and the yowlers, and sucking mud. All the things that can breathstop you — how did you get by in the big wideness if you didn't know about those?" Surely she must have had some guidance for the time she was free.

"The only thing that will breathstop you is a sire. We had one, he lived on our farm and we knew not to get near him. As for all the rest, they are just myths. Stories. Some tell them up and down the aisle, just to make themselves heard. You don't believe in all of that, do you?"

She was too precious to contradict. I told her some tales about our big wideness, not to make her wrong but to divert her from the maw mouth, which was frightening her again as it went back and forth with its dirty loads. She fastened her ear and her eye to mine, and then she was led back to her own cage much too soon.

One by one everyone else on the old farm was also made to go away, including my own mother. Roughly said he saw her leave. But that was the same time that Tinglefoot and I were taken to a new pasture and hungried from our mothers' milk, and after that we never really thought about our mothers because we had each other. As the herd of youngsters we ran with grew smaller, and there were fewer new ones coming along, others of different sun-cycles and sizes were introduced to the group. That was when I met Roughly and Samsam, who fit in well. Megara was more of a problem. They had to take away Fancy, the other lead mare, and give Megara her place or they might have torn each other apart. Gradually we were able to settle into each other's ways, we did less biting and fighting and made a kind of pact for living among ourselves.

When we were at the old farm Megara and the managers likewise had a kind of agreement. She was the one who would go away in the horseswallower, and then come back again the most often. We were always so glad to see her return, the whinnies would ring up and down the aisle and through the paddock every time. There would be a lightness to our managers for a while; they made many fond noises over her and all the bright coloured strips that came home with her. For Megara's part, she was permitted to always be the leader other than during her managing times.

Once I asked her how she could do that. "Megara, you are so good at leading us but at the same time you follow their orders. Does that not make you wild inside sometimes?"

"Sonoro," she said, "our managers have a different set of reasons for being. Even though we work well enough together, we are not truly meant to understand one another. Enough that we each make our peace, and get what we want."

"I don't know if I can ever make peace with what they ask." I made my voice rumbly because I didn't know if she would understand.

But Megara was thoughtful, even soothing. "It's true that you are more of a puzzle than most. You never have a quarrel with anyone in the herd, but you find reason to resist whenever the managers ask something new of you, anything the least bit different or more difficult than what you've done before. And yet you enjoy what deliciousness they give us more than anyone I know."

She was right. Often I couldn't find any part of managing agreeable but I couldn't wait for the deliciousness that came after. I would brace my teeth against the hard jointed jangly bar and my back against the manager or straddler. It was better when our high-talking manager took over towards the end of our time on the old farm. Through those long and tedious sessions she and I found a place where I could accept her direction most of the time. Once I started to know what she wanted before she did, I felt less of the urge to push back just for the sake of it. But I couldn't do that for anyone else, she and I had a language that no one else shared.

All kinds of comings and goings happened on the old farm. We stood watch during the silent night-time arrivals of foals that were greeted with amazement by the managers in the morning. From time to time there was a breathstopping, sometimes out in fields, other times in the company of horsehealers and managers. We all knew the way the horseswallower could make someone disappear, usually never to be seen again. We were the five who stayed on at the old farm when there was no one else of our kind left.

Through all those sun-turns we breathed and worked and sweated through the energies that preceded our managers' actions. Every manager has a kind of aura, a mixture of their always-self along with the urges that drive them in a single sun-turn. We didn't mind an aura that we could understand, one that clarified the message. But more and more, in the changes that happened before we left the old farm, we were clouded and confused by what passed between them and ourselves. The place had become crowded with the spirits of who our managers used to be, and the puzzling selves they had become. When they were finished with us and we were left in our paddock to stamp and sigh in the lowered light, we had to help each other settle so that we could face another sun-turn with them. Roughly, Megara, Samsam, Tinglefoot — all through the last five sun-cycles of my life we were together. Now I am nowhere, and without them.

*   *   *

Today something small and furred came into my cage. I can't remember what it is called but there were some of these creatures back on the old farm. This place is still new and strange but every now and then I have a memory-flash, and it is like I am back there. Thinking back, I couldn't say how many of these small furpieces there were at the old farm because they always prowled the shadows around the barn, and along the edges and in the corners of our managing area. We often complained amongst ourselves of their lurking during our managing times. They could make even the steadiest ones like myself have a fear-surge, and then there was pressure and correction to contend with through no fault of our own. We never had anything much to do with them.

But today that furred thing came into my cage, and it wanted nosing. Usually they only come near in order to scour for scampery mice, always underfoot as they try to eat the fallen oats. I complied, even though it was strange to do it with such an odd thing. I hovered my great flat nose just above its tiny pink one. After a while I became curious and started to feel the creature all over with my lips, which is also how I come to understand if something unknown is safe and able to be part of my world. As I did that the furred thing made its body into a wave, and pressed itself against my lips as I passed over it. The hair on it was very soft, much softer than any of my kin, and its back and tail moved in an unfamiliar way. Then something very strange happened — the furpiece began a thrumming deep inside, both a sound and a sensation as I pressed against it with my muzzle, something I'd never felt or heard before. We went over and over the same space, my lips on its back, the creature's small self doubling around so I could do it again and again. Neither one of us could get enough, and that bit of contact became our whole universe for the time that we had it.

Then there was a noise, a kick from another cage, and we both looked up. Our moment was over and the furpiece sidled away. From its walk I could recognize it as a hunter. We should be far apart and intolerant, for our kind is the hunted and as Megara taught us, we must always be wary. Yet the furpiece and I had shared something that was a consolation to my lonely heart, and already I missed it.

*   *   *

Back at the old farm, our managers had a problem. Although Megara tried to explain it to us, I could never really understand and perhaps it was not meant to be understood. I could tell

Megara had to make some of it up because of the way her blind eye would roll when she spoke, looking for something that wasn't there. Like a leaky drinking trough that tries to satisfy our thirst but can't unless water is dumped into it faster than we drink, she tried to pour out words to describe what couldn't possibly make sense. But she had to lead us through the confusion, that was her job. I know this much: the problem in our manager family is the reason I ended up in this cage and far away. For all her skill and strength, Megara couldn't stop the imprint of the managers' mistakes on our lives. For all her defiance, Tinglefoot could not overcome the ever more tense way their hands and voices would work us. Samsam was so dear to them, but he too had to part from the manager family with the rest of us. All of Roughly's grace and good manners couldn't save him from being given up. We knew we were the favoured ones, because for a long time we were the only ones who didn't leave the old farm, and when we did we went together. During the last sun-cycle we lived through at the old farm, sometimes the high-talking manager would bring me into the barn, and the air about her would be dense with her energy. She seemed to need me for nothing more than someone to lean against so she could shudder and cough until it was all through. She would put me back out in the paddock again without even a managing time.

Megara was able to explain this much: among our managers the ties are different than those among ourselves. There is a blood bond, but it only brings on a certain kind of loyalty, one that is brittle. Unlike our family, who stand together against the wind and the yowlers and the scant times when we have to show each other where the grassy nibbles are, the managers' loyalty can be broken, it would seem at the times it's needed most. Because of that broken loyalty we had fewer managing times, which most of us liked. But it also meant a lengthening of the feet that tripped us because the hammerer didn't ever come. Sometimes hungrytimes were missed, which made Roughly get the gutwrap and we nearly lost him. He was pacing and patchy for two hungrytimes before he was noticed. And then in a way that even Megara couldn't have imagined, the horseswallower came and made us five live in the big wideness for that whole sun-cycle. We saw our high-talking manager every once in a while, and we continued to trip on our feet but at least they wore down with all the walking. We loved it there because we could choose our place and our pace and we could be together.

We had to learn how to be that free, though. To start with, there were a great many green and growing things we didn't know. From the tender golden willow branch to the delightfully bitter milk of the yellow flower, there were many new flavours to enjoy. We tasted the life in timothy and sweet-scented alfalfa as growing things, instead of just dried flakes in bellyfill. But we also had to learn to tell the savoury from the sickly. Megara knew of a tiny white flower that could take you down quickly if you ate it, and a small yellow one that would do it more slowly, and she made sure we could recognize them. Once we knew what to avoid, we loved eating whenever we wanted. Roughly and I became ever so good at delicately gathering a whole thistle together with our thick strong lips before biting it off in a bunch. Then we would enjoy every bit, even and especially the prickles. Oh, and those clumps of luscious clover that appeared in highest-sun time, which Megara warned us against over-eating or we would be gutwrapped for sure. "And no one but us will know you're breathstopped for days out here," she would say. Still, she had to chase Samsam out of it daily. We learned how to test the footing around the water hole so as not to get stuck and sunk — as Megara described, I thought, in far too much detail. Tinglefoot would only put her hooves exactly where mine had been after she heard Megara's warning. There was a rocky sand patch for rolling, and low hills for wandering, and time in the field for play and scratching and sun warming. All of these we made our own.

I remember all of this, now as I sleep-stand in my cage in the dark, a time when peace should be all about and within me. But I am not really here in my cage, I am in a kind of hollow space that curves me backwards and forward in a spiral like the managing exercises we were often made to do. Only this kind of work gives me no chance to stretch, no way to relax the grip of the memories.

*   *   *

Today the managing time here at my new home did not go well. So many of my memories would be better left behind, but when I need to recall something in order to perform my job, I remember so little. I wonder if I ever learned anything at all, and my confusion and over-reaction are discouraging even to me. I must seem more like a barely-managed youngster than an eight sun-cycled adult to my new manager. He says pull, I say push, he left, me right. He wants curve, I want straight. And when we argue like that the bar is made to sit heavy and hard on my gums and the pokers dig sharp into my sides. Today I wanted to do my free onetwothree because I can roll along in that gait so easily, but he only wanted onetwo-onetwo on and on and on. I never thought I would wish for my high-talking manager the way I do now. Towards the end, though, we did something different: another manager got on, the first one set one pole between two others and I was asked to go over it in onetwothree. When I did what they asked I found I could make an arc of my body and suddenly everyone was happy and everything was soft. I had never been asked to do such a task before; although it was odd it was also a satisfaction I'd never known.

Afterwards I had scratchy circles of drying sweat on my sides and an ache in the crest of my neck from the strangeness of that exertion. I let my legs crumple and I lay down in my cage's softness. The itchiness of my back and neck and sides was so unbearable I decided to carefully roll in order to scratch all those places. I really tried to stay as small as I could but it felt so good that my back leg stretched upward and I started to go over in pleasure. As my flank touched the wall, my hoof banged against the cage's bars and I got stuck. The bars grabbed my hoof and wouldn't let go. I did my best not to panic. I thought I knew what was happening, for Megara had explained something like it along with all her other lore. But I wasn't outdoors in the big wideness, up against a hill or a bank or a fencepost with a friend nearby to talk me through. This was my cage and the lights were out which meant no managers till the next sun-time, and I was fully against a solid wall with my foot caught fast.

I waited and thought. I didn't thrash and kick the way I know someone down the aisle did the other day, and I fought the fear-surge spinning so naturally out of the place that keeps us alive. This wasn't a time when that instinct could help me. I held still and tested my back against the ground, I tested each of my free hooves, then I began to make small grunty movements to gradually gain a better pushing place. The foot that was caught wanted to make me frantic, but instead of pulling I made a small twist and it was given away by the bars. Now I could use the weight of that free leg to make myself go further towards the wall, but also more onto my side. A front leg was now worked under me: together with my back hoof it gave a great force and I was up, safe but now even more sore than ever. I didn't think I could possibly be more uncomfortable or lonely.

Then I felt a back sensation and a memory-flash. The picture that I saw and felt was the sharpest kind of death squeeze, only it was much tinier than the memory. I was meant to run or spin but I couldn't do that in my cage. I swung my head to see, and that was when I understood: it was the furpiece, sprung upon my spine, finding a place to settle up there but having to use its sharps to stay aloft. Strange indeed, especially that vision of a quick cutting death. Once again I pushed my mind to a calmer place and let my ears soften and my head droop, so that the panic could leave the center that tries to control.

The furpiece was where it wanted to be, finding its comfort in my warmth. I felt it gradually settle, I sensed the softness of its belly fur and then its little throb that radiated into and through me. I found I wanted it there too, as a consolation against all the hurt.

*   *   *

After the last time the high-talking manager came in and shuddered against me, and I was put back out with the others, Megara said something unexpected. "They should take away the parts of all of them, those who call themselves our managers. They cannot manage themselves, for they are too many stallions. They cannot be at peace when they are all of them living together."

Samsam and Roughly and I had, of course, all had our parts taken, that was why we could be a family with each other, and with Megara and Tinglefoot. Megara insisted that our lives were much simpler because of it. We geldings have no idea what could be or could not be, we only know our lives as they are. Megara said she wished there was a way her own parts could be taken. This time her blind eye was looking like it was able to see the wind, and not rolling.

"In a way I understand our managers, because I am also a slave to so many unseen commands. I would sooner be more steady," she said quietly.

It was true that she could be impossible when the high sun-time came and her body wanted something it couldn't have. Tinglefoot was the same, if possible worse. But I thought Megara was forgetting something important. "Think of all your wondrous foals," I pointed out. "Surely they must be reward enough for the cycle you say is such a wrestle."

All she allowed was a long sighing breath.

I cannot forget that moment — Megara, so wise and strong and ferocious in her love, and in her leadership, wishing she was otherwise. And wishing the managers were otherwise too. That was nothing new; from time to time all of us wished our managers would be more reasonable. Like when they would leave a bucket of deliciousness in sight but out of reach, then go away and come back only to loud-talk us for banging to remind them. Megara's wish was different. That they could somehow be put together in another way, organized more sensibly, follow each other more closely. That, or leave us to manage for ourselves in the big wideness as we had during that sun-cycle.

Cavalier — Glossary

This glossary can be used to enhance the comprehension of this story. However, there is sufficient context for most, if not all, of the invented words to make their meaning clear if the reader prefers not to interrupt the storyline.

bellyfill	hay
big wideness	prairie
breathstopping	death
cage	stall
deliciousness	oats
family	herd
fear-surge	startle or flight reaction
furpiece	cat

gutwrap	colic, intestinal obstruction
hammerer	farrier
head-holder	halter
high-sun time	summer
horsehealer	veterinarian
horseswallower	horse or livestock trailer
hungried	weaned (from the mother)
hungrytime	time between feedings for stabled horses, about six to eight hours
hunter	predator
jointed jangly bar	bit
littlebig	pony
manager	trainer or advanced rider
managing time	training session
maw mouth	tractor, front end loader
onetwo	trot
onetwothree	canter
straddle	beginner or inexperienced rider
sun-cycle	year
sun-turn	day
yowler	coyote

GRATEFUL MIGRATION

"We're never single-minded,
unperplexed, like migratory birds."
Duimo Elegies, Fourth, R.M. Rilke,
tr. M. D. Herter Norton, 1934
"We are not in harmony,
our blood does not forewarn us, like migratory birds."
Duimo Elegies, Fourth, R.M. Rilke,
tr. Stephen Mitchell, 1980

Clenched, abdomen and jaw, Roberta dissects the day as she makes the bed. She tosses aside pillows, stretches sheets to perfection and tugs on blankets even though it is almost time to get under them. Once a degree of symmetry is restored, the cream coverlet turned down, pillows casually and plumply arranged, her bed looks good enough to be an ad for a hotel room — the promise of perfect sleep, or sex, or best of all, both. She never used to bother making the bed, but with all the axis-shifting changes of the past year — breast cancer and chemo, her husband Dawson's departure, today resuming her medical practice after a sick leave — she has found that she needs an invitation at the end of the day, an inducement to let go of her burdens and be open to oblivion.

The bed frame's four tapered mahogany posts almost graze the ceiling. Along with other artifacts from the ancestral farmhouse out East, the quality of the wood and the workmanship of the tongue and groove fittings are not common here on the Prairies. The furniture belonged to Roberta's great-grandparents, who had operated a profitable tobacco farm in southern Ontario. Both the farm and the furniture passed through the generations until the arrival of a plant virus. The ensuing crop failure devastated the family's financial and psychological outlook. Only her mother, the oldest daughter, could still manage to plan for their survival. At twenty-two she had moved her parents and her sisters to Winnipeg where she managed to find work with an accounting firm. They moved from the gentle climate and manners of a place where Loyalist sentiment still reigned, to a region as prone to drought as it was to flood and the whorls of devastation both left behind, where names and faces were a confusing array of pronunciations and colours. Starting over again in a new province, with only a few heirlooms to remind them of their previous existence, they were immigrants in their own country.

The four-poster bed and its companion pieces dominate the room. An oval floor mirror of the same darkened grain occupies the southeast corner, though Roberta moved it to a different angle during the past winter to avoid seeing the corporeal reality of her recent illness, surgery and reconstruction. A heavy armoire stands opposite, dignified and unconcerned, quietly asserting status and era. It had to be disassembled to be moved up the stairs and into the bedroom when she and Dawson bought the house fourteen years ago. The chest of drawers has more than enough space in its five large drawers, now that only her clothes are stored in it. Each piece of furniture has a single midline fleur-de-lys to acknowledge its Quebec origin.

There was a running argument about the bedroom set, mostly taking place between Dawson and the furniture itself. He felt it was too big, too dark and oppressive for their small-ish, second-floor bedroom, and frequently said so from his side of the bed. The massive pieces replied through their continued solid presence, while Roberta made little effort to take a side. Only one of the debating parties was self-propelled, though, and one day the side in possession of that quality made the most of it, and left. He left her with a last name that she didn't want but couldn't easily get rid of, a house that she wanted but wasn't sure she could maintain, and an unexpected need for conversation. Dawson had always been the more talkative one, spilling over with observations, complaints and stories, especially at the end of the day. Roberta didn't mind being a passive listener, she often felt that her words and solutions to problems were used up after a busy day in clinic. She thought she wouldn't mind the absence of his evening chatter. But the silent house could exert its own pressure, and she hadn't realized how much even the exchanges she'd shared with Dawson had been a valve that couldn't be opened otherwise.

Today, her first day back at work, brought back many of the frustrations and idiocies that she recalled from before her medical leave. After hospital rounds this morning, she had spent a few minutes flipping through paper files and then emails, reading only headings and subject lines. It was as though she'd never been away, for here were nearly all the same issues that had been active when she'd left off. Then her clinic was over-booked, which she'd specifically asked it not to be, not the first week at least. But their internist, Dr. Mustafa Gregor, had taken an unexpected leave, so along with all the other clinic doctors some of his patients had become hers. Given the shortage of specialists there was little likelihood he would be replaced any time soon. She could accept the added burden more readily if he hadn't been the one member of their group who was especially hawkish about his patients' management, and given to publicly humiliating other doctors when he disagreed with their treatment decisions.

When the bed is ready she sits on its edge and attends to her fingers. The cuticles are ragged, and especially the skin around the thumbnails is irregularly textured and punctuated by small scabs. She carefully snips off all the stray skin with a pair of nail clippers. Then she makes use of two skin creams and a waxy substance from a shoe store meant for conditioning leather, which she keeps on her bedside table beside the stack of poetry books she means to read some day. She works the combined lotions along the length of each digit and into the thinning skin on the back of her hands. Her fingers were almost completely healed during that brief quiescent period after the chemo was finished and before she started to anticipate her return to work. She tells people, if they notice, that her hands are this way because she washes them so often.

But that is not the truth. On a day like today, her first day back at work, she has a habit of tearing at her cuticles and hangnails. She cannot stop doing it, but she can detach herself enough to analyze the process step by step: first a picking motion liberates the little dry pieces that surround the fingertips or thumb, then bit by bit she grasps them with her stubby nails. She will shred the skin and discard the flakes of waxy translucence, far enough away so as not to cling to clothing, with a flicking motion. She continues until either her absorption is interrupted, or the bleeding starts. The slight periungual ooze is evidence of ritual and cleansing, such that healing and renewal can begin.

In fact it is an old habit recently revived. When she was a science undergraduate, studying for exams during pre-med, she would make use of a small scalpel taken from the biology lab to extract blood from her left inner arm. It was always a relief to remove the most recent scab and for her arm to achieve again that deep scarlet ooze. When exams were done Dawson would come in his old roadster and they would roar away to the nearest and loudest party. If he saw her bandaged arm it was easily explained that she'd had a skin cancer scare, and it needed to be repeatedly biopsied. Dawson was in business school, and on an athletic scholarship. He was kind and humorous but she could easily outpace his vocabulary and comprehension in matters of the flesh.

*　　*　　*

As she stood in the sway of a city bus this morning Roberta wished she had selected a smaller book. Her hand and forearm strained slightly against the resistant bulk of pages and binding. She had given up her seat to a pregnant woman and was trying to read while holding on to the overhead bar. She had taken the bus to the cancer center many times during the past year, when the campaign made her weak and occasionally double-visioned. Even before Dawson left he was frequently away doing contract work and that was when she started using public transportation. She decided to continue taking the bus for at least her first few weeks back at work. The routine of catching the 162 Express was familiar, and the absence of combative drivers and elusive parking spaces might make a small but noticeable improvement in her anxiety about the whole transition. There was further comfort in the pulsating humanity of public transit: nearly everyone able-bodied, not ill or complaining, wanting and needing something but not from her. Conversations would ignite and extinguish all around. On one trip a Kenyan man saw the medical journal she was reading, and told her about his challenges in qualifying to work in a pathology lab before he got up for his stop. Another day she took the only free seat at the back of the bus and two graffiti artists continued to talk around her, expletively discussing a resplendent new tag that encroached on someone else's. Often she couldn't help but overhear a half-dialogue into a cell phone, anything from a pleading request for a refund to a loud complaint about a co-worker. Once she would have found such an onslaught of problems and issues of trite, now all this evidence of life was invigorating.

This morning she stepped out of the bus and onto greasy grey late March slush: the overnight precipitation had combined with road salt, packed snow and black ice to form an unpleasant and slippery porridge underfoot. April may be the cruelest month, Roberta thought, but March is certainly the messiest. She carefully walked the half block to a set of glass doors that opened into her hospital's lobby, unchanged in its minimum of signage and absence of charm. Today Roberta had been particularly aware of her facility's deficiencies, having spent the past year appreciating the indoor water garden and vaulted skylights of the cancer center's atrium. Fortunately for all the unsteady and unsure pilgrims who ventured into this older hospital there was Edward Yau, the retail pharmacist. His store opened directly into the lobby and he often stood at its open door to offer greetings and directions, a faithful and unobtrusive postilion.

"Good morning, Dr. M., and welcome back," he said this morning, with a small bow. "You are well today?"

"Very well, Edward, and how are you?" Roberta paused on her way through the lobby.

"Excellent, Dr. M., excellent. You are ready to get caught up at the clinic?"

"I think it will be a while before I'm actually caught up. Somehow there are a lot of things that no one but me can do." Roberta tried to make light of the workload she knew awaited.

"Ah, that's because there *is* no one like you. Surely you know that." Edward's smile was as luminous as ever.

"Maybe there's no one else who wants to do what I do. I promise I'll start getting those prescription reorders to you today. I'm sure there are a good many."

"I know you will, I'm not worried." He ended his sentence with another small bow, and Roberta felt permitted to hurry away, ahead of further solicitude or inquiries.

She would have preferred to take the stairs up to the ward, but energy and breath had been scarce lately so she pressed the elevator button. When the doors opened she was face-to-face with the entire housekeeping day shift; they must have just finished their first break. There were deferential smiles and shuffles as they made space for her, and numerous greetings acknowledging her return.

"Glad to see you back, Dr. Miecznikowski," a woman to her right said. Carla was one of the few co-workers who routinely called her by her full name, being of Polish descent herself.

"Thank you, Carla. How have you been?"

"Pretty good. Actually not so well. I've got an appointment with you soon."

"Okay, we'll see you then." Roberta was glad the ride was only two floors up and that the elevator doors would be opening soon. She didn't want the conversation veering any further into confidential territory.

Rather than the usual hospital hierarchy of physicians down to maintenance and cleaning staff, in their small facility relationships were often bridged by familiarity and even a degree of affection from years of working together. For Roberta, the ties were further complicated by the fact that many of the female staff were her patients. She knew that her own strengths and frailties were observed at close range, here in the elevator and during her absence, in casual conversation and at coffee breaks. Now that she has been on the illness side of the equation it is inevitable that she will be, and surely already has been, subject to extra scrutiny. She was aware that her hair was thinner, though there is still enough of it to maintain the cut and style she likes. She decided to wear grey tights today instead of nylons because so many veins now mar the surfaces of her legs. As always, her cranberry jacket is free of lint and dusty rubs against vehicles, and she made sure to replace a missing button last night. She never used to mind the casual observation of her appearance, but today Roberta kept her eyes down to avoid eye contact. Doing so made her take note of the knit skirt she chose for her first day back. She wouldn't have worn something so short and close fitting before she was compelled to consider the finite aspects of her existence. Now she savoured these small bodily satisfactions, and indulged in them whenever she could.

It was 8:35 am by the clock over the nurses' station when Roberta arrived and rounds had already started. Several of her colleagues were there reviewing lab results and writing out orders in the staff room. Roberta took the nearest swivel chair and again received many greetings from all sides of the room. Paula, the charge nurse, and Caroline, the ward manager, had gone through the first few patients on the list. For her benefit they went back over the ones she had missed. Roberta was again acutely aware of all eyes on her, and grasped for familiar medical territory. This had always been a place where she felt comfortable, but today she was the foreigner, ill at ease with the language and customs.

When they were finished and the physicians dispersing, she took note of an absence and asked, of no one in particular, "Where is Mustafa? Has he already done rounds?"

Glances were exchanged, and Caroline was the first to answer. "I guess you haven't heard. There's that war in Syria, and he still has family there. When he heard the bombing was near his home town he decided he had to go back. We haven't heard from him since."

"You're right, I didn't know. What are we doing with our cardiacs now?" Roberta inquired.

Again a slight pause, and this time Paula answered. "Nothing, really, we have to transfer most of them. All the doctors feel out of practice with managing them. First time we've been without Dr. Gregor for any length of time since he came to work here."

It was true: whatever else one might have to say about him, Dr. Gregor was a tireless worker who almost never took a vacation and was always available for consults. Although the group had been glad to recruit a cardiologist, he and the family physicians had often been at odds. In her own dealings with him Mustafa had criticized Roberta's indecision and hesitancy in trying new medications on her patients and in following his recommendations; she knew that he considered her cowardly and backward. They disagreed about everything from drug dosages to end-of-life discussions during rounds and sign-out, though they made an effort to avoid outright argument. And whenever there was a meeting between the medical staff and administrators, Roberta would arrive on time and try to make helpful contributions even though she didn't necessarily feel the gathering was worthwhile. Mustafa would show up late, if at all, leave early and only interject the occasional rumbling criticism during his brief attendance.

"The frustration of the hyper-intelligent," one of the other physicians would mutter when Mustafa strode yet again out of the boardroom before a meeting was adjourned.

During the past year, whenever Mustafa came to mind, she recognized how little she looked forward to resuming their professional relationship. But away from the immediate discomfort of his abrasive manner, Roberta could sometimes find a degree of empathy for him. He had been an interventional cardiologist before he came to Canada, and she recalled him saying that he had had his own angiography suite and cath lab in Damascus. He would have been accustomed to working with highly specialized nurses and equipment, in a sphere where his word was law. In that setting he was the hallowed practitioner who brought back to life the near-dead by stenting a coronary artery, inserting a pacemaker or ablating a troublesome focus of aberrant electricity. But here in Canada he was licensed as a mere general internist at a small community hospital, occasionally reduced to groveling for referrals from the family doctors and always working long hours to make his overhead payments and support family still in Syria.

*   *   *

The hospital cafeteria's furnishings were limited to a small stretch of scruffy chairs, information-laden bulletin boards and fluorescent lights a few watts short of full illumination. Midday attendance had already passed its peak by the time Roberta arrived, and there were only a few people waiting for either an appointment or a day surgery pick-up. She was content to sit alone and eat her lunch. Unaccustomed to so much interaction, her first four hours back at work already had her feeling quite worn. Within a few minutes, though, Mackenzie from lab seated himself across the table and a few chairs down. At times loud and provocative, Mackenzie tended to make his tablemates vacate the staff lunch area more quickly than they would otherwise.

"How about that snow last night — I suppose your drive in today was bad," he said as an opener.

Roberta thought she could handle a neutral topic like weather, though she would have preferred not to talk at all. "I took the bus today, so I just had to make it through a bit of slippery stuff on the sidewalk," she said.

"Oh. Car in the shop?" he asked through a mouthful of shepherd's pie.

"No, I just thought I'd give it a try," Roberta replied.

"I can't stand the bus, always full of creeps and weirdoes. No way I'd give up my car."

One time she would have felt the urge to reply, which might have escalated into an argument of some sort. Today she simply blew on her spoonful of soup, a thick tomato dill with plenty of macaroni noodles. She considered telling him exactly why she took the bus in order to prevent some kind of embellished gossip from germinating and eventually making its distorted way back to her, versus simply leaving the topic alone. She could easily imagine the rumours arising from this simple exchange: that the chemo had damaged her vision, or, no, it's because she's too weak to even drive a car, she probably shouldn't be working at all. Once she would have avoided the cafeteria altogether and eaten at her desk. Now she didn't care nearly as much: let them talk, or not, she knew why she did what she did. Or she didn't know why she did what she did, and neither did anyone else, so it didn't matter. At the moment all she really wanted to do was enjoy her soup. The kitchen staff still made it nearly every day from scratch and it was always delicious.

But Roberta's appetite still hadn't returned to its pre-cancer state. Today when she looked down at the food before her she had to remind herself that this was nourishment, and that she needed it. Along with her soup, she had asked for whole wheat toast and a small carton of milk, and she had a grapefruit brought from home. The grapefruit was at its seasonal peak: when she held it she appreciated the sensation as much as the sight of its skin, shiny and when rubbed producing a small squeak. She had borrowed a knife from the kitchen, and used it to run quarterly incisions through the skin. Her thumbs pushed along the knife's lines to strip away the peel. She broke the grapefruit apart in segments and bit into its red flesh, making the juice run. It stung the flayed skin of her fingertips, which by now had had the healing balms of the previous night washed away. As much as she disliked the disfigurement of her hands, she found it easy to accept her habit as a form of punishment for her sins of omission and commission. Like the time she forgot to call a patient about an abnormal potassium and he had an arrhythmia because of it. And her refusal to accommodate Dawson and move with him to Calgary for his new job. She only had to look down to see the corporeal reality of her mistakes and inadequacies. The discomfort in her fingers made the pain of regret palpable, her obsession damaged her most accessible body part.

Roberta slouched slightly in her chair with a pressing sensation inside her head and wished she could take a nap. She hoped she could keep herself going through the rest of the afternoon. The week. The month. She could have stayed on disability, the insurance company was willing to keep paying. But last month she talked her oncologist into allowing her to return to work. It wasn't hard to convince him she was mentally and physically competent, able to withstand the rigors of a busy general practice with hospital privileges. Not someone the oncologist would be tempted to report as — what did they call it? — a physician at risk. The slightly skeptical arch on one side of his face was balanced by a knowing camaraderie issuing from the other: *"If it were me..."*. He completed the Return to Work date on her form and said she could call his office anytime if she ran into trouble.

She needed to be the duty that defined her. She had come to realize, in the time she had to take off work, that being a physician was both a reward and a payment for the privilege of being a healer; as much an invoice for her shortcomings as a remittance for her strengths. She was glad that she was back to being a hardened linebacker for patients like Josie, her borderline. Not surprisingly, she was the first patient booked in this morning's clinic. Although their particular negotiated truce had lasted a good three years, there had been many difficult moments. She was also ready to have her clinical judgment questioned yet again by Josie's sister Iris, as unalike as a sibling could possibly be and Roberta's only physician-patient. And the sooner Roberta got back to prescribing for patients like Vania, who never left the office without an argument about whether the pills she was taking for her blood pressure and her depression were doing her any good, the better. This morning she had surveyed Vania's current concoction of medications as prescribed by other physicians with a sinking heart and resigned herself to months of sorting out. And what about Gerhard, incurably cheerful, uncontrollably hypertensive, stubbornly impotent Gerhard. Who actually brought her flowers for her first day back. She had it all again, along with a genuine, practice-wide gladness at her return. She had noted a few stealthy glances from those who were checking to see if she had returned intact. Wondering if she was now more like them: partial, something lost in the self or the soul, broken but still beating. Roberta could imagine her patients hoping that their doctor's own guardian angels and wound-watchers remained on alert, so that she could continue to be there for them.

"Code blue, 3409. Code blue, 3409."

The imperious voice made everyone in the cafeteria look up. Code blue, Roberta thought. What kind of crisis was that? Was it a cardiac arrest? Or was that a code red? Something medical, she was sure, though there were alerts for everything from tussling patients to tornadoes these days, and it was hard to keep them all straight. She had better go.

She was gasping for breath by the time she finished the fourth flight of stairs. There was no need to ask where to go because she could see the crash cart just ahead of her. Please no, she thought. That's Mr. Maendel's room.

Among the people and equipment that had arrived ahead of her Roberta looked for someone who might know more than her. Jeff from Emerg, already stationed near the head of the bed, thank goodness. He could run a code. And Paula, who often knew what to do before the doctor did.

Mr. Maendel was alive but struggling to stay that way. Respiratory arrest, Roberta thought, the announcement eponymous in this case for whatever had brought on the dusky colour to his lips and fingers.

"Get a twelve-lead on him," Jeff barked. Mackenzie was already sorting out the wires on the ECG machine while the nurses undressed the patient's heaving chest. Feeling herself redundant, her mind a blank where there should have been a recipe for resuscitation, Roberta took the patient's pulse while she looked at the heart monitor: fast but not necessarily fatal, so something else had to be amiss.

"He's having a big anterior infarct," Jeff scanned the ECG before it had even finished printing. "We need to thombolyze. What's his weight?"

Roberta felt the urge to interject, though at first she wasn't sure why. What was it she'd read about him as she looked through the myriad results this morning? She struggled to visualize the consult letter she knew she'd seen on her long-time patient. To read it in her mind the way she used to be able to see her own lecture notes when she wrote exams in medical school.

"Hold on. Didn't he have a subdural bleed from a fall and a head injury?" Roberta said above all the human and machine-generated noise. "I'm not sure when, but he's still being followed up by neurosurgery so it can't be too long ago."

Jeff paused. "We'd better check. Is there anyone around to give consent?"

"His wife's just outside the door, I'll go talk to her. And his level of intervention is medical, not full resuscitation. I remember that from his first heart attack."

"Hold on, Paula, don't draw anything up. We might be forced to save the system a few thousand." Jeff unhooked his stethoscope and draped it over his neck to signal the most urgent efforts were on hold.

"I'm sure that nitro and morphine would be appropriate, why don't you go ahead with those," Roberta said as she left the room.

*   *   *

At the end of the day Roberta stopped by the emergency department. She found Jeff in the charting room dictating a letter and waited for him to sign off before she spoke.

"Thanks for your help with that code," she said. Jeff turned around when he heard her voice.

"Oh, hey, Roberta. Yeah, sure, but I hear he didn't make it. That was too bad. Good thing you knew about the subdural, though. Nobody else did," Jeff leaned back, stretched and yawned hugely. "I lost a patient once to a stroke when I thombolyzed her, and it was pretty bad. No one wants to go through that."

"If Mustafa was here I wonder if he would have given it," Roberta couldn't help speculating.

Jeff nodded his head but his expression was noncommittal. "Maybe, and it might have saved the guy, but more likely he would have died anyway. Sometimes you just have to be a healer, and not a hero, and that's okay." He turned back to his paperwork and Roberta accepted the signal that the discussion was over.

"You're right. Anyway, thanks," she said. "See you around."

"Yeah. And good to have you back, Roberta," Jeff paused and looked her way again. "So many patients who pass through here mention you, and how much they miss you."

"Nice to be needed," Roberta replied.

*   *   *

"What more could we have done?"

In the quiet house Roberta surprises herself with the sound of her own voice, especially in the evening. The ongoing internal conversation bursts through her lips at unexpected intervals. Tonight she talked it through while she straightened the edge of the duvet.

Already it seems like quite a while ago, but it was only yesterday that Roberta made the effort to be especially nourishing to herself when she went for a walk in an outlying park. The forest paths and the bending river were still frozen but the sky was a softer blue than its midwinter brilliance and the sun warmed her face. When she stepped out into a clearing she heard a hoarse but familiar two-note call overhead. One, then another in counterpoint that merged with the first. She looked up and saw a small angular formation of Canada geese. Seems early, she thought, though the birds were known for their hardiness and even a bit cheeky about it. She could recall laughing with Dawson in this very park as they watched them waddling about on thin ice, falling through at intervals and being completely unperturbed. Then Roberta heard another sound repeated from above, that sounded more like the voices of excited children. This time it was a flock of trumpeter swans, their long necks perfectly aligned with their purpose. Roberta felt a slight apprehension for the graceful birds. What if there was an early spring snowstorm, something the area was well known for? Surely there was some instinct guiding their decision to arrive now, a trustworthy inner compass as certain and mysterious as the signal that directed their flight. The swans only staged here, en route to some destination further north. It was always a thrill to see them as they briefly made the river or a flooded field their way station. Roberta finished her walk and drove home, aglow with the privilege of that encounter.

It was just as well that she had tried to be balanced before all of today's upsets. Besides Mr. Maendel's death, she was confronted with the same problems she could only vaguely recall from just before she'd had to stop working. At the time they had caused her teeth to ache with frustration and her chest to compress with the recoil of outrage, and she would have thought they would all be resolved by now. But there among the papers thickening her bulging inbox was yet another draft of a protocol that she remembered as having been especially contentious. The physicians were being exhorted by the administrators to adhere to a new cardiac protocol and its strict timelines. There was debate over the resources that the doctors felt they needed to do so, as opposed to what the hospital actually made available. The physicians proposed the hospital acquire equipment that they could use themselves, quickly and with little training. The managers argued that would be a duplication of services and a capital expense they couldn't afford, that lab techs could be called in when needed.

At the last meeting, Mustafa had made no attempt to be diplomatic. "This is ridiculous. You're creating all kinds of contradictions. Calling in the lab makes for a delay, so you're not going to meet your own timelines. And the lab tech isn't free. We are. In your eyes, at least. We would actually save you money by performing the test ourselves."

"That would be a different budgetary line, one we can't access." The facility director's way of remaining calm, even slightly condescending, in the face of Dr. Gregor's combative style only increased the tension.

"Can you at least put it in next year's budget?" Roberta suggested. She seldom agreed with Mustafa, but this time she was glad he gave voice to her exact thoughts. Perhaps for once the doctors could present a united front and effect a change in their favour.

But arguments had stalemated, agenda items were tabled, everyone left unhappy. And now half a year has passed and nothing has been resolved. If Mustafa couldn't force through the necessary changes then no one could. She's not sure she really cares, one way or the other, and she knows how one set of irritants at the hospital can be so quickly replaced by another. Middle age has only heightened her sense of injustice; it seems there is no peace in wisdom. When she lies awake at night with her brain unnaturally busy, all the perfect responses, analogies and connections she wishes she'd made during the day come to her. If only she could have her say, make use of those exact words, she is certain she could convert everyone to her point of view.

The bed is finally ready and Roberta is glad to climb into it. Once she is finished with her hands she takes a book from the top of the pile beside her, a paperback collection of poetry by Rilke. She smiles as she reads the inscription from an old boyfriend — *Let these days begin our years. All my love, Nick* — and flips the pages to find a short poem. *God or goddess of the sleep of cats*, it begins, and she herself is asleep before she can finish reading it.

SNOW

The winter of '07 Lisa's mother turned seventy-five, and all of a sudden the formula that described her life had so many variables it could no longer be solved. Lisa was good at math, and logic, and so was mother. They should have been able to figure it out. Failing that, Lisa wondered if she could just blame it all on the snow. There was so much of it that year, clogging the sidewalks and streets like never before. She couldn't have possibly known what would happen. While she was at it, could she also blame Mel, her supervisor at the time, who made her that offer. Circumstances accumulated, and like the snowbanks and drifts that impeded progress and blocked perspective, they obscured certain truths about the landscape.

It all started (if Lisa didn't think about it too much, because if she did the cascade of events changed entirely, as did the spectrum of responsibility), it all started in the featureless Winnipeg head office where she worked. The previous senior managers, unimaginative except in their greed, had been so proud of that building, all poured concrete and reflective glass. It was the day of her team's February quarterly meeting, if she recalled correctly. Which had escalated to a monthly gathering as audits and court appearances and other ominous deadlines approached.

On her way to the meeting Lisa noticed herself in the polished brass that framed the elevator doors in the lobby. She liked what she saw, and allowed her reflection to smile back ever so slightly. She wore her new, beautifully fitted burgundy winter coat, trimmed about the hood with sumptuous fox. She had splurged on it during a company trip to Montreal last November, feeling expansive after both a promotion at work and being freed of daily parental responsibilities in the past year. In particular, her son Kevin wasn't around to tell her that she shouldn't wear fur. Still, she felt slightly self-conscious. She was unaccustomed to attention, and she missed the reassurance of her daughter Meredith's advice on how to dress for the day since she'd gone away to university.

While she waited for the elevator, Lisa mentally defended her divergent positions of wearing the elegant coat at the same time as a pair clumsy old boots, ones that Meredith would never endorse except to wear while shoveling the driveway. Lisa chose them for their warmth, aware that they could garner a different kind of attention (once when she was grocery shopping and the princess coat was at home, a little girl had pointed at her and cried out "Mommy, is that a man? But look at her boots!" in the produce section before being shushed). Practical versus pretty remained an unresolved debate, even now that Lisa had time to indulge in the latter. Meredith had moved out a year ago, and Kevin last fall, but Lisa often found herself mentally engaged in conversation with one of them. It was only a problem if someone saw her making a particularly eloquent hand gesture or facial expression, then she had to quickly come up with a diversion.

She murmured thanks to the man who held the elevator door for her, and rewarded him with another brief smile. Several of the elevator's occupants nodded to her in greeting but no one smiled. The typical expression lately was either dour, or downcast, or both. Humour had all but disappeared. Lisa restrained a sigh. Unlike everyone else these days, she was both generous with smiles, and in no hurry for winter to end. She had a genuine love of the cold season, with its glittering snow by day and cascade of stars by night. And now she felt like the daughter of a Russian tsar every time she donned the new coat. Whether it was just the winter, more dire than usual this year, or the number of ongoing pressures at work, she noticed that people's mood deteriorated with each intemperate weather system and with every revelation about the company that appeared in the news. She wished she could get a forecast for today's meeting: the last one should have had a wind chill warning.

From the back of the elevator Lisa counted the floors: ten, eleven, twelve, no thirteen but count it anyway, fourteen... Counting had always been soothing for Lisa. Still, her apprehension followed their upward progress. Before this promotion, her desk had been in the acreage of cubicles on the building's lower levels and easily reached by stairs. Moving up in the corporate hierarchy meant her own office and a much better view, but no way to avoid the elevator.

Samara, administrative assistant to the CEO, greeted people as they entered the boardroom. Here was someone who still smiled. Like Lisa, she had not only survived the recent corporate shakeup, but had seen her career advance because of it. Lisa noted a deferential camaraderie evolving between them in the past six months; she found it curious how people noticed her more now that she had a title and not just a job.

"Hi there Lisa. How are you?" Samara said as she handed her a revised agenda along with a sheaf of attachments.

"Hello, Samara. I'm well, thank you," Lisa replied.

"Did you get much snow out where you live?" Samara asked, although she was already looking at the person behind Lisa and offering him a package of papers for the meeting.

That was one. In this country, at this time of year, people liked to talk about snow. If it was a winter when there wasn't much snow, they talked about that. Lisa found this preoccupation, bordering on an obsession, with snowfall and its aggregate effects to be tedious. She counted as an antidote for that, too, tracking the number of references to snow over the course of a day. So far the record was seventeen, from morning radio banter, through a day of meetings and greetings at work, then during grocery shopping and dry cleaning pickup afterwards.

"Enough to make me slow down on my drive here. Hope I'm not late," Lisa answered as she began to unwrap herself from her warm clothing.

"Oh no, everyone's still arriving. Say, Mel wanted to have a word with you before we start. He's over by the coffee," Samara looked at Lisa again as she gestured with her free hand toward the cluster of people around the refreshment table.

Mel Mahovitch, interim CEO, cycle and ski enthusiast, wore his light grey suit, red tie and Oxford striped shirt as a kind of standout fashion statement among the otherwise interchangeable, dark blue financial crowd. Coming within range of his slightly breathless enthusiasm, Lisa found herself wishing, yet again, that he wasn't interim, and that he wasn't gay.

"Lisa, how are you? Please, can you come over this way a bit, there's something I want to ask you." He placed a hand on the back of her upper arm and they maneuvered away from the coffee corner. The usual throng of middle managers, hoping to make a favourable impression, grudgingly moved aside for them.

Mel made his pitch without preamble. "How would you like to be the one who goes to that course on the new accounting system? It's in Vancouver, and you'd be away for about three weeks. Mo had to cancel, perhaps you heard."

"He was subpoenaed, then?" Lisa had heard, but had not altogether believed, at first. When there were so many rumours, and the newspaper's financial section read like a scandal sheet, it was best to get one's facts from the source.

"Yes, and of course that has so many implications in itself. But we have to get someone up to speed here or we'll be left in the dirt when the upgrade happens. I realize it's short notice, but what do you think?" Mel smiled engagingly as he spoke.

"It is a bit sudden. I'm not the one who usually gets asked to do these things," Lisa replied cautiously.

"They told me that. You have your kids to look after. Of course, if that's the case we completely understand." Mel's empathy made his plea all the more enticing.

"Actually, that's behind me now. Just. They've both moved out," Lisa said.

"Excellent. So you'll go?"

"Can I check on a few things? I still have a couple of dependents, an elderly mother and her dog. I would have to make sure those bases are covered." Lisa felt she could be honest with Mel, that he wouldn't deny her this opportunity just because she was hesitant.

"Certainly. Could you let Samara know? And would you mind doing your own bookings? The way things are right now, you know how it is..."

"That would be fine."

"Just send her the receipts. We'll put you on the following meeting's agenda, and you can teach the rest of us. Something positive for a change, right?"

Mel had a wandering eye that took a moment's adjusting. Lisa used his steady eye to maintain her focus. Even so, she found herself noticing that his tie was not solid red after all, but a tone-on-tone paisley imprint. A glimmer of anxious excitement made her both attracted and averse to this proposal, the same way she felt the impossible delight of being drawn to Mel. Recently a kind of renewal surged through her at times like this, making her feel entirely out of step with the usual view of midlife as an inexorable downward slope.

"Oh, Lisa, just one other thing." Mel's tone changed from persuasive to one of concern.

"Yes?"

"You weren't comptroller while Conner was here, were you?" he asked.

"No, I was appointed by the courts after he left. Then the company made my position permanent," Lisa answered.

"'After he left.' That's a nice way of putting it. Anyway, good. They'll be doing more forensics in the next few weeks. Between that and the weather," he made a jerking motion with his head towards the frost-edged window and sent his wandering eye further astray, which Lisa found altogether endearing, "you'll be better off in Vancouver, even if it rains the whole three weeks."

If there was need of another scapegoat for the way that winter unfolded, here it was: the collapse of their biggest client, and how it changed everything. Without it, Lisa never would have been promoted, she would have had no opportunity for corporate travel or training. For years she had been in the holding pattern that an overburdened solo parent must assume, declining or ignoring opportunities until they stopped presenting themselves. She had truthfully begged off added responsibility, and therefore the chance of a promotion, on the grounds that kids needed to be picked up, fed, raised and there was no one but her to do it. Middle age should have seen her fade gradually to the level of an office clerk until retirement obscured all remaining ambition. But that previous reticence had sheltered her from the early, high-level company scheming, as well as more recent, covert shredding sessions. Now, instead of seeming to lack corporate commitment, she was free of the taint that clung to so many, and had sunk more than a few. Who would have thought the profession of accounting would find itself portrayed as a menace to society? Lisa discovered a hunger to be part of the avenging forces that overcame her more natural tendency to blend in and just do as she was told.

As the meeting ploughed on, Lisa began to reflect on whether she could manage to be away from her mother for three weeks. Last summer mother's deteriorating state had been conveyed to Lisa in letters and emails from concerned friends who still lived in the old neighbourhood. At least that way it didn't come as a complete shock when Lisa arrived in Regina to survey the squalor and disrepair of the little house she had grown up in. From the freely swinging storm door, to the abundance of partly opened tin cans, tea towels crumpled and stiff with spills, kitchen sink marinating in its clogged contents, it was obvious that the age of autonomy was over for mother, even as it was just about to begin for Lisa.

"Seems like you're having a hard time managing here," Lisa observed once she found a place to sit down.

"Yes, it got ahead of me and I never could catch up." Mother's hand made an automatic gesture meant to straighten a pile of magazines, but caused them instead to slide sideways onto the floor. They were hardly noticeable among the general clutter. At first Lisa couldn't reconcile this mother with the one who had raised her, who had always known how dirty and disheveled life could be and made such an effort to keep its edges from visibly fraying. She was forever knitting a new dishcloth that would replace the one in use before it started to decay, as though she wanted to be sure no one read anything private into the weakening fibers.

Lisa had begun to formulate her approach even before she saw the state of mother's house. "You know, Kevin's moving out of the basement suite at the end of summer," she said gently. "Has its own bathroom, and a walk-out door in the back so you won't have to go up and down the stairs."

There, she'd said it: Kevin, nineteen and staunchly loving but aching to leave, would be in a different hemisphere by the following month, likely not back again until the spring. "We could have you moved in by September," Lisa said when mother didn't immediately reply.

"That would be nice," mother said, and clasped her hands between her narrow knees as if this would prevent them from doing anything else incriminating.

If mother did move in, it would mean not having the house to herself, as Lisa had anticipated, and not having to face an empty home, as she had feared. On the long drive between Winnipeg and Regina Lisa had thought through all possible options, a process that helped her make this decision the same way she did most: with a minimum of discussion and an absence of visible emotion. She and mother both had abundant experience in taking action alone, given that they had both been their children's sole provider. Although they had done a generational inversion through their parallel years of loss and grieving, with Lisa a widow and mother divorced, Lisa found she could stave off self-pity by reminding herself that mother never asked for help or complained. She and mother had only ever had one prolonged period of disagreement, when Lisa was in her late teens and had wanted to know more about her father. But it was only a phase and she had long ago made peace with mother's refusal to say anything about him. Which made it unsettling when mother became preoccupied with her long-gone ex a few months after she moved into Lisa's house. It started with the containers of urine. Lisa imagined their kindly housecleaner choosing her words carefully when she left the note.

Dear Mrs Dutoit:

I'm sorry but seems like your mother has been using yogurt containers instead of bathroom, and then she put them under the bed. Maybe it's a kidney infection. Sorry.

Angelique

"What have you been up to, mother?" Lisa could hear that parental tone in her own voice, the one where anger gets converted into disappointment, as she knelt and searched for more indiscretions in the suite. Why should she be so mortified?

Mother wasn't embarrassed. And aside from Angelique, who seemed to pass no judgment, there wasn't anyone else around to know. "Go on, Dash," Lisa said irritably to mother's Dachshund, pushing his firm body aside.

"I can't go in the bathroom. Donald's in there," mother declared.

"Donald? Donald who?" Lisa straightened up and felt dizzy, both from the squatting and the surprise.

"You know, Donald. Your father."

"Mother — Donald, my father, you know he's not here." Lisa tried not to sound as exasperated as she felt.

"Yes, he is."

"Now?"

"Yes."

"Can you show me?" Lisa asked, even if she wasn't sure she wanted to know.

Mother pushed herself to standing from her armchair, declined the offer of her walker, and shuffled forward with an arm outstretched. Her finger pointed as unreliably as a wayward compass in a magnetic storm well before she reached her destination. At the threshold of the bathroom she stopped. Swaying, she directed the erratic finger towards the tiled floor.

"See, that's his face. It's pushing through the floor, right up through the floor. I can't go in when he's there like that." Mother's voice wavered along with her general unsteadiness but seemed sure of its purpose.

"So how do you manage if you never go into the bathroom?" Lisa asked as she did her best not to imagine what might be happening in her own house.

"Oh, I can go in when he's not there. He only comes when it gets dark," mother declared.

"Then you use the containers."

"Yes, I found them in the storage room over there. I'm glad you saved so many. You never know when things like that might come in handy."

Mother was a little less gaunt, and Dash noticeably less plump, now that they were both sensibly fed and regularly walked. The two newspapers that Lisa brought down every morning looked like they had been read, and seemed to be the only company mother needed besides Dash. Now Lisa needed to reconsider: she might have to humble herself and ask for help.

"So, are you thinking about all the great food you'll eat while you're in Vancouver? It's become quite the culinary mecca." The meeting had adjourned and Mel was leaning forward against an empty chair next to Lisa. Samara was right behind him. "Samara thinks she'll have time to do some of the arrangements. She's already looking into changing the course registration to your name. You'll confirm with her as soon as possible?" Mel asked. Samara smiled in affirmation; this time Lisa found it harder to return the gesture. Just as there had been elements of her single parent life that no one save another solo parent could understand, now only those who had a deteriorating elder of their own could grasp the situations she faced. There was no point even trying to explain. "Yes, and thank you," was all she said.

She left the office building in a thoroughly swaddled state, with hat and muted floral shawl further protecting her within the burgundy coat and hood. Her sturdy boots made a hollow resonant sound crossing the parking lot on the packed snow, affirming that the temperature still hovered around minus thirty even though it was mid-day. Her afternoon client was a twenty minute drive out of town through a treeless Prairie vista. Along the way she took note of a huge snowdrift, one that had been forming all winter. She saw that it had grown even larger since she had last made the drive. A shelterbelt of tall Lombardy poplars kept the prevailing northwesterlies from ravaging the small farmhouse nearby, but it also resulted in a regular deposit of snow and ice crystals on the leeward side. The enormous wave was an eye-scalding white on a sunny day like this. The only visible feature, besides sheer size, was the way the top of the drift curled into a crisp and delicate lip, making it look even more oceanic. It was now almost equal in height and width to the adjacent bungalow. Lisa wondered briefly if a house could get buried in snow; then she was past and she didn't think about it anymore.

*   *   *

The evening before she was to leave for Vancouver, Lisa made a tour of the entire house including mother's suite, ensuring that all the details were as firm as the check marks she'd made on her To Do list. Dog walkers were remarkably hard to come by so Dash would just have to be let out in the back yard at intervals, which mother ordinarily did in the daytime anyway. The commode sat discreetly in its corner; mother had managed quite well with emptying it every morning and there had been no more unpleasant surprises. Angelique, as it happened, was going away on her winter vacation at the same time as Lisa's trip. With only mother at home the cleaning could easily get caught up once Lisa returned. There had been no more mention of Donald, no other distorted versions of reality or passages into frames of reference best forgotten. The home care service would continue to come for mother's bath, and they were accustomed to using the back door so mother could let them in.

"Well, mother, I think everything's all set," Lisa said as she finished her survey.

"Yes."

"Neither of the newspaper carriers will deliver to the back door, so I've had to cancel both of them for the three weeks."

"I don't mind."

"And you know I've left you lots of food in the freezer, you just have to take it out to thaw and then heat it in the microwave like you always do."

"Yes," was all mother said.

"Come then, Dash, time for your walk." The little dog, relieved of the fleshy rolls that used to corrugate his back, lifted his short front legs up off the floor as best he could and yipped in happy agreement. Lisa carried him upstairs and proceeded to bundle herself against the cold night air. Dash himself was dapper in the little sweater knit by mother when she was still quick enough with her needles and her mind. Out on the front porch he dropped himself down the front steps in a sideways fashion in order to keep his back end apace, which made Lisa smile. She never would have thought she could grow so attached to such a creature. He had an odd little squint of a body and a deeply suspicious temperament, and yet she knew she was going to miss him and their outings while she was away. For one thing, apart from the necessary interactions with her co-workers, she talked more to Dash than anyone else. And if it wasn't for their nightly walks, she wouldn't get to see Orion stand guard over their house during the coldest winter months. She wouldn't have been startled and amazed one night by a large form that swooped past, silent and low; it must have been the barn owl she so often heard, querying her existence at close range. Being out after dark meant she could indulge her covert fascination with her neighbours' lives if they left their curtains open: movement, lights, televisions, pictures. The neighbourhood was abandoned and lifeless by day, but at night there were many manifestations of home. While she walked Lisa sometimes imagined herself in a different world, having a sit around the samovar in a tavern or a roadhouse, the way they were always doing in the Russian stories she read lately. In the company of other wanderers, they would warm themselves with tea, and loosen but not remove their outerwear as they maintained a defense against the dangers of the cold and the world. She could see a black and fragrant brew being dispensed from the low-bellied device, a little slip of steam from its vented end, cups being passed between fissured and reddened hands, the surreptitious addition of spirits as evening pressed in. There would be conversation, about things exaggerated and concealed, inquiry and confession, and it would last until the storm outside abated or the candles inside guttered out. Like mother, sometimes she didn't so much feel the need to talk, as to listen and not be alone.

"I'll see you in three weeks, then, mother," Lisa bent towards a light embrace.

"Yes."

The passive responses, much diminished even for mother, caused a pang in Lisa's throat. Mother's voice, like her person, seemed folded in on itself, the crease being the divide between who she used to be, and who she was now. As quickly as she wished she wasn't going, Lisa corrected the thought and aligned her purpose. She had to repeat that process almost daily while she was in Vancouver, at the same time trying not to call too often or mother would become anxious, convinced something must be wrong for Lisa to be phoning long distance.

"How are you doing?" Lisa would make a casual and cheerful start to her calls.

"Fine."

"How is Dash?"

"Fine."

"You let him out today?"

"Yes. Why do you ask?"

"Just checking. What have you had to eat?"

"Something from the freezer."

During her time in Vancouver, conversation with her colleagues had likewise been a restrained experience. Before leaving on this trip, a pleasantly intrusive image saw Lisa engaged in animated banter with the other participants, perhaps with one who was not only interesting but unattached. Maybe they would go for drinks (although that made her wonder, how exactly do people go for drinks?). For the first few days Lisa pushed the limits of her introversion and made small talk. It was exhausting, it made her feel loud and noticed. But aside from desultory greetings, and the obligatory assignments done in groups, no one reflected her aroused interest in the world. Instead, there was a tendency for everyone to form an alliance with a particular part of the room, often with exactly the same chair, day after day, and to be absorbed in whatever electronic device they had at hand. When she visited the Vancouver branch, it reverberated with shattered faith in the head office. She noted a degree of suspicion about her very presence, as if the previous leadership's bad behaviour — or at least the risk of being caught at it — might be contagious. At the end of the day Lisa felt no desire to keep up with the news and only turned the TV on to watch the yoga station. She eschewed newspapers in favour of the thick Russian novels she'd taken out of the library. They were so absorbing she didn't even remember to count the pages she had read. On weekends she took long walks or bicycle rides along the seawall; she at least saw a good many people on these outings.

At the end of the three weeks Lisa was relieved to be back in Winnipeg and to be driving in the direction of home, even though it was still unseasonably cold. The taxi driver's voice was as gentle as his foot was firm on the accelerator. Going around corners he steered skillfully through all the skids, and only fishtailed briefly when he pulled away at green lights. Still, Lisa was not used to being driven by anyone, and she gripped the door handle tightly.

"Is it next light I turn, ma'am?" the driver asked.

"Yes, turn left, then go to the end of the street and make a right," Lisa directed.

"Thank you, ma'am."

It was hard to believe there could be so much more snow than when she left. During the drive, Lisa was determined not to say anything. But when her house failed to appear, she couldn't hold back.

"How much did it snow while I was away?"

"Yes ma'am. It has been a bad winter. Some people cannot get out of their houses."

"I'm — but..." Lisa tried to think: straight ahead there was a mountain of white, and the side path to the back door didn't look any clearer. The driver, for all his skill in navigating the snowy streets, was wearing only a lightweight jacket — fine for a car's heated interior but unsuited to the kind of cold that made one's teeth clench rather than chatter. Taking note of his Sikh headdress, Lisa wondered aimlessly whatever possessed anyone to come to this country if they weren't born here.

By now the driver had politely opened her car door, so Lisa fumbled about for the fare and told him to keep the change as a sort of abeyance for the error before her. Her suitcases looked small and useless beside the socked-in driveway and porch; the base of the mound's snow pack surrounded her tall dress boots. She advanced by another step, and immediately felt a cold sprinkle about her ankles as snow cascaded over the top of her boots and down inside (how pleased she'd been when she bought them, the way they made her legs look longer). Now that the taxi's headlights had swung away, and the motion detector light remained dormant despite her flailing attempts to activate it, she realized she was outdoors in the cold and dark, closer to midnight than she cared to contemplate, without a way into her house.

"Need some help?" she heard a voice call.

It was her neighbour, she wasn't quite sure of his name, the one who stood outside on his doorstep to have a smoke even in the worst weather. When she happened to see him there as she went out with Dash, she would choose the opposite direction, saving herself the embarrassment of sending forth a greeting, or not.

"I've given myself a hernia keeping my driveway clear. Thought you must have been away 'cause I never saw you out with the dog. These last two storms have been doozies," he said. He came over carrying a shovel and with the cigarette still there between his lips. He cursed the weather and apologized and then cursed it again as he carved a narrow path. As soon as he sidled out of the aisle he'd created Lisa quickly thanked him and made her own way in. "I'm Dan. Dan Engel. Good to know your neighbours, eh?" she heard him say behind her. Lisa was sure she would have shaken his hand if she hadn't already tunneled so far into the drift.

When she opened the front door, the house's interior mocked her fluster by looking exactly as she'd left it, warm and quietly lit by a table lamp. Snow fell out of her boots as she unzipped them while walking towards the basement, and she nearly banged her own face opening the door.

A fecal smell, then the pitch darkness of the basement (what about all those night lights, the ones that weren't supposed to turn off?) threw Lisa's panic from fast idle into full gear. She missed the last step and almost fell into the stew of soiled newspapers and distressed books. She groped for a light switch and when she found it she saw that a sort of literary hurricane had roared through the suite: scattered covers and spines of books, pages that seemed to have been torn out one by one, mingled with newsprint in loose sections and crumpled wads that covered every square centimeter of floor.

Seeing mother in her corner chair, a mistreated kitten came to mind. A thread of sound seemed to emerge with each breath, although Lisa soon realized it was from Dash, there on her lap. The matted hair, the pastiche of dried food throughout mother's clothes, the glazed look from Dash, above all the horrible stink, shamed Lisa to a quick and brutal conviction. She shouldn't have gone away, she was wrong to lay claim to her life. She fumbled in her coat pocket for her phone and dialed 911 for the first time in her life.

When no voice was able to penetrate mother's silent shroud, the paramedics decided to lift her onto the stretcher. They picked her up with barely a contracted muscle, so gently and respectfully that Lisa wanted to sob, to be beaten down with guilt. "Donald?" was the only thing mother said as the swarthy and round-faced paramedic straightened her legs and did up all the buckles and straps. "It's fine, missus. It's all going to be fine," he said.

Sitting through the dull hours in the hospital's emergency department hallway, Lisa worked at calculating the number of tile perforations along the ceiling's entire length. At the same time she considered how it came to be that she had so badly miscalculated in relocating mother to her basement apartment. It had seemed like such a reasonable collaboration of needs. She had never forgotten the time when Kevin and Meredith were about ten and eleven, and her sister's family had taken them both on a ski trip for a week during Christmas vacation. Although the gesture was as much for Lisa's benefit as it was for the children's, Lisa hadn't been prepared for the mathematical paradox of their absence: the house was three times larger with two thirds of its inhabitants gone, and all her good intentions and projects could not fill the extra space. She had spent the week floating from mending to sorting photos to catching up on filing, unable to settle on anything. She couldn't even decide what to eat or when to go to bed. Unpracticed in the habit of spending time with friends, she called no one, and no one called her. Without the scaffold of work and children to frame her time she fell into lonely purposelessness, counting down the days, then the hours, till the children got back. Mother's presence in the house seemed to offer a balanced equation of not being solitary, while still being private. Should Lisa ever, for example, meet someone, and should she and that someone wish to be at her house together for the night, it could be achieved without intrusion, or even awareness, on mother's part. It all seemed to make sense, and yet there was some coefficient she hadn't considered. For the life of her she couldn't figure out what it was.

A fitful stirring of sheets and creaking of metal made Lisa get up stiffly from her chair at the foot of the stretcher and walk to the opposite end. Mother asked to have her head raised. While Lisa was doing that, mother's voice suddenly intoned more solidly than it had for a long time.

"I caught him."

"Who?" Lisa asked.

"Donald."

"Your husband." Lisa came to the side of the bed and steadied herself by holding onto the rails.

"My ex-husband. I told you that he keeps coming back, finding us. Every time we move he shows up. I thought I'd better report it," mother said.

"Report it to…?"

"To you. I was told I should report all the things he's done. I suppose I shouldn't tell you but he raped me."

"He raped you?"

"Only once. That's against the law, isn't it? Maybe not? You look doubtful. Maybe you need to look it up."

"Who am I?" Lisa risked asking.

"You're that police officer. I can't remember your name, but I remember you. I'm glad they sent a lady police officer," mother nodded.

"You said that you'd caught him."

"Yes he was back and kept coming up through the drains and the cracks and every little space he could find so I set a trap. And when he came through the only place I'd left open I had a box ready and I shut him in it and I carried it outside and I buried it in the snow and since it was so cold and from the way my hands and face and feet hurt so much I can tell you that he's frozen in the backyard if you need to see for yourself." While she said this, mother sat herself upright in the bed to project her truth more forcefully.

"Did he say anything...?" Lisa ventured after a pause.

"I didn't let him talk. I had to work fast or he would confuse me."

"Did he say anything about me?" Lisa tried again.

"Why would he say anything about you?"

"I mean, did he say anything about Lisa."

"That is a good question." Mother slumped back onto the stiff mattress. When she did that Lisa could no longer smell the bit of sour that clung to her despite the generous sponge bath given just before she was parked in the corridor.

It occurred to Lisa that she could move her chair up from the foot of the stretcher and sit beside mother. She paced a hand on top of mother's and went back to her counting.

CRITICAL

Roberta can't sleep. Even though the house is dark and still, lately the combination of middle age and middle of the night brings on a flurry of doubts, regrets, tentative plans and half-made lists. They bind themselves into a kind of crazy quilt that is more suited to strangling than comforting. She lies in left-facing fetal position and tries not to look at the clock, but she knows it's a losing battle. The past month has been particularly bad, ever since she gave that treatment to Valerie — terminal, palliative, tenacious Valerie. Roberta is resigned to the inevitable hour of 3:15 a.m. when her inner voices make a clamorous continuum. Her mind springs into action and she is ignorant of fatigue. Twenty years of medical practice, she thinks, and still I question my own judgment. There is nothing to do but get up, find something to do, and hope to fall under the spell of sleep again in a while.

Roberta is about to put on her paisley silk housecoat when she decides it isn't warm enough, and chooses the flannel one instead. Once in the kitchen she goes to empty the dishwasher, but then remembers that she only puts it through every few days now that she cooks and eats alone. The silk dressing gown should have been enough of a reminder. Dawson gave it to her just before he left a few months ago, perhaps in hindsight as an apology for finally making his break. But by now she has put it on so often — preferring its soft caress and jewel tones to the practical weight and solid colour of the flannel — that the association is weakened. Roberta looks around the kitchen for something to do. Mail lies unopened on the kitchen counter, and there is the usual clutter about the phone nook that needs straightening. Once these are dealt with she flips through a stack of medical journals, gathers up a small afghan, and makes herself comfortable in the old brown armchair. Eventually she finds herself yawning as she reads the same paragraph over and over without absorbing any of the information, and she heads back up to her bedroom. She makes a fitful return to the lighter stages of sleep around 4:30, still wrapped in the housecoat. When morning comes she greets it with less clarity than her nighttime awakening.

At least there is a reason for last night's disturbed sleep: today is the day of reckoning. Then again, she could think of it as *a* day of reckoning, since by now she has wrangled her decision about Valerie through so many internal conversations that she is her own judge and jury. But today is undeniably different, because her choices and conduct will be formally held up and scrutinized by others. Despite her lethargy she flings back the covers and sits up; she had best not be late.

She is glad she laid out everything she was planning to wear before she went to bed last night; it saves her having to make any decisions while less than fully alert. She knows she should do her exercises but there is no time.

Roberta goes into the bathroom and picks up the hairbrush. As she leans sideways to pull it through her hair, she recalls the day she gave Valerie that treatment and how she was reeled in towards the nurses' desk the moment she exited the hospital elevator. Nadine, the ward clerk, was the first to speak. "Good morning, Dr. M. You're just in time, the nurses are finishing report. They'll want to let you know about Valerie."

"I called in yesterday, so I know some of it," Roberta said briskly.

"Paula was her nurse on days all weekend, she's probably the most up to date." Nadine nodded towards the staff room door as Paula came towards them pushing the metal cart loaded with ward charts. Lean, minimally adorned, not one to waste time or words, Paula started to speak without greeting Roberta.

"Dr. M., you're here, good. I have a lot to tell you. Valerie's developed a fistula, it made her right lung collapse and she had to have a chest tube put in Saturday night."

Roberta was accustomed to brusque manners in her workplace; she could be like that herself when the world condensed around a sick patient. It helped to focus on the problem at hand, and sometimes it was a relief not to have to make small talk.

"Yes, I know. I called here on Sunday morning and you were busy, so they put me through to Valerie herself," she replied. Roberta hadn't come in on Sunday, though. Without it being said, everyone who had ever worked with her recognized this as a change. She had been off work six months for a localized breast cancer, and although she usually she didn't talk about herself at work, in this case she let enough people know the cancer had responded well to surgery and chemo in order to quell the rumours that would inevitably circulate. Still, when she resumed work a month ago Roberta decided to divide herself differently, to exercise restraint in her dedication to work. So far that resolve had been variably expressed: sometimes she still stayed late at the clinic, but she rarely came in to the hospital on weekends any more.

"That's right, they asked me to talk to you." Paula paused in her task of sorting the charts with new orders written in them to look directly at Roberta. "Sorry I couldn't take the call, we were run off our feet yesterday. Valerie's doing well, considering, but she keeps going on about whatever it is she's got from a native healer. Something you're supposed to be giving her. You know about that?"

"Yes, she and I have discussed it several times," Roberta nodded.

"I don't know what it can do for her now. You'd think it was going to cure her, the way she gets so excited when she talks about it," Paula shook her head slightly as she resumed going through orders.

"Did someone bring it in from the reserve?" Roberta scanned the nurses' desk for the object of their discussion, not sure exactly what she was looking for.

"Yes."

"Where is it?" Roberta asked.

"The medicine man potion?" Paula allowed a slight sigh. "It's in the pharmacy fridge. We didn't know where else to put it, and we thought it might be disrespectful to dump it in the sink. You know she can't take anything orally now, and it's some sort of tea. So I guess it's useless."

"That depends. Do you know where I can get one of those IV filters?" Roberta said casually.

"In the supply room, middle shelf, to the right. What for?" Paula looked up again from the charts.

"In case she still wants it."

"You're not serious. You wouldn't give that stuff IV."

"I was hoping you would, actually. My clinic starts soon." Roberta tilted her head slightly and smiled. Paula did not return the smile. Instead she stood up and took Roberta's arm, then propelled her briskly across the hall and into the supply room. Roberta couldn't ever recall being apprehended this way in her professional life.

"Roberta Miecznikowski, you must be crazy — I could lose my license. I bet you could too. Do you even know what's in it?" Paula made Roberta face her and did not release her arm.

"That's not the point." With an effort Roberta maintained an even tone.

"What *is* the point? The woman's dying, for Pete's sake, and not very nicely. Can't we just make her comfortable and leave it at that?"

Roberta tried to assume a deflective, even authoritative, stance, and merely hear Paula's words without actually listening. But there was too much resonance between this conversation and Roberta's own ongoing ricochet of argument and rebuttal. In the week since Valerie's admission to palliative care she had mentioned taking a traditional medicine for her lung cancer every day. Paula released Roberta's arm with a *tsk* of exasperation. Roberta proceeded to rummage through the plastic baskets, looking for the device she might need. She found the filter but fumbled with the mechanism that allowed it to connect to a syringe, even though she knew it to be quite simple. Paula did not offer to help. Instead she continued, "Sam from pharmacy's not very impressed either. Good thing you weren't at report this morning to hear him. He said the policy revisions on alternative therapies haven't been approved since the last incident in the region. And that was when he thought Valerie was going to be taking it by mouth."

"Tell you what. I'll go see her, we'll talk it over, and together we'll decide what's best." Roberta had managed to unite the syringe and filter, after which she laid the unit on the edge of the shelf. She noticed that holding it emphasized the slight tremor in her hands.

"Just leave me out, okay? This is way too far gone." Paula pushed past Roberta and crossed the hall, where she became very absorbed in unlocking her medication cart.

When Roberta opened the small pharmacy fridge there was a small mason jar with Valerie's name on it on the top shelf. Roberta carried it, along with the filter and syringe, down the corridor to a door with a sign saying Palliative Care — Please

Inquire with Nurses before Entering. She knocked gently and entered the large and bland, if comfortably furnished, room. She had come to think of it as a place that concentrated transit from this world to the next, where between the dun-coloured synthetic flooring and the firmament of styrofoam ceiling tiles the end of living was honoured with extra space and comfort. Across one wall a series of plaques were aligned, acknowledging donations made either out of gratitude or in continued bargaining with eternity. The sun often brightened the corner near the head of the bed on morning rounds, as it did that day. Sitting in a recliner at the foot of the bed, her beading always nearby, Valerie's sister Martina raised a hand in greeting. But it was Valerie who spoke first.

"Hey, it's Dr. M. — how are you today? Are you late, or have I just been hoping too hard for you to get here?" Valerie's slight weight made a gentle imprint on the stiff hospital pillow, and the acute angles of her face still tallied an expression of hope. A blue and orange star quilt that Martina had brought on the day of admission was draped over the hospital-issue bedding. Now it had a few darkened spots on it that Roberta recognized as dried blood.

"I suppose I might be late, and my apologies if I am," Roberta said. "How are you doing, Valerie?"

"Great. I feel like I could run a mile now that they've put this thing in." She pointed to her right side, where thick plastic tubing passed discreetly from beneath her hospital gown and over the striped flannel sheets that were bunched around her upper body. The tube curved downward and emerged again from under the star quilt, then made its way towards an apparatus on the floor. It ended by connecting to a big black rubber stopcock in the neck of a large and ancient receiving glass. Within the graceful shape of that bottle there was, finally, an equalizing of air, fluid and pressure between Valerie's chest cavity and the outside world, a nominal reprieve of her suffering.

"I think it could be difficult to drag all this gear along," Roberta smiled as she crouched down to check the device's settings and contents. "Still, I'm glad you're feeling better. I hear from the nurses it was a tough weekend. Paula's especially concerned about you."

"Yeah, but I made it. That Paula, she's the best. Anyone would pull through with her as their nurse. The other doctor, though, he doesn't talk as much as you."

"Maybe not, but he got the job done." Roberta straightened up and held Valerie's wrist for a brief pulse check.

"You're right about that. Now, what about my stuff. Am I going to be able to take it?" Again, that spark in Valerie's expression, her radiance gone but not yet replaced by despair.

"I see everything she eats come straight out of her and into that jar," Martina said. Standing, vigilant, Martina was now so much more than just a sibling. She was her sister's longest life companion, a sentry in her last illness. "So it must be coming from her chest. I don't understand."

Roberta alternately addressed Valerie and Martina. "I know, I heard about that from the nurses too. I guess no one has had time to explain. There's a fistula inside your chest, an abnormal connection that the cancer has made. So you can't take the medicine the way you wanted to, that is, by drinking it."

"But we could still do it, right doc? You could put it in through here." She held up a frail forearm and the IV tubing moved along with her gesture.

Roberta spoke without hesitation. "As long as you're ready for the possibility of a reaction."

"What kind of reaction?" Valerie said eagerly, the way someone does when they have nothing left to lose.

"Really, I don't know. It could give you an allergic reaction, like some people have when they eat a nut or get stung by a bee." Roberta noticed she was tapping her fingers on the bed rail and willed herself to stop. "It could harm the kidneys or the liver, it could make you confused, all kinds of things. I have no experience with this kind of medicine, I told you that on Friday. You have to be ready for anything."

"You know me, I'm always ready for anything. I'd be hoop dancing if it weren't for all these tubes holding me down."

Roberta found herself reflecting on the fact that so much simpler day-to-day scenarios existed in the world of medicine, especially in her chosen field of general practice. Work that didn't involve cancerous fistulas and painful invasive procedures, requests for doubtful interventions and the whole grey and choppy sea of uncertainty in between. What if I had taken that job at the walk-in clinic, instead of coming back to this, Roberta thought. A straightforward, suburban practice, a whole community of employed, literate patients who ate fiber and knew the names of their pills.

Roberta brought herself back to the task at hand and accepted Valerie's consent to proceed. "Okay then, I brought it from the med room. Give me a minute and I'll draw it up. Good thing you have an intravenous line, even though I know you didn't want one. I hope it wasn't too uncomfortable going in."

"It took them a few stabs," Valerie admitted with a grimace. "Each time I thought about my little granddaughter and that helped. Are you going to be giving me the medicine, Dr. M.?"

"Yes. The nurses don't feel comfortable giving it, seeing as it's not one of their usual meds."

"No problem. Fire away." Again Valerie offered up the arm with the IV, while Martina frowned and at the same time nodded in agreement.

While they had been talking family members quietly materialized in the room, as they had so often in the past week. Valerie's enthusiasm generated a wave of chuckles, the softly inscrutable faces serious until the instant before laughter. Then a momentary disappearance of stricture and betrayal and two centuries of belittlement, until the usual suppression was invoked again.

The combination of syringe plus filter was almost too big for Roberta's hand, but it readily locked into a port on the IV tubing as if eager to do its job. She positioned the apparatus so that it was supported by the bedrail and applied a steady amount of pressure while looking at her watch, although in fact she had no idea how quickly she should give the medication. Usually she carefully followed medication delivery rates as they were spelled out in the hospital's IV manual. But for this product there were no such instructions, therefore she had no need to watch the second hand and she could let her mind roam as she slowly depressed the plunger. What if thoughts and words could be so cleanly issued, actions so fluidly absorbed, she wondered. Then: *Paula's right. I must be crazy.* As the amber fluid approached the bottom of the syringe's barrel, she was struck by how disarmingly simple the act has been. The combined forces of her own muscles contracting and laminar flow had taken the unknown substance into Valerie freely, without blame.

Roberta looked at Valerie and asked, "How are you feeling?"

"Great." Valerie also raised her eyes. She had been watching the solution enter her body even more intently than Roberta.

"Any sensation in your arm? Your chest?" Roberta untwisted the empty syringe and then watched to ensure that the IV fluid resumed its usual rate.

"A little burning there in my arm, that's it."

"I don't see any urine in your catheter bag, so your kidneys might not be holding up so well." Roberta knew this to be another harbinger of the inevitable, but Valerie didn't seem troubled by, or even interested in, the information. She was smiling and talking animatedly to her sister and other relatives, the mood in the room had become quietly celebratory. A few women began chanting softly and children were being allowed off of laps.

Roberta knew it was time for her to leave even though she would like to stay. Now there would be a tense hour, two, maybe more. She would have to go to her clinic, keep busy, be her own distraction, try not to over-think.

Once in her office she quickly became absorbed in the morning's patients and their problems, and was surprised to notice that it was 12:45 before she thought of Valerie again. As soon as she did, though, an anxious twirling sensation overtook any feelings of hunger. In spite of that, and the fact that there had been no calls from the nurses, she decided to cross the road and get something to eat at the hospital. On the whiteboard outside the cafeteria cabbage borscht and cheese biscuits were listed as the day's lunch special, ordinarily her favourite. Nicole in dietary saw her coming, her ladle was already on its way to serving up a bowl when Robeta waved her hand and said, "No thanks, Nicole, I'll just have toast and a yogurt today."

Before she sat down she called up to the nurses' desk and let them know she was in the building. Nadine told her there was nothing to report about Valerie. No news is good news, Roberta thought. She sat down and reminded herself not to rush while eating, and read a section of the newspaper that had been left on the dining room table. Brenda and Michael from the business office came in and joined her and they chatted about weather and vacation plans. Roberta was glad that the strain of the morning had eased. She was on her way back to clinic and almost at the hospital's main entrance when she was startled by an overhead page: "Dr. Miecznikowski, call 359 stat, Dr. Miecznikowski, 359 stat."

Roberta was closer to the ward than she was to a phone extension, so she took the stairs and walked in the direction of the nurses' desk. The corridor seemed unusually shiny, solvent-smelling and much too long. Her stride length too short, her mind too active. I am wrong, I have transgressed, forgive me.

She could see Paula walking towards her with the chart held open in both hands. She moved briskly but wasn't running, always a good sign.

"They told me you had just left the lunch room so I thought I'd meet you halfway," Paula said. "I brought the chart, that way you can give me orders and sign them straight off. Valerie got really short of breath all of a sudden. Otherwise she's been having a good day."

They entered the room, unacknowledged except for the expression of relief that briefly crossed Martina's face. It was clear that that in spite of the urgency of the overhead page, the angels were not yet assembling and Valerie was still firmly tethered to this world by her suffering. Her chest seemed to grasp at the air with every breath's excursion. There was a fearful animation in her eyes, and the tendons of her forearms were exposed with the exertion of gripping the bedrails. Nothing is going to be subtle about the final innings of this rout, Roberta thought. Sheets and star blanket and tissues were in a tangle at the foot of the bed.

Quickly Paula and Roberta went through the diagnostic possibilities. They had worked together long enough to know how to speak their thoughts aloud, helping each other stay on track in the face of a failing patient. Even so, Roberta had noticed that her memory was a sluggish beast since coming back to work from her sick leave. It needed to be prodded, and occasionally whipped, back into responsiveness. Algorithm, guideline, protocol, mnemonic, where are you when I need you?

"You gave her that traditional medicine this morning," Paula said as she manipulated the hissing oxygen mask to fit more securely against Valerie's face. Paula spoke without inflection, or even eye contact, making it difficult to detect whether the statement was an affirmation or an accusation. She told herself that this was Paula: always at, and on, the patient's side. Despite the way they disagreed first thing that morning, surely Paula understood how much Valerie wanted not just the treatment, but the hope that came with it. Roberta knew her own struggle to be no different; really they were all on the same side. Suddenly Roberta felt more confident. She was willing to be the conscience, and live with the consequence, of her actions.

"Yes. It was ready and so was she," Roberta said as she put her stethoscope to her ears.

Paula nodded and counted respirations while Roberta listened to Valerie's lungs. The bell of her stethoscope could barely make contact with Valerie's chest wall because of the way her ribs formed a ladder of bony ridges. Even so, it was impossible to miss the gurgling and muttering of substances that were where they shouldn't be, the cacophony of insatiable cells fighting for nutrients and space. By now nearly every principle of function and homeostasis had been violated by the cancer's incursions and the sophistication of its weaponry: hormone-mimicking chemicals sending confusing signals to other, still unaffected organs; contaminated passages forcing their way into clean ones; various humours and solutions mingled into a chaos that could no longer be overcome. The body was compelled to follow the cancer's directives the way a charismatic but corrupt dictator makes his people believe they want what he wants.

Paula checked the catheter bag. "Very little output."

"Yes, I noticed that this morning." Roberta unhooked the stethoscope and dangled it from her fingertips, thinking.

"No signs of anaphylaxis," Paula said.

"It's five hours since I gave that medicine this morning. I'd say we're out of the woods that way. Unless you've been shooting something up on your own just now." Roberta sent a small smile towards Valerie, who shook her head behind the sea-green of the oxygen mask. Roberta still needed to remind herself of first principles — talk to, not over, the patient — even after her own hospital experiences in the past year. It was so easy to become immersed in the details of diagnosis and therapy, and forget the ultimate purpose of comforting the ill.

"Maybe a delayed reaction?" Paula made an uneasy adjustment to the IV site, anxious to be of use.

"Maybe. Valerie, you remember we talked this morning about possible reactions to your medicine?" Valerie made a small nod over the struggling mechanics of her breathing.

"I can't say if this is a reaction or not, but you need something to help you feel better, right now. Can I give you some of our usual medicines for it?"

This time Valerie communicated by a single thumb, raised from its clasp of the bedrail.

"Let's see if we can mobilize some of this fluid, hopefully your kidneys have enough left in them to do that. And we'll open up the airways with a medication through that mask you're wearing."

Roberta gave the orders to Paula, who was immediately activated by her purpose. Quickly the neck of a vial was broken and medications were given, to Paula's relief as much as the patient's. The mist from the nebulizer drifted upward like incense, and within a few minutes Valerie's upper body relaxed. Roberta continued to stand at the bedside and consider her next step when the hospital chart, opened to the order sheet, was thrust in the direction of her right hand.

"Can you write down those orders now, and I'll sign them off straight away?" Paula asked. Once again, the indifference of her tone was at odds with the implication of her words. The busy work of charting and completing verbal orders, co-signing and documenting, was usually left for after the patient had settled.

"You don't trust me?" Roberta asked. The usual tone of their exchange had been altered by something other than the severity of their patient's condition.

"And did you make a note in the chart of what you did this morning?" Paula's question had the same anxious quality as her earlier aimless fiddling.

"Of course I did." Roberta's charting has never been questioned, in fact she had always made a point of defying the illegible and insufficient scrawl that was the professional stereotype.

"And I renewed her morphine order while I was at it, so go ahead and give her that too." Roberta balanced the chart on the bedrail and did her best to write on the order sheet. She passed the binder back to Paula who put her initials alongside Roberta's writing without looking up.

"She looks like she's coming around now," Roberta said after a few more minutes of observation. "I'll take the chart back to the desk and finish with it, if you'd like. Then I better get back to clinic. Call me if anything changes."

*   *   *

Three weeks later, Roberta had to leave a patient in her examining room to take a call from the CEO's administrative assistant. Cecilia used to be in medical records at their hospital; she and Roberta exchanged pleasantries before Cecilia's tone dropped slightly. Roberta was silent through the carefully-worded delivery. "The meeting's next Wednesday," Cecilia said. "The provincial coordinator is coming to it for support, and learning. We've already talked to your receptionist and she's rescheduling your patients for you."

"Really?" said Roberta. That last comment from Cecilia seemed like one boundary too far. "And what if I declined to attend?"

"They're calling it a critical incident, Dr. M," Cecilia continued, sticking to her script. "Not that anyone's being blamed, but we're obliged to investigate once it's been reported."

"Obliged by whom?"

It didn't matter, of course. Power comes in many forms, in this case a manifesto within an algorithm upon a legal-sized flow sheet. It arrived with the inter-office mail the next day, and Roberta spent a while considering the complicated series of arrows, pastel-coloured geometric figures and bifurcating decision points. Apparently they were at the juncture marked Investigative Phase.

Professionally, Roberta could understand the structure, substance and sense of what had replaced not just rumour and accusation, but also the possibility of covering up someone else's mistake. Viscerally, she experienced a cold sway of nausea just looking at the diagram and its accompanying cover letter, and felt not unlike days three to nine of her chemo cycle last year. Valerie wanted it, Roberta gave it, it shouldn't have been given, is what it seemed to come down to. A foregone conclusion despite the health region's appearance of adhering to protocol.

Now it is the day of the meeting, and Roberta wonders yet again: who instigated this? Not Paula, surely she's not a squealer. But no one is a squealer now. Whistle blower, they call it.

If half of life is showing up, the other half must consist of not making excuses, with a bit left over for out-dressing your opponent, Roberta thinks as she carefully pulls on her tights. In the month since Valerie died, Roberta has spent many nights besides this last one, sitting up in her armchair, trying to read the most tedious and sleep-inducing material she can find but often unable to stop ruminating. After her initial thoughts of boycotting the meeting, certain at first that her medical association would back her up, gradually she accepted the fact that she might be left unsupported. And besides, what was she avoiding? If she did what she thought was right, she should be able to defend it. She will attend, she will do her best to explain but she will not make a single excuse — not for herself, not for her actions, certainly not for the inadequacy of every possible medical intervention in the face of erosive death. For that there is no excuse. She will wear her favourite burgundy silk shirt-dress.

The representative from the province has clearly thought like Roberta in dressing for the meeting, or perhaps he never thinks otherwise. He enters the boardroom tidy and assured, in a tan cable-knit vest beneath a tweed jacket. His camel brown pants and leather brogues suit him equally as well as the jargon he has acquired for this position. Once they are all assembled and introduced around the conference-room table — nurse manager, hospital administrator, pharmacist and Roberta — he begins to summarize the case and the process. Roberta tries to remain silent, but when he starts to outline how medical interventions alter the natural course of disease and outcomes, sometimes to the patient's detriment, Roberta cannot hold back.

"I thought it had been established by this time that doctors are not stand-ins for God," she says. Sarcasm or satire? Criticism or caricature? This could hurt her more than help her, and she knows it.

"Of course, all of us are only human, including physicians," the coordinator affirms.

"Then how do you know what I did caused her harm?" Roberta inquires.

"We don't know that, and that's why we're here. To learn and to share."

"She was about to die of her cancer, that was well documented in the chart. We wouldn't be going through this if no one thought I killed her. If it was clear to you, or anyone else here, that she was terminal and in her last few days of life, and nothing was done to alter that, there wouldn't be any need for this process."

"Yes, well that's what we're here to find out about, aren't we." He speaks in a confident tone, strengthened by his own convictions and backed by generous public funding. Roberta senses her own words and actions to be trivial in comparison. Her vocal range, versus his. It wasn't meant to come to this, she had meant to help. She might have wanted the same from her own doctor, had she been in Valerie's place. Still, she knows she doesn't go easy on herself, or on anyone else. She peels at her hangnails the same way her mind peels away at the insufficient platitudes that layer the possibility of truth. Then, seeing what remains, naked and diminished, painful and bloodied, no wonder she is dismayed. An implacable integrity is never satisfied. Now she is the one who stands accused and aware, caught and condemned by forces even more righteous than her own, if that is possible.

In the end, does it matter who told what to whom, how many players saw, knew, divulged or didn't? Probably not. Much like dying, the administrative process becomes self-propelled after a while, and nothing is likely to change its course. Medicine has always moved forward the way blocks of cathedral stone and increments of scientific knowledge have advanced civilization for all time: slowly, often misdirected at the outset, achievements brought about through some form of enslavement or suffering. Decisions need to be made and the world has little patience for the doubtful. To be of two minds is to halve one's capacity for action: better to take a wrong course confidently than stand at a crossroads and achieve nothing. Roberta has little to say for the remainder of the meeting; the rest of the participants are also largely silent. They finish early and there are handshakes all around.

*   *   *

A week after Valerie received her treatment, Roberta awoke to a phone call from the nurse on nights. The voice on the line was more declarative than inquiring: "We need you to come and complete the death certificate on Valerie so we can release the body," was all he said. Roberta forgot to ask his name; staff turnover had made it difficult for her to identify nurses by their voices since she had come back to work. She hurried through breakfast and managed to catch an earlier bus than usual.

With so many people in the room Roberta felt uncomfortable being the focus of attention. As quickly as possible she performed the ritual to verify that breath and heart had ceased to function. To affirm that the suffering of the dying was over, and the suffering of those left behind could now truly begin. Roberta hugged Martina awkwardly; it seemed like a trivial gesture alongside the palpable sadness all around. Martina sat down and resumed massaging Valerie's stilled hand. Her upper body pulsed back and forth to the soft rhythmic sounds from a far corner of the room.

Roberta made a discreet exit and walked slowly back to the nurses' station, giving her tears a chance to subside before she reached her destination. A blank death certificate was clipped to the front of Valerie's chart. Robert began to carefully fill in the required information, describing both immediate and antecedent causes of death in reverse chronologic order. She had always found it difficult, in the limited space on the form, to fully account for the combination of circumstances, microbe or mutation, bad habit or bad luck, whatever it was that brought the deceased to this juncture. The form contained no space for any reflection on endurance, resilience, regret, rage.

"Hi, Dr. M.," Paula said as she sat down beside Roberta.

"Hey Paula. How are you?" Roberta hoped she was past the visible stage of crying.

"Okay, I guess. Sad to see her go. Such a spirit," Paula looked down as she spoke and Roberta noticed that her eyelashes were wet. In this death more than usual there was also the dissipating spirit to account for: immeasurable, transcendent, undeniable if impossible to document.

"There aren't many like her," Roberta agreed.

"They said in report she went really fast at the end, she just closed her eyes after her last dose of morphine and that was it."

"Most cases with a fistula like that don't last more than a day or two. An hour or two if there's aspiration," Roberta kept her own eyes down as she printed her name and address beside her signature.

"I hope we did everything we could. I think we tried."

"Thanks, Paula, for everything. You were good to her." Roberta didn't want to cry again so she looked over the completed certificate. Her mind found the fragile shape of Valerie's face, as it had so often during the past week. Just yesterday Valerie had still been able to perceive the stimulus of life as long as it was at close range, and had given Roberta's hand a slight but sentient squeeze. Now it seemed to Roberta like she was having a parlay with an apparition, right here at the nurses' desk, because she suddenly felt a hand around her own. It was Paula, and this time Roberta felt the strength come in her direction from the other side of the clasp.

LAST RESORT

Seated at the marble-topped hotel room desk, Sonia tries to write. The few square inches of space on her postcards should be easy to fill with the buoyant and happy language of resort travel: the beauty of the beach, the wonder of the weather. Buoyant, like the brightly-coloured buoys nodding on the depth-deceiving surface of the ocean. Happy, the way she would like to feel about being here with her family, surrounded by warmth and sun in February. About seeing her brother Marcel for the first time in eight years. She stares out the window at the fading bird of paradise flowers in the hotel courtyard. The morning light shifts and deflects its way through palm fringes and into the sitting area of her room. It illuminates her hand as it remains suspended above the surface of the desk.

A paralytic began to seep inwards two days ago, during the drive from the airport to the resort. It took them past clustered homes made of corrugated steel and found plywood that were overlooked by ochre- and papaya-hued villas, their walled perimeters topped by razor wire and protruding shard glass. In between those extremes, the driver navigated precarious washed-out sections of road still under repair from last year's hurricane. Sonia's husband, Ross, and their two children,

Nathalie and Alex, were able to thrive on the joy they had accumulated in anticipation of this trip, and were charmed by everything they saw. For them, the experience was so novel it was beyond the range of question or doubt. They rejoiced in the seeming lawlessness of the traffic, and waved as they narrowly passed labouring chicken buses. Even Nathalie was able to squeal gleefully as they dodged their way through roundabouts. "Whoa, look at that, Dad!" Alex exclaimed more than once as a pickup truck marked POLICIA passed, with three or four uniformed men and their substantial firearms draped about its open box.

During the drive Sonia kept her reactions to herself, although she almost gasped when she saw a couple with a baby embedded between them skim by on a motorbike. Finally, a set of iron gates parted to reveal their resort. The gentle curve of the cobblestone driveway calmly refuted the chaos and inequity they had just negotiated. Sonia made the smile on her face stick while they were still on the bus, then found reason to walk alone to the edge of the parking lot as their bags were being unloaded. Their resort topped a rise of land that descended on its eastward side to the ocean. Looking west, she could see the city's dirty exhalations had coalesced with the haze of the evening sky to make the sun a floating tangerine disc.

Now that it is their third day at the resort they have established a kind of rhythm that allows Sonia an hour alone in the room before the others return from their breakfast. She picks up one of the postcards and turns it over to look at its picture side. If she angles it a certain way, the tranquil image disappears in the sun's glaring reflection. She bought the postcards on her way to the dining hall last night, lingering over the choices, hoping the evening meal would proceed peacefully. But her brother Marcel was just as unlovely on their second night as he had been the first. Following an afternoon in the bar he spoke loudly to the staff and demanded a hamburger when their table was invited to the buffet. While they were eating he needled

Ross with questions about money and taxes. Alex, nine and infatuated with his recently revealed uncle, already understood when he should focus on his dinner. Late in the meal, Marcel became more muted and shifted his gaze to the Mayan centerpiece. Eventually he reached for it with a hand ambivalent to its purpose. By the time it dropped he had upset everything, and everyone, even more. Sonia had flinched, and she could see from his face that even Ross acknowledged defeat. Nathalie had been slowly making her way through the few things she found appealing; Alex had left his salad to last but could have been persuaded to eat it, especially if Marcel had eaten his at the same time. Now everyone's appetite was over, and when Sonia stood up the children were quick to follow. Still, Ross did his best to intervene with his brother-in-law. "Marcel, why don't you get yourself to bed? Here, I'll take you, make sure you don't get lost."

Sonia sees all this in the space between her pen and the pile of postcards. A small fasciculation under her eye has started again. She first noticed its tiny flicker on awakening this morning. Although she hadn't meant to, she disturbed Ross slightly when she got out of bed. He reached for her but she moved quickly enough to get past his grasp, and she put a pillow in the place that her body had warmed. When she did that a tiny worry doll left by the evening turn-down service fell onto the sheet. The bits of fabric and the eyes in asymmetric stitches recalled her mother's handmade toys. She picked it up and put it on her bedside table, behind the lamp so she didn't have to see it. Ross didn't fully awaken, and after she'd dressed she saw his arm around the pillow.

Now it is eight forty-five and soon they will be coming back to the room. She taps her pen on the table, and traces shapes among the marble's pocks and veins. Focusing on it, she can appreciate how nature turns randomness into beauty. But like the children at supper last night, she can't be distracted. Yesterday evening merges with another scene, and she sees her father seated at the head of the big wooden table. His always-infected finger festers in its salt-water broth on one side, while his left hand clasps a mug of wine that is never allowed to be empty. From her place on his left Sonia's four-year-old legs wrap around those of her chair, as a pile of something white that she cannot bring herself to eat cools on her plate. She imagines her stomach contains a solid mass of black bugs that does not allow further entry. The smell of her father's drinking breath diffuses towards her and mingles with, then becomes, the smell of supper. He sits there unshaven, absorbed in the mystery of the tableware, beyond the animated stage of drunkenness. Suddenly it all comes hurtling towards her in a kind of noisesome cluster: rage, projectile force, the ferocious thing that stands for love, and his voice breaks as he shouts: "What kind of kid doesn't eat everything that's put in front of them?" It sends her hurtling from her chair and onto a tiny snap in her wrist. While she is sprawled on the floor she is aware that there is something unfamiliar about her left arm, and when she sits up she needs to cradle it with her right one like a doll. Marcel is instantly at her side. He picks up her chair and helps her hold the arm, then positions himself between their father and the remainder of her limbs. He stares down the enemy, this unholy marriage of neglect and nourishment, arranged nightly to offset so many other vacancies.

Whenever she is reminded that she came from such a place, Sonia doesn't deserve, can't stand, won't allow herself to be touched. So this morning she moved away just as Ross made his still-sleeping turn towards her. In the last few days she has often been startled awake by a dream — this morning it was a wasp stinging her between the shoulder blades, palpable. She had to get up to shake herself free of it, and once up she might as well get dressed. She is the first one at breakfast, not just from her family but among nearly all the guests at the resort. It gives her a chance to try and speak to the waiters in Spanish without the children around to tease. "*Numero de habitaçion ciento viente*

143

cinco," she says carefully as she signs her bill, certain that the waiters like her better for at least trying.

Nine o'clock, the hour when the breeze starts to move off the ocean. At any moment the stiff spears of the yucca plants, charming in their spiky homeliness, will begin their anxious little sway. In the courtyard the gardeners make their patient ministrations before it gets too hot. The invisible bird that cried out through the early part of the morning has quietened with the mounting heat and sun. Green parrots take up their chant; every morning they have a boisterous reunion with endless gossip and squabbling in the tops of the palms. Can she not just write about that? But the bit of blank space on the postcards before her can neither ignore nor convey the space within, so she pushes them away and lays down her pen.

Behind her is the sound of a card in the lock, then footsteps running. Small hands cover her eyes as people rustle into the room.

"Guess who I am!"

"A mako shark?" Sonia tries to recall details of the last documentary she and Alex watched.

"Nope, way bigger."

"A great white?"

"No, bigger."

"Okay, how about a whale shark?"

"That's right!"

"Oh no, don't eat me up!"

"C'mon Mom, you know whale sharks are filter feeders. They only eat plankton," Alex says impatiently.

"How could I forget? Good thing you're along as shark guide and advisor."

"Am I going to get to see a shark?" Alex climbs aboard the side of her chair and wraps his arms tightly around her torso. It is much more difficult to dodge the affections of a nine-year-old boy than those of a sleepy spouse. Alex already smells of sun, and his skin has the geography of a boy's life: a fine overlay of grit, occasionally interrupted by scabs and calluses. "Now I'm a ball python and I'm going to squeeze you to death."

"It sure feels like it. Was Uncle Marcel at breakfast?" She wants so much not to ask, but she needs to know.

"No, but I think I might have seen him coming down the hall," Ross says as he gropes for his glasses and spreads a newspaper out on the bed. "Don't worry, I'll deal with him." Sonia wants the pulse of guilt and gratitude that she feels to flow noticeably in his direction and be acknowledged, to make amends for her distance, but Ross is reading the paper and doesn't look at her.

Nathalie appears at her other side and kisses the top of Sonia's head in a way that seems odd and tender. At thirteen she is about to become either a moody tormentor or a merciless rival. "What are we doing today, *maman*? Did you finish writing your postcards?"

"I don't know yet, Nathalie. And no, I didn't even start my postcards. I couldn't think of what to say," Sonia admits.

"What do you mean? That's crazy — you don't really say anything on a postcard. I just messaged my friends on the hotel computer." Nathalie turns so that she now projects toward her father as well. "Hey, I saw a sign, they're teaching how to do the beading like we saw. And body art, hennas and stuff. I want to do that."

"I want to go scuba diving!" Alex manages to generate a pumping action while still hanging partly from the chair and partly from Sonia.

"Careful there, now I think you've been transformed into some kind of monkey. How was breakfast?" Sonia turns herself from side to side as she speaks, to include both of her children.

"I had thirds!" Alex pulls up his T-shirt as proof.

Nathalie frowns slightly. "My stomach hurt. I couldn't eat anything except the fruit, so I just had that."

Sonia slips her arm around Nathalie's waist. "My little grand-mother, are you worrying again?" Nathalie shrugs and pulls away. Sonia has been close to telling her daughter, in recent months, about how she herself felt the blackness in her stomach when she was young and often found it hard to eat. She wants to share that with her, but whenever she tries there is a tightening in her throat and she stops.

Sonia rotates in her chair away from Nathalie and speaks in Ross's direction. "What does Dad want to do, besides read his paper?"

Marcel appears at the door but remains at its threshold. "Hey, there's a guy giving para-sailing rides. Who's gonna come with me? I always wanted to fly."

"C'mon in Marcel, we're just getting organized. I want to do a bus tour of the old city," Ross says without actually looking up.

Marcel emits an odorous thread to last night as he makes his way in. His voice is still half an octave higher than usual. He sits down on Ross's paper.

The children shift towards the desk and align themselves with their mother. Sonia has a sense that Nathalie is making some kind of sound, though there is nothing to hear. Alex makes himself straight as a soldier on inspection, capable of watching a hero fallen face-down.

"I'd be happiest just staying here, doing some reading on the beach," Sonia says, grounding herself in a mantra of neutrality.

"Looks like it's everyone for themselves, then, for today," Ross says as he lifts his eyes, their benevolence magnified by his reading glasses. He smiles as he scans the room and completely conceals what Sonia knows to be his real desire: to put the *Por Favor Non Molester* sign on the door, and for them to have the room, and each other, to themselves for the day. To be her pursuer, as she had once loved him to be.

"So I get to go scuba diving?" Alex's enthusiasm prevails and he lunges toward the bed then climbs on his uncle's shoulders.

"Actually, snorkeling is the first step, and I saw that on the activity list," Ross replies genially. "I'll get you signed up, then Marcel and I will get on our way."

"Cool! I'm going to get my bathing suit on, 'kay, Dad?" Alex nimbly clambers down and heads for the adjoining door.

"You already have it on," Nathalie points out. "You slept in it."

"Did not!" Alex yells.

"You did."

"Just 'cause I don't change my clothes three times a day." Alex pauses at the door to make a face at his sister, then disappears.

Now everyone except Sonia is moving. The last one out, Ross pauses. He and Sonia are both in a half-turned stance, almost facing each other. "Are you sure you don't want to do that bus tour with us?" he inquires.

"No, now that I'm here I'd much rather stay put."

"Okay, I'll do it with Marcel, then. Keep him from killing himself."

"Thank you, dear."

"I'll give him a bit of a talking-to about the drinking. That ought to help." He winks at her and is gone.

Ross is such a good man that it is easy to forgive his magical thinking. Sonia will eventually have to pull on the cords, haul the scenery back up and out of sight, and make reality their backdrop again, because it is the only thing she knows solid enough to stand on.

Still, why reject him? Without wanting to think about it, she can tell where the weight of his arm would have landed, had she not moved away this morning. There, on the curve just below her waist, towards her back, where she used to love to be stroked.

Alone in the room, Sonia packs her shoulder bag and reflects that if she has just turned forty-three, then Marcel will soon be forty-eight. In the years since she last saw him, he has taken to shaving his head close. It reminds her of the crew cut he would always get at the beginning of summer as a child, the way the short hair would emphasize the strength of his cheekbones and the blackness of his eyes. They were the youngest of nine. All their older siblings had either run, or been taken, away. She and Marcel lived a life parallel to that of their parents. The day Sonia's arm broke their mother was out looking for pain pills; it was two more days before she came home.

But Sonia didn't mind because she had Marcel, who could cut the mouldy bits off the bread and make her a mustard sandwich when the black bugs stopped their swarming and a space opened up in her stomach. Sonia couldn't use her left arm at all so he made her a sling from a scarf he found in their mother's drawer. The first night, while their father snored on the couch, Marcel told her a story about a man and his horse and the ground they covered and the woman the horse turned into. Late the next morning their father roused himself enough to stamp about and swear, but by then Marcel had found Sonia a place in a closet and he told their father she was gone for a sleepover at Auntie Di's. Eventually he got shaky and left them in peace, and for the rest of their time alone Marcel made Sonia feel safe because he knew everything: where to put the buckets and basins when it rained and the ceiling leaked, how to write a note from their mother to say Sonia wouldn't be at preschool, what poison ivy looked like when they went outside for a picnic with crackers and cups of water and a few of their homemade toys. Usually the toys, with their primitive features and lumpy bodies, never left the house, but everyone else was at school that day so there was no one to see. Only old Auntie Rose next door noticed them, and when she did she stomped off in search of their mother.

The first thing their mother said when she got home was "Who's hungry?" When she saw the scarf around Sonia's neck and arm she said "What's wrong with Sonia?" They had beans on toast before they went to the hospital because by then Sonia's stomach was empty enough to eat.

"The chair tipped," their mother told the nurse, who yawned right at them and said their health cards needed updating. Twice more the doctor asked Sonia what had happened, after she'd told him the first time. Then he let them see the fracture on the bluey black films. Inside the itchy skin of her cast, Sonia wondered if the bones would cross over like the ones she's seen on a bleach bottle.

*   *   *

Sonia hopes she has packed everything she needs for her day on the beach, and that she can be completely undisturbed. She feels her face relax as she makes her exit through the French doors of the dining room and gazes out toward the sea. A coral-coloured stone wall borders the path as it curves its way downward to the beach. Half way along a woman is seated on the edge of the low wall. Her hair is a sandy blonde that must have come from a bottle, but it suits her despite the lines around her mouth and the eyes that belong to an age well in advance of the hair colour. Surrounded by the crimson throats of hibiscus flowers, she is quite still except for the wind luffing her loose white blouse and generous skirt. Contrary to her desire to be alone, Sonia slows her pace as she approaches the bend in the wall where the woman is seated.

"Be sure to get an umbrella. The sun is hard on us Canadians," the woman says before Sonia can decide if she should utter a greeting.

Sonia smiles. "How do you know I'm Canadian?"

"Just about everyone here is. No doubt we're a good target for their marketing," the woman smiles back.

"Well, you're not wrong to be giving me advice, seeing as it's my first time doing this kind of trip. You?"

"My second. I love winter but I don't mind leaving it behind for a while. My name is Vera," the woman holds out her hand with graceful confidence.

"Sonia," she replies.

"Sonia. That's a beautiful name. French?"

"My father was French. My mother was Ojibway-Cree."

"That's a story, and a history," Vera nods.

"You're right about that." Usually Sonia never says anything about her origins, even if asked about the long straight ebony of her hair. Somehow this woman is both absorptive and reflective in her soft flowing sail of an outfit. Still, Sonia feels she has revealed enough and is ready to continue towards the beach when Vera says, "I died on this day last year."

"Pardon?"

"Mmm-hmm. I noticed the date on the calendar at the front desk this morning. I was having day surgery. The anaesthetist said it must have been a reaction to one of the drugs."

"What happened?" Sonia asks, suddenly transfixed.

"My heart stopped. Just like that, it didn't pump any more."

"Do you remember anything?"

"Not really. I was counting backwards for the anaesthetist. The next thing I remember, I was trying to pull the breathing tube out and they were telling me not to."

"But you were actually dead for a while?" Sonia sits down beside her and lowers her shoulder bag.

"Yes, they had to shock me and pump on my chest and do all those things like you see on a TV show to bring me back." As she speaks Vera makes a stroking motion along the grain of her skirt, smoothing the already loosely draped surface over her right knee. Sonia finds herself mirroring this gesture along the length of her sarong. She pictures her own life ending and restarting, and wonders what if any difference it would make.

"Do you do anything differently now?" Sonia asks.

Vera pauses in her stroking. "This trip, actually, although it hasn't worked out the way we'd planned. And we made an agreement, my husband and I, that when the time comes for one of us to go, the other is allowed to go too."

Sonia is confused, but not for long. "You mean a suicide pact?"

"If you want you can call it that," Vera shrugged. "We aren't telling anyone because of course the family would never stand for it. I'll never see you again so I can tell you. It's sort of a relief to let someone know."

"How do you know I won't report this when we get back?" Sonia blurts, instantly sorry to sound like she would betray Vera.

"Who would you tell? And what would anyone do?" Vera just smiles. She leans back slightly on the stone wall, and embraces her own knee to keep her balance in that position. "Besides, you've got far too many problems of your own. I've been noticing you, this is supposed to be a break and it's obvious that it's not. You'll forget all about me and my husband and whatever goes on between us before you even get to the beach."

This proximity of awareness and insight, so lacking in judgment, is surprisingly easy to accept. Like Vera, Sonia is relieved to know that someone knows. The woman's voice is calm and her words are slightly clipped at the end, as if a long-forgotten language was her mother tongue but its memory still makes an imprint on her inflection. Vera continues, "So we planned this trip, paid for it and then two weeks ago my husband had a small stroke and the doctor said he couldn't go."

"You came alone then?"

"No, I'm not that adventurous," Vera shakes her head. "But there were so many rules — we couldn't cancel, or be refunded, and no changing dates either. Finally they agreed to let me bring my sister instead."

"That's good."

"Well, we haven't always gotten along, over the years. But I guess it's a test of whether I learned anything in coming back to life," Vera replies.

"Maybe." Sonia smiles. "It's family, after all."

Vera laughs. "You're right, maybe. There's what we resolve to do, and there's what we actually do."

Sonia nods and stands up. They part, after another brief clasping of hands. Sonia removes her sandals when she reaches the end of the paving stones. She feels a bit buoyant, after all.

*   *   *

The hall adjoining the dining room is oval-shaped, and ringed by small rectangular windows set into deep valences high in the vaulted ceiling. Like the soothing breeze off the beach, they moderate the strength of the equatorial sun so that it always seems to be just the right temperature in the hall. Beyond the French doors of the dining room, Sonia sees that a peach-coloured aurora is suspended along their stretch of horizon. After just a week, she is surprised at the strength of her own colonial attachment to the place. The temptation to stay and never leave is undeniable.

It is the migratory hour between drink time and supper time, when guests drift through the hall towards the dining room and candelabras everywhere come to life. They flicker gently with the air currents, in synchrony with a scattering of half-melted pillar candles. A burrito table begins the evening meal with an abundance of colourful and sometimes enigmatic choice of fillings. Manolo, who also presided over the morning omelet station, gently corrects Sonia's Spanish as she makes her choices. Next to him are platters of steaks, their crimson juices pooling to the edge of their dishes. Sonia finds the tang of chimichurri sauce especially enticing. The top note to her ardent and aroused senses, though, is seasmell, coming in through the fully opened French doors along the eastern wall of the dining room.

Ross, Nathalie and Alex have spent the day out on a boat and Sonia smiles at their equally sunburned noses when she turns to check for them in the lineup behind her. She gathers the children near and guides them through the tables of food, coaxing Nathalie towards steamy chafing dishes in hopes that she will find something agreeable. Alex is too tired to speak and passively allows his mother to load up his plate. He has seen his shark. After a period of dignified bartering with the boat operator, he purchased a tooth from a great white; he can go home happy.

"This is our last supper, Mommy," Alex observes with a sigh, and falls silent again.

They settle themselves at a table and Ross begins a desultory exchange with the couple already seated there, when a popping sound comes through one of the open French doors. So precise, and so belonging to some other setting, that there is only a brief pause in conversation at the table. Until the men and their guns enter the room. Even then, Sonia's first thought is that they are being treated to an impromptu performance.

"Are those real, Mommy?" Nathalie's hand grasps her forearm, making Sonia's forkful of salad fall.

The men shout in Spanish, or perhaps it is Mayan, how would she know, and fan around the edge of the room. They start to pull the doors shut and round up the staff centrally. One diner makes a break for a still-open door. A breach of sound painful to all senses causes the fleeing man to dive forward, then lie flat on the patio outside. Sonia can neither look nor localize, but from somewhere in the room there is a distinct sound of vomiting.

With one gun carried in both hands, and another slung across his back, a tall man makes the commands of his stocky leader understood. "All you rest, lady and gentleman, you will be safe if you be quiet and cooperate," he shouts.

"Where's Uncle Marcel?" Alex's voice, despite its still-unchanged timbre, makes a surprising projection into the room.

"Hey there, my little hammerhead, I'm right here. It'll all be okay." They see Marcel with the twitching group of staff in the center of the room.

"*Callate!* Quiet!" The tall man's scanning eyes cannot identify the speakers, but he achieves his goal with a single arc of his gun. "All men, this way," he makes a further gesture with the gun's muzzle end.

Sonia to Ross, Ross to Sonia: a glance for a half of a half of a second, a movement of her hand, and then the gesture is gone with him. Sonia squeezes herself into stillness to keep herself from running after him. She is helped by her children who hold onto her arms, everyone pressing themselves to a point beyond pain. That same sense of noiseless sound coming from Nathalie is now near a shriek. Sonia is aware of sweat in every intimate place while at the same time her mouth is parched and frozen.

"Him too." A gun in Alex's direction.

"He's a child." Sonia speaks as though through a dry and fibrous substance. It is possible she only mouthed the words.

The leader looks at the taller lean man. A brief exchange between them ends with a burst of laughter. Seeing another arc of the gun, Alex makes his own decision and moves away before Sonia can reach for him.

The group of staff is being moved in a different direction, and once again Marcel's voice defies the previous directives. "I'm with them." He points to the group of men and boys being corralled through the doorway to an adjacent room. They have their hands on their heads and are bumping together like animals afraid of their handlers.

"Vamos." A gun gesture makes him part of the herd.

All Sonia can think is how glad she is that Vera seems not to be here in the room. How can she care about a stranger in such a situation? But all that is sane and good and honourable has been stripped from her consciousness. Whatever is meant to happen to her husband, her brother, her boy occupies an inaccessible part of her mind, surrounded by a wall of fear that bristles with regret. She had wanted a trip that would bring together the people she loved most. Could they please just start over and try again? By now she and Nathalie are seated on the same chair, completely wrapped around each other. She would rather they be shot right through than let go.

But they are not allowed to remain in that position long. Soon all the girls and women sit together on the floor, after having been made to push several tables aside. Their captors lounge and eat from the buffet, laugh and occasionally point at the women. The staff have left the room, the candles are sputtering out and the smell of fear would be even more pungent except that it is the smell of themselves. Nathalie and Sonia are still entwined, but more loosely now. A woman on Sonia's right utters occasional sniffled sobs. Her thigh is pressed against Sonia's through the forced closeness of the group, but Sonia does not feel the least bit close to anyone: she senses herself alone in a time of resolve.

"Mommy, why are they doing this to us?" Nathalie whispers into Sonia's neck.

"They want money, I imagine," she replies, her own voice barely a whisper. "We're probably hostages."

"But why us?"

"It's not us, really, they're desperate and we happen to be in the line of fire."

"Don't say that!" Nathalie pulls her head away.

"Sorry, I mean they're desperate for money, maybe to get rid of a load of drugs, I don't know. This place is the target. We just happen to be here," Sonia strokes the side of her daughter's head.

"But it's us, and it's Alex, and Daddy, and Uncle Marcel, and..." Sonia can feel Nathalie try to cover her knees with the sunflower print dress she chose for their last evening, to try and shield every surface of herself from this suddenly malicious world. Sonia begins a small rocking motion to soothe and distract.

"We told you be quiet!" The stamping of cracked and unlaced leather boots emphasizes their captor's dissatisfaction. A masked man comes from the adjacent room where the men have gone and walks toward the group of women.

"Come with me." Sonia cannot mistake the signal, she is only glad that it is a finger, not a gun, pointing at her, or the resolve might disappear.

Sonia transfers Nathalie limb by limb to the sniffling woman so that she can be nudge-marched towards the door the men went through. As soon as she enters their room she knows why she is there. Marcel is in the grasp of another masked man. "Hey, Sonia," he says as soon as their eyes meet. The scattered droplets of blood on the floor are not immediately apparent on its inlaid stone pattern. The tall man with the emphatic gun points it at Marcel as he addresses Sonia.

"I say you tourists not know what hunger is, he say he know."

"Sorry, sis, you know how I am." A jab in Marcel's side makes him huff slightly. An abraded area on one side of his face is clotting into a scab but he manages a grin with the unhurt portion.

"So, tell. What you know of hunger." The tall translator peers keenly at Sonia.

Sonia's mind is a rapture of not wanting to understand what is laid out before her, at the same time needing to register that Alex and Ross are here, alive, obedient, in the center of their group.

"We grew up on a reserve," she says, her voice flat. "It's not like the rest of Canada. Our mother was indigenous, Ojibway-Cree, we say Anishinaabe. She had nine of us. Sometimes we were hungry, yes."

The men guarding the women watch from the doorway. Sonia counts only five men holding them ransom, somehow at first it had seemed like so many more. She is aware of a chanting, throbbing sound. She can't tell who it is for or where it comes from, whether it is a good thing or a bad thing. It is only with the appearance of the black bugs at all the doors, swarming, human-sized and at first not at all reassuring, that she realizes it is Marcel, singing the way he used to when he was a drummer at pow-wows. As he launches himself away from the man holding him, she can see it is the flight that he's always wanted to take.

*   *   *

At the front desk Sonia makes one last attempt. The clerks are standing instead of sitting in their wingback chairs the way they usually do when graciously conversing with guests.

"*Pardone*, I wonder, have all the guests been accounted for?" she asks.

One clerk is twisting a lock of hair around her forefinger; she looks at her colleague before she answers. "You are the one who lost a brother, *si*?"

"Yes, that's me. I'm wondering about one of the other guests, if she's alright."

"The police just gave us full verification. Besides your brother, there was one guest killed on the patio, and two of our hotel guards were shot at the gate," the clerk replies.

"*Los sientos*, I'm sorry, this is so hard for everyone," Sonia says quietly. "But can you check your list for a woman named Vera? I only know her first name, but I wanted to make sure she was okay, and say goodbye to her. I didn't see her in the dining room last night."

The two young women seem glad to have something to do. Together they hold up the computer printout and confer in Spanish, too quickly for Sonia to follow. Sonia sees that when they get to the bottom, they return to a higher point and go through the list again before they meet her eyes. The young women both shake their heads.

Sonia is not ready to give up. "We only exchanged first names. She was tall," Sonia holds her hand above her own head, "and she had light brownish blonde hair. She was older than me and she had a beautiful smile."

Sonia searches for some other distinguishing feature when a third clerk, hovering in and out of a side room, speaks. It is Samantha from Illinois, who came for a month to learn Spanish and has stayed on for two years. Sonia remembers speaking to her the first day.

"You're talking about Vera, the tall woman, right?" Samantha ventures.

"Yes. You know who I mean?"

"I do. We first met a few years ago, when she got married. I was fifteen and here on vacation with my family, she and I ended up talking quite a bit. It was her first trip with her new husband, and my parents' last trip together, 'cause they weren't getting along very well. I actually asked her why people bother to get married right on her wedding day — can you believe it? Only a fifteen year old would do that." Samantha is able to smile slightly at the memory.

"Can you help me find her? I haven't seen her since, since... the day I met her," Sonia entreats. "I want to know if she's okay."

"Oh, she's not here now," Samantha says with assurance. "She got a call from home and had to go back. Thursday, I think. Something urgent about her husband. I didn't even get to say goodbye."

"I wish I'd had a chance to talk to her again." It takes an effort but Sonia manages to keep her voice even. Her face must register her dismay, though, because now all three clerks look as though they might cry.

"I know what you mean," Samantha's voice is now much less steady. "I always felt like she'd known me and loved me all my life. I'm sorry."

Carefully Sonia turns away. There is a sense over her entire body that a layer of crackling glaze has been applied, and is about to diffuse into a topography of fissures. She directs herself through the lobby, when suddenly before her are Ross and Alex, a little further away Nathalie. And though they have only two arms each, between them it feels like enough to hold the world.

DRIVE

Occupying the exact center of Josie's gaze, the highway converges on infinity. Its surface shivers into a mirage even in the cold of December. Hands at ten and two o'clock, radio tuned to her choice of pre-sets, Josie keeps her focus. It is the first day of a long road trip and already the discomforts of a small car interior are maddening. Worse, a troublesome hollowness has taken hold, the one that makes her wonder if she were to die right now, who would come to her funeral. Would it be worth taking her own life to make everyone who has ever known her, care that much more about her and her suffering. She knows she needs some kind of distraction so she reminds herself about the stacks of prints and canvases in the trunk: they are all that really matter. Although there's also the issue of managing her brother, Blake, sprawled on the passenger seat beside her. His turn at driving ended early.

"I'm not comfortable with you following that car so closely, Blake," Josie said during the first hour of the trip, less than a hundred kilometers out of Montreal.

"No, eh? Then just go to sleep," he replied casually.

"Go to sleep? How can I sleep when your driving scares me?" her voice rose.

"How does my driving scare you? I'm perfectly safe. Never had an accident."

"You did so. We were nineteen, it was just before we left home. You ran Mom's car into a tree and totaled it. She was furious. Never let either of one of us drive any of her cars again. "

"That was the other guy's fault. I was avoiding him. Doesn't count," Blake shrugged.

"Oh sure. You were lucky you lived. By the way, you remember passing that truck a little while ago? That was terrifying. You know you didn't have enough room." Josie crossed her arms and stared straight ahead.

"Look, if I'm driving I'll make the decisions. I'll extend you the same courtesy."

"Then pull over and let me drive," she ordered.

"You said you were tired," Blake looked at her and raised both hands as he shrugged again.

"Not since that near-death passing experience. I'm wide awake now. Keep your hands on the steering wheel, please."

"You're not right all the time, you know, Jojo."

"Actually, I'm — keep your eye on the road, will you?"

By now Josie has done five of their six hours of driving. It used to be that Blake was as easily pushed as pulled, but he is more difficult to maneuver now that they are twenty-four. Josie wishes they were going to New York — so much closer, and such an easy place to ditch Blake until it was time to move along again. They'd be at the outskirts by now. But there's too much risk of getting caught at the border. Besides, the market in New York is too hot, she heard that all of a sudden everything that sells in a gallery or at an auction gets tracked online. The only way to offload a haul would be to sell directly to a private collector, and she needs money now, not in a year or two. So instead they are heading all the way to the West Coast. Once they get there, she'll look up her contacts, make her way around the Gulf Islands, go all through Vancouver Island and then up the Sunshine Coast.

Business is so much more laid-back there, and she knows galleries that will take pieces on consignment without any fuss about provenance. They will have to stay on a strict schedule, though, if she's going to be back in Montreal when winter term starts. She is certain she's thought it all through, at the same time annoyed that Blake didn't bring along better music for the trip. Josie shifts her position and tries to find some comfort for her back and legs.

Now that she is away from Montreal she can begin to relax. In spite of Blake and the distance they have to cross, this is a remarkably easy way to get ahead. And it has all come about because of her good planning, which started last summer. Along the cobblestone streets of Old Montreal, Josie had been careful to select galleries that were crowded and charming, rather than ones that were sparsely furnished and hip. She visited them weekly, always with her portfolio along on the pretext of sketching from established artists. They really should have more security in these places, she often thought as she smiled at the proprietor on her way out.

She also has many of the excellent pieces that she and Natasha jointly created, which by rights are half hers. More than half, considering the money she'd contributed up front. Blake didn't ask a single question as they carried all the paintings down from the studio, and many up from the basement storage locker, and stashed them in the trunk last night. Natasha had left the studio a few hours earlier in her fury, and showed no signs of return when Josie and Blake made their getaway this morning. Josie saw that her joint account with Natasha still had a healthy balance before she made a withdrawal on their way out of Montreal. Of course, it's almost the end of the month which means many payments would soon be due, but Josie's pretty sure there is enough left in the account for Natasha to cover them. Josie is quite pleased about making such a clean break. If only she could stop thinking. The sound of the tires hitting the seams in the asphalt affirms the dullness of the trip with an insistent stun-ka-thunk, stun-ka-thunk, stun-ka-thunk. Annoying, but at the same time more agreeable than her everlasting internal thrum. Can I please just stun-ka-thunk, Josie thinks, and not actually think.

The monotony of traversing the vast and unpopulated boreal forest is nearly delirium-inducing. Josie decides to count the roadside crosses and memorials from highway tragedies as a way to pass the time and distance. Along with Blake and her two other siblings she used to travel this stretch of highway every summer to reach a relative's cottage. Some of the markers are from that era and seem like familiar landmarks, others acknowledge more recent deaths. The large cross at Highway 240 is still standing and appears to be wearing a fresh wreath, its bright colours incongruous against the blanketing snow. Farther along she sees a series of posts, each with plastic flowers attached, encircle a hydro pole adjacent to the ditch on the other side of the highway. Half an hour later they are at Parson's Siding, site of many infamous wrecks. On the northeast corner a threesome of crosses cling together, the larger middle one leaning in a protective embrace over the other two. It has a name in block letters — Freniere? — painted on its horizontal arms, but it has always been hard to read at highway speed, and no one ever stops to take a closer look. A few hundred meters further there is an ad-hoc shrine with a statue of an open-heart Virgin Mary on their side of the highway. Josie considers making a cynical comment about exposing one's charity to an indifferent world but Blake beats her to it and guffaws. Josie checks herself and decides instead to bring Blake in line.

"Don't you think people would need their church and their faith even more after someone dies like that?" she demands. Blake just grunts.

Josie had attended church during the last few passionate months, although she only went because Natasha did. The ritual of their life was ordered around such a reverence for painting that it seemed possible to make a show of worship, spirituality even, allowing her to be that much more aligned with Natasha. Every service included a time for silent prayer and that was when Josie noticed her friend was especially absorbed; it often took a while before Natasha was able to chant responsively or stand again. Josie would mirror Natasha's posture and timing, and absorb her goodness.

When they first agreed to collaborate in September, Natasha already knew of a place in the old city that had space for rent. It was just past an upscale area on the waterfront, in a neighbourhood not yet given over to high-end condos and tourism. As the rental agent nasally described the structure's evolution from an office building to one now occupied by artists and entrepreneurs, Josie knew it was right even before they crossed the lobby. A stairway made of marble slabs rose elegantly in an ascending sequence of rectangles, triangles and squares, and the ironwork of the balustrade was fashioned into an intricate pattern of leaves and branches. The steps were worn on their medial side into a foot-finding gulley by a century of dutiful workers, the polished wood of the handrail had been clasped so often its grain was blended with the oils of a thousand palms. They were shown a single large room with fourteen-foot high ceilings and eight-foot tall windows, its only other feature a small bathroom with two-fauceted sink and ancient but functional toilet. They could lease by the month, on the assurance they were not planning to ever stay overnight. Josie paid the deposit that day.

Once they had purchased their supplies, they pledged themselves to canvas and plywood board, rapidly-crumpled tubes of acrylic paint and sable-tipped brushes. Pigment-stained in their extremities, they worked without talking. As the weeks passed the studio became chilly despite the flannel shirts they wore by twos and threes, while the clanging radiators struggled to keep ahead of the cold. The only other sound was from the tinny speakers of a ghetto blaster that played Gregorian chants or Bach partitas on repeat and was changed every few days. They ate in accordance with the scope and portions of a penitent — raw, vegan and toxin-free — to match the purity of their output. They brought in narrow cots one Sunday morning when there was no one around to see, and set them up at right angles in a corner they called the cloister. The beds remained peripheral, unmade and empty until Josie and Natasha could barely stand at the end of the day. In the brief time that they lay awake before their sleep-scapes ascended, it was agreed that this was when they could speak freely. Childhood would often make an appearance for both of them. It was a wandering and desolate waif, inconsolably charged with keeping the past alive. Josie usually spoke first, and most.

"They died in a head-on collision when I was eleven — they were always travelling without us. My first thought was that it served them right," she said one night in the cloister.

Natasha lay on her back and spoke to the rectangle cast on the ceiling by the streetlight. "I understand how hard it must have been for you, Jo. It was the same with my father, when he went to fight against the Serbs. He didn't have to go, and he left without really saying goodbye. Our neighbours had become our enemies and he had to do battle with them. They called him a hero, but to me he was just selfish. I too was eleven when he died, but maybe I already told you."

"It was as though they expected it," Josie continued, "the way they had everything laid out for us in their will. The trust fund, the accounts already set up, who does that?"

"And yet how would you have established yourself as an artist if it wasn't for them? You are provided for, sometimes that is all that matters. You yourself are like a gift, Josie, the way you have helped me. It all reminds me of when my mother and I first came to Canada as refugees. It was Christmas time, and we had nothing, absolutely nothing. Suddenly a stranger appeared at the apartment door. She had two children at her side. Each of them had their arms full of bags, cardboard boxes, a big frozen turkey, they could hardly hold on to everything."

"Sounds like what we call a Christmas hamper," Josie said. Natasha usually didn't go on like this, but Josie decided to allow it in order to deepen their alliance.

"Yes, that was it, but we didn't know at the time. Our refugee coordinator had arranged it for us, and for everyone in our group."

"My mother would have been the type to go around doing things like delivering Christmas hampers. She always had to make herself seem better than anyone else." Josie tried to direct the conversation back to her storyline, but Natasha was not to be diverted.

"There was everything in it — or so it seemed to us. Cookies, a scarf and hat set for my mother and one for me, a doll with a whole wardrobe — she even had her own winter clothing — pens and paper, some books we couldn't read. We didn't know what to do with the turkey. We had to phone the coordinator to ask."

"They knew what to do with a turkey in our house, someone did anyway. And how to give presents, there were so many gifts under our tree. Then they'd be off again, to some party or other, or on a flight down south. The left a nanny in charge, a movie on the TV to keep us company and away they'd go. I didn't cry at their funeral."

"I understand, Josie. We didn't have a funeral for my father for a long time. After the war my mother and I went back, as much for his service as to decide if we wanted to live there again. It was easy once we saw all the destruction, heard of all the hatred. We realized our life had already started over again. I knew that even as a child."

Josie felt a rush of attachment towards Natasha in these moments of confession and remembrance. When that happened her empty center was filled with the transplanted beauty of her friend's suffering. Even in the dark Josie could see before her the clarity of Natasha's eyes, the dynamic of her hand gestures and high forehead when she was making a point, the definition of her collarbones: Josie wanted to be her, and to match her in painful recollection. And Josie found it increasingly easy, the more often she did it, to make up a story about her parents that made them at once guilty and inaccessible. She would take from her own life a particle of truth here, one of her imagining there, and bring them together like colours blended together on a canvas into something more beautiful than any of them alone. A sudden highway death generated immediate absolution and empathy in a way that was especially satisfying.

Falling asleep with Natasha in the cloister reminded Josie of the days when her younger sister Iris would climb into bed with her. They would hold hands and Josie would make up stories for her sister until they fell asleep, finding warmth, and safety, in their intertwined selves.

*   *   *

After two more hours of driving Josie knows she needs a break. Traffic volumes are much reduced, by now she accepts that she will just have to take her chances with Blake's driving. She lowers her speed outside a town called Near Falls, and notices that clumps of snow from the last storm have been ladled onto all the forks and branches of the aspen that border the highway. The small trees are uniformly bent into supplicant arches; Josie imagines them doing this in anticipation of her arrival. The town itself is an unattractive conflagration of corrugated steel buildings, plain bungalows clad in post-pastel siding, cement trucks rotating and steaming. Josie finds it hard to believe that to some this is a community, and that they would choose to live here. A low bridge takes them across the churning foam of a river that flows between the encroaching snow and ice on either bank. Dirty ivory and greengrey trucks occupy the closest parking spots at The Dynamic Garage and Gas Bar where they pull in. Visitors are exhorted to remember Souvenirs. Tackle. Bait. Ice. Licenses. Taxidermy. They secure gas and snacks and take bathroom breaks with barely a chance to stretch. Josie reminds Blake not to engage any of the locals in conversation. They depart with Blake behind the wheel, and are exhorted to Report Wolverine Sightings on their way out of town. Within a few kilometers there is no reception on the radio, and the last CD is stuck in the player. Josie prods her brother into conversation to distract her from the loop that insists on playing and replaying the past four months of her life.

"How come you hardly ever say anything?" she begins.

"I guess I'd have to believe you were interested in listening, Jo. Of course, I..."

"I don't really care if people listen to me, as long as hear me."

"I suppose that's what most people want. I like to just think."

"Think of something to talk about, will you?" Josie says impatiently.

"Hell, I don't know. Hey, wait, here's something. You see that gap coming up, where a bridge might go over top this road?" he straightens his position and points ahead.

She looks. There is raised earth on both sides of the highway, as one would expect to see for an overpass. "Yes. What about it?"

"There was a bad accident here last year. I remember reading about it in the paper and thinking I knew the place from all our drives along here," he continues. "It was stupid, really. A trucker was driving a semi, drunk. Hit the cement divider coming up to the overpass and flipped his truck over it. Hit another truck, landed right on top. That one was a fuel truck. Huge explosion. Pretty well wiped out everything, including the bridge. Only a few pieces here and there to gather up."

"I guess they were both killed?"

"No kidding. Fuel truck driver had his wife or girlfriend in the cab with him, so she was gone too. They say you could see the explosion in Toronto."

The story and the glimpse of the blast site, already well behind them, shocks her in a way that seems out of proportion with the deaths of people she has never known, and doesn't really care about. What marks the tragedy is a blank, a gap, an absence. This must be why people erect all their little crosses and memorials, however tawdry, along these lonesome stretches. It frightens her to recognize the same emptiness inside herself, her own unoccupied center that can never be joined. It makes her wish she wasn't alive.

Natasha had filled that void for a while. By the end of the third month they had finished several dozen paintings, and there was increasing pressure to be ready for the opening. The studio had become silted with clutter and waste, making them pause more and more often from their work to find what they needed. They would stop painting and Josie would write the show's testament while Natasha cleaned the cloister and studio area. Coming from such a disadvantaged background, Natasha was more accustomed to that kind of work. Josie made sure that their division of labour flowed naturally from their respective strengths. If Natasha raised any objections Josie would point out that she had tested at the ninety-fifth percentile for expressive language: her parents, for all their faults, had at least recognized her as gifted. In the last month of living with Natasha, Josie noticed these differences in their status more and more often. Living very nearly the same life, she found the weight of their overlapping selves was becoming too great to bear, the shading too subtle to be able to situate boundaries. They were friends, conspirators, sister-selves. Increasingly, Josie couldn't stand her.

Josie noticed that it was winter solstice — a date she had always felt particularly auspicious — when she decided it was time to leave. There weren't many clothes in her wicker laundry basket in the cloister, and since she never bothered to iron, Josie simply poured them into a suitcase. The gesture made Natasha pause in her mopping. "What are you doing?"

"Packing." Josie replied without looking at Natasha.

"I can see that. I repeat: what are you doing?"

"I'm going away. I need a break."

"What about the show? And the sales? The opening's in a week, you know."

"You'll manage," Josie said as she pressed down on the lid of her suitcase.

"What do you mean? We're one hundred per cent collaborators — remember?"

"Do you have that in writing?" This time Josie looked in Natasha's direction and wished she hadn't. Natasha's beautiful face was contorted as though she might spit.

"I didn't know you were this kind of person. Bitch." The word came out like spittle.

"Look, Nat, I'm going to be away for a while, not necessarily forever. I need a break. You'll manage. You're so much better with pressure than I am," Josie softened her tone.

"Meaning I'm capable of responsibility and you aren't. Like I said: bitch."

"I'll pick up where I left off when I come back."

"I wouldn't bother." Natasha flung the mop in Josie's direction and fled the studio. That was the last Josie had seen of her.

Natasha was right: Josie wouldn't be back, either. Not with everything she had stashed in the trunk. There were still plenty of blank canvases left in the studio, and some board in the storage locker. Nat could put the pedal to the metal and be ready in time for the opening. She'd always loved that expression once Josie explained it to her.

Josie thinks she might try and doze when Blake speaks. "Day after tomorrow's Christmas, you know."

"Do you have to remind me."

"Just saying, Jo. Don't care for it myself much anymore." Blake slouches and has only one hand on the steering wheel. Josie debates whether or not she should correct his driving again.

"I hate Christmas," she says instead.

"Get out, Jo. You do not."

"I can't stand it."

"You made that big castle or palace thing once out of ginger-bread when we were in grade twelve. You were right into it, more than anyone else I ever knew," he counters.

"Abbey." On this point she does need to correct him.

"What?" Blake asks.

"Abbey," Josie says. "It was an abbey, one of my imagining. If I could go back in time that's what I would be, a twelfth-century abbess. In a perfect community, completely under my control."

"Whatever, it was amazing," Blake says. "What happened to it? All I remember is you wouldn't let us eat it."

"I donated it to the Department of Fine Arts when I got in. They let the Faculty of Agriculture feed it to the pigs during summer session, I heard. The Philistines."

"Well, you couldn't expect them to keep it forever."

"I could expect them not to make it into bacon bits," Josie says and is surprised how strongly that betrayal still tastes. Blake finds this story hilarious and chuckles for quite a while. Now she wishes he would just drive, and not talk. But he seems to have warmed to it in their tenth hour of travel. "Do you suppose we should call Mom?"

"Call Astrid? Whatever for?"

"'Cause it's Christmas." Blake's suggestion is as casual as his driving position.

"You must be kidding. She'll be even nuttier than usual. You know how she gets this time of year. Besides, we both just said we're ignoring Christmas. Let's stay true to that spirit."

"Aw, c'mon Jo, don't be so mean. You know it's lonely for her."

"So why doesn't she just call her big hunky boy Marcus over for a little Christmas cuddle then. Seeing as she always liked him so much."

Blake rouses himself enough to sit upright and send her a look of vague alarm. "Pretty weird, even for you, Jo. That's our brother, and our mother, you're talking about."

"Don't I know it. So we're agreed, then: no phoning home. Right?"

Blake shakes his head and slouches back into his preferred driving position.

We all had to endure our older brother Marcus, Josie thinks, his bully and his bravado. We all heard Astrid's coy refrain, over and over, whenever he was around. Anyone could see the way Iris, the youngest, tiptoed about if Marcus was home, and cringed if he came close. Astrid so jealous of her. It was obviously some kind of triangle. If Blake couldn't read anything into his family's behaviour beyond the level of dinner theatre, that was his problem.

Even though they were twins, Josie had often noticed how life had shaped her so differently from her brother. Like the experience of their father's death. They were toddlers when he fell from a ladder to an untimely, and unheroic, death. Blake could make the story amusing, even affecting, when it had to be told. But Josie had made Blake swear he would never talk about it when she was around. She saw it for what it was — a pathetic way to go, a misstep while cleaning dead leaves out of a gutter at a wife's nagging — and never told anyone. Not the truth, anyway, and she included her mother in the fatal event that finished him off whenever she could.

They stop for groceries and gas on the outskirts of Sudbury and Josie decides she is ready to take the driver position again for their last stretch. Winter solstice claims its right to darkness and makes the late afternoon light fade fast while at the same time a low pressure system begins its descent. It blends the earth's darkening surface with the sky as blinking tips of communications towers ease into condensation and cloud. The windshield is briefly scattered with tiny raindrops that change to icy pellets within a few kilometers, and then the weather settles into its true purpose: a blasting tunnel of snow. Josie tries her high beams but they only illuminate more of the mesmerizing bits of white. Low beams reduce her visual distance by half but make less impact on the skittering flakes. Although it is difficult to maintain attention this late in the day, Josie pushes herself to keep the conversation going. When they pass a particularly tall cross Josie is glad that an occasional structure is still visible in the headlights.

"I wonder how close those crosses are to where the crash actually took place," she says without daring to glance at Blake.

"What do you mean?" he replies lazily.

Good, Josie thinks. Sounds like I woke him up.

"Obviously, if the accident happened right on the road they can't put a memorial there," Josie points out. "Maybe it's hard to know exactly where the person died, so they have to make their best guess."

"They get those collision experts out to analyze it all — stopping distances and point of impact and everything," Blake says. "I bet they know pretty well what happened."

"Do the families want to know, is another thing," Josie muses.

"I bet if I died you'd want to know exactly where it happened," Blake says as he yawns and stretches.

"Do you think so? Maybe, maybe not."

"You'd be sunk without me, Jo."

"I think you should let me pay attention to my driving. Or they'll be hunting for a spot to put our cross." Suddenly she doesn't want to talk any more, or to think about death in such concrete terms.

Now the world is a swirling dervish. The more she looks, the less she sees. She follows the fluorescent-tipped resin posts that hug the curves, but even with their guidance driving around a bend is particularly vertiginous. The snow falls at a slant into the road's turning radius, something like a physics problem involving vectors. It makes Josie just as dizzy to think about it as it does to peer into it. She tries switching radio stations. No help: music is just more noise to enervate, or else there is static where a station used to be. When she turns the radio off she can hear a distinct howl. It must be the wind going through the roof rack, she tells herself, although it sounds more like the netherworld calling, wondering.

Here are two more crosses, a larger one standing resolutely above its smaller companion. Blake says that means they are at St. Sebastien, and only have twenty more kilometers to go. Luckily she can expect a substantial structure marking their turnoff, or she might drive right past. It was always known as the Masonry, its size and stone construction unusual for these areas. Although the Shield has an abundance of granite and limestone, few in these reaches have the means to build with it.

The visibility is so bad Josie puts her four-way flashers on, maybe that will help. If she can't see, she can at least hope to be seen. Headlights approach from behind, glowing through the whorls and gusts. Loud and long and bright a semi-truck passes, much too fast. Its backdraft expands the twists of snow into a moment of oblivion and adds further sway to the small car's alignment in the lusty wind. Josie's breathing is shallow: this is why so many crosses have taken root along the highway. This is how people die. The steering wheel feels like it has expanded to twice its usual diameter in her grasp. She glances down and it appears completely normal, but somehow she can't grip it tightly enough. Her voice cracks while singing — the only alternative to the radio, making Blake groan in dismay — and she urges herself back up to sixty kilometers an hour. She knows the car is nearly as great a hazard if she drives too slowly as it would be if she went over the near-invisible yellow line. Angled snow is again at odds with the road's surface and gives her a sense of driving off into space. It is suddenly clear to her that mass times acceleration equals a force that can alter fate, and that she doesn't want to die.

The light at the Masonry has never been so welcome. For all its solidity and size, its outline can only be seen dimly through the nearly horizontal snowfall. As soon as she makes the right turn onto the secondary road that tracks along the lakeside, a weight is removed from her shoulders and chest. The snow here is loose and she accelerates gently for fear of getting stuck. She hears the whirring of the front wheels as the try to grip the powdery surface beneath them. Still, the road must have been plowed not too long ago, or else they would be pushing the car out of a drift by now. Her jaw is stiff from being clenched through the terror of the highway. She finds it an effort to open her mouth to speak. "I wonder if the Allards still live in their place year-round. I hope so or we won't get through."

"We staying here for Christmas, boss?" Blake sits up straight, his voice animated for the first time today.

"I wish you wouldn't keep bringing that up. I was hoping to just skip the whole thing," Josie mutters.

"I always thought the cabin would be a great place to spend Christmas," Blake says. "Anyway, we've just put a thousand clicks behind us, and we're not going any farther now with this storm on the go. Stay in low gear going up this hill, okay?"

"Shut up, Blake."

The car scrambles and skids up unmarked roads towards the new properties that border on the provincial park. Some are bravely lit against the storm with strands of coloured lights, some still have construction company signs out front. As she catches glimpses of timber frame and stonework down some of the driveways, Josie registers her approval of these structures compared to the frugal little cottages clustered along the lower roadway. She can see herself in this kind of country home, some day. She almost misses the post marking lot 6456 and has to back up. She churns through a small drift and finally comes to a stop in a circular driveway. A stone obelisk and a carved bear standing on its hind legs flank the double door. With all its windows illuminated, Josie has to suppress the feeling that the house is staring down at her. She opens the trunk with the last of her strength. Blake carries a portion of the artwork through the door while the house's occupant hands Josie an envelope, all without a word. There is no need to look at him, and her scarf is up over her own face — after all, it is a cold night.

Josie lets Blake drive down the hill and around the familiar curves to the little rusty red cabin. They haven't been here for five or more years but the key is still on the nail under the porch, wood is neatly stacked against the east wall, plaid wool jackets occupy all the front hall pegs as always. Josie sets down her smaller suitcase and sees how lowly the cabin is, a place visited only by those who cannot transcend their past and improve their position in life. Its only future is to be the brunt of a contested will, then demolition in favour of a structure more worthy of the winner. Right now it is simply a place that allows Josie's larger purpose to unfold, nothing more.

Blake hums as he hauls in Josie's larger suitcase and then squeaks open the wood stove to get a fire started. He has already brought in the groceries and located a cooler so they don't have to use the generator for the fridge when Josie realizes she has been standing in the same spot for quite a few minutes, and that her legs are shaking. She finds her way into the cramped living room where she sits on the edge of the old crimson couch. Her legs are numb and her peripheral vision vibrates. When Blake drops a piece of wood her exaggerated startle response makes a spasm across all her limbs. She leans back but continues to feel a sway in the room. If she holds herself perfectly still the fearful drive through the storm recedes. As she uncoils, she takes further stock of her surroundings. There is the carved loon that acts as a doorstop and stubs everyone's toe. Above the wood-stove is the light fixture made out of deer antlers, even uglier than she remembers. Every item in the small living room forces her to swim through old tensions and the tendrils of hardening positions from late adolescence. The worst fight happened with Astrid sitting right where she is now. Josie remembers how her mother didn't even follow her outdoors when Josie left the room, threatening to run away into the woods. Or perhaps it was drown herself in the lake. The combined effect of surging memories and receding stress hormones makes Josie both more aware and less alert.

She must have been asleep, because she is suddenly awake. Almost afraid, faintly nauseous, wondering what there is to be so worried about. Nothing is wrong. But she only feels alive when she is on the edge of a crisis, in the midst of an essential imperative, or doing something that overwhelms the ordinary and swarms the perseverance of her thoughts out of existence. A rough grey woolen blanket is draped at the opposite end of the couch and she pulls it over her shoulders like a shawl. It provokes less reaction from her skin than it did when she was younger. If only I could be that much less reactive, she thinks.

Josie notices Blake's voice, and another, and a scrabbling sound. She makes her way over to the side door that opens onto the porch, where they first entered.

"Josie — I didn't think I'd ever see you here again." An elderly woman wearing skidoo boots almost up to her knees and a beaded parka stands just inside the door.

"Hi, Mrs. Allard. Yes, I'm back to haunt the place."

"I had to come over and check, I hoped you weren't thieves or anything like that. You're spending Christmas at the cabin, how nice," Mrs. Allard smiles even though Josie doesn't.

"Well, we're just on our way somewhere. You have a dog now." Josie directs the conversation downwards. Anything but their journey is a better topic.

"Actually, you remember old Mr. Belanger, farther up the road? He stayed here year-round like us. He was killed in a car accident and now we have his dog."

"I'm not surprised. It's terrible driving out there," Blake says from his position at eye level with the dog's shaggy blonde face.

"It was ten days ago actually. Very sad, he pulled right out in front of a truck coming along the Trans Canada, down at the bottom of the hill. You would have passed right by the spot on your way in. We will have to put something up there to remember him by when the snow melts," she shakes her head and is no longer smiling.

"Was it stormy?" Blake looks up and asks.

"No, it was perfect weather, middle of the afternoon, we can't understand it. The RCMP said maybe it was a blind spot, maybe he wasn't paying enough attention. It might even have been a suicide, if you can imagine. They say he had put all his affairs in order just before it happened. So sad. Anyway, he's gone, and we have his dog. Who is making our cat's life miserable. I was wondering, you guys always came up with a dog — how would you like to have Molly here for a few days?" she holds the dog's leash towards Josie.

"Sure, Mrs. Allard. We'd love to," Blake replies instantly and reaches up for the leash. He had already found where he should scratch to make the dog's hind leg ignite with pleasure. Wiry blonde hairs drift about.

This is not in the script. She has been taken advantage of in her exhaustion, it should have been her decision. And yet here she is, trudging about with the animal in the snowy clearing behind the cottage. There is still wind and falling flakes, and occasional snow djins make their way, gaunt and gyrating, through the open area. But among the spruce they don't send themselves in aggressive trajectories across her path, and sometimes there are sparkling instants in the snow. The dog doesn't mind the weather at all. She mashes the snow joyfully, burying her head up to her ears, scooping up mouthfuls for thirst and for fun. The wind still has its chill, but there is neither the menace nor the malice it brought down upon her just an hour ago. How could there be such a configuration of storm and serenity, such stillness and beauty in the center of rage? She isn't prepared to believe these conditions can co-exist if her own life doesn't allow them to.

*   *   *

Josie drives into painfully bright winter sunshine. The last sign said Thunder Bay 212 km. Three days delayed, first by the weather then by the twenty-vehicle pileup it caused. Stupid drivers.

Miraculously she finds clear radio reception, rare among these steeply blasted rock faces that abut the highway as it curves its way along the north Superior shore. She recognizes the music as a movement from a Sibelius symphony, the second time she's heard it since the start of the trip. Now she understands what the radio announcer said the first time, how the music is congruous with the surrounding broad expanses of land and water, the roughed-in rocks and lichen, the little conifers grizzled by the harsh continental climate. It's all there in the repeated lament of the horns, the query in the strings' pizzicato, the sadness and breadth of the full orchestral scoring, held to silence in the final bars.

Natasha told her how the orchestra in her city continued rehearsing and performing during the war. The players knew they could be ambushed by snipers on the way to, or even inside, the concert hall, as did their audience. Still, they kept coming to play and to listen. When the concert hall was bombed and burned, they moved to a church sanctuary. Candles would be lit and lights dimmed to make them a less obvious target. Natasha recalled the intensity of the assembly, the defiance and illogic of sharing such an indulgence in a time of terror, which made it all the more essential as homes and friendships were ravaged.

It's over, and Josie will make Natasha — and any chance of a sequel — part of the past. Just like her scare during the storm the other day, she will detach and leave it behind. She, Josie, has made all of this come about. She didn't just plan it, she did it, and she is justifiably exhausted. Once again she should be able to relax and be oblivious. Instead Blake is enjoying that privilege: he and the dog are snoring in the back seat. She could cry, but she still has to concentrate on driving, and besides there's no one to notice. There isn't much point if she has to keep it sotto voce, and not be credited for the effort.

FORTY

On his way to the clinic Gerhard made his usual illegal U-turn, only this time he got caught. As he braked to the flashing lights behind him he felt the pill bottles click and jostle in his coat pocket. He had finally remembered to have all of them along, as Dr. M. half-patiently asked him to do at every visit, and now he wouldn't be on time. He had postponed this appointment, and refills for one prescription in particular, as long as possible. It seemed like a needless expense when he hadn't dated anyone for over a year. But lately he had glimpsed the occasional flash of hope in the periphery — nothing definite, just a few possibilities — and it was too anxiety-provoking to be without.

He tapped his fingers on the steering wheel as he waited for the police officer to come up to his window, and resisted the urge to scrape frost from the inside surface of the windshield. That would only make it worse. In this kind of weather, everything seemed to make everything else worse. Forty below with the wind chill, the radio announced this morning, making it sound like an accomplishment when it wasn't. Here in Winnipeg, in January, that wasn't even close to a record.

"I'm so sorry, sir. I didn't see the sign," Gerhard eked out a smile between clenched teeth. It wasn't just the frustration. His little car was doing its best but the vinyl seats remained stiff with cold and siphoned all warmth away from his core. Now he had an open window to add to his discomfort.

"The one on the boulevard, that says NO U-TURN, or the one on my vehicle, that says POLICE?" the officer replied amiably.

"Neither, really, I'm sure I wouldn't have — oh, just sorry. I did the wrong thing," Gerhard said as he proffered his license and registration and tried not to appear nervous. He remembered his ex-brother-in-law the policeman, redolent with aftershave and self-assurance the way he usually was off-duty, mentioning once that he was less likely to hand out a ticket for a minor offence if the driver seemed truly contrite. Humiliating, Gerhard now realized, but worth what one could get out of it.

This particular officer, however, didn't reply and was already back at his vehicle. Through his side view mirror Gerhard could see him radioing the command center, and he appeared to be taking his time about it. He probably wanted to make their roadside delay a warning against whatever driving sins others might contemplate. The police officer was actually making his call from outside his cruiser, as if to spite the cold. His moustache, the hairs of the rabbit fur that lined the flaps of his hat, even his eyelashes, were quickly accumulating frosty dollops from the bit of moist warmth that escaped with his breath. His robust frame leaned casually against the door of the cruiser, the coiled handset wire stretched to its maximum length to accommodate his height. He's even got one of his gloves off, for God's sake, Gerhard thought. What's he trying to prove? We all have to be tough to live here. We don't have to risk frostbite to show it.

*   *   *

Josie cursed again: already slow lines of traffic were being forcibly merged to avoid the icy slough of a water main break in the curb lane. The cars themselves remained indifferent while their drivers progressed through various stages of irritability. Now it'll be slippery and heavily salted here for the rest of the winter, Josie thought. Corrosion was already making mortal flesh of her car. She had been nearly on time leaving the house, but none of the lights changed in her favour, and every time she finally got moving it seemed like another stalled car emerged through the ice fog in the stupefying cold. Her only consolation was that it was peak 'flu season so the clinic would be running equally late. As it was, parking might be enough to induce another arrhythmia. Just now — was she imagining it or was that the flipping sensation in her chest that had started this whole chain of appointments, anxiety and inconvenience? So far it only ever happened when Drew phoned to talk about finalizing their divorce. Their last two such conversations had ended with her in an ambulance — she made sure that he knew she'd called 911 on her landline before they hung up. It was three months now since they'd spoken.

A paralyzed traffic light, flashing amber in her direction, made its contribution to the traffic's slow progress. Its hue and winking frequency reminded her of the echocardiogram she'd had last week, the very study that was meant to be interpreted for her today by her doctor — if she ever reached her destination. The echocardiogram screen had been enhanced to non-lifelike tones — sky blue and cherry red in addition to the yellow glow — making it easier to believe this was not really a part of her body being analyzed. But when the cardiologist had to page a colleague after she'd squinted at the same area for the third time, and the two of them stood discussing and pointing for what seemed like an eternity, Josie knew it wasn't just an image of her inner workings but an implication of her mortality. Lying on the unyielding examination bed with the flimsy blue hospital gown flung open, she was fully inside-out, undefended. She could even see the problem for herself if she lifted her head high enough without disturbing the probe on her chest. She wanted someone to page Drew, her ex, even though he was nowhere in the building and unaware of her vulnerability. Now that she thought of it he hadn't given her his new cell number, so she didn't even know how to contact him during the day. Under the circumstances — and aside from her bare chest — even her twin brother Blake would have been a measure of companionship. But he'd gone off to teach English in some forgettable country, so he was no use either.

Non-laminar flow was the term Dr. M. had used to describe the way blood churned as it made its way past a faulty heart valve, when Josie asked what exactly a murmur was. It seemed, once she understood, as good an analogy as any for her life: swirling eddies and vortices of blood getting mixed up and clotted instead of moving smoothly forward the way it was supposed to.

*　　*　　*

Gerhard wondered how long it could possibly take to write a traffic ticket, even in the cold. He thought back again to the days when he had a police officer for a brother-in-law. Rob always had a story from the trenches of law enforcement to share at family gatherings. His anecdotes had an invigorating effect on pre-dinner conversation, especially when they caused a collision of opinion between those who found him hilarious and the hand-knit sisters who had a passion for the downtrodden. If the exchanges became too provocative and Gerhard knew they might be overheard in the kitchen, he would try and inject a story from the front lines of his own workplace, a small factory that made farm machinery parts. Somehow, his observations and wisdom always got sidelined by the onslaught around him. Only the summons to the carved turkey would quell the debate, according to his mother-in-law's suppertime protocol for mealtime civility. Despite her frail shuffle, Gerhard admired how she was able to wield such power over her combative tribe. He didn't miss his ex-wife Cherie or her extended family since their divorce twelve years ago. But he was left with the lingering paradox that he missed his ex-mother-in-law.

Despite the public shaming of the present ticketing incident, Gerhard could appreciate it held certain kind of clarity: manly dominance, one male more invested with power and righteousness than the other. He was the loser this time, but maybe in another encounter he would be victor. By contrast, could anything match the humiliation of a man on his way to see his female doctor for a prescription so that he could have an erection, an event that he didn't know for certain would come to pass any time soon? It seemed like the differential made for so much confusion that he didn't even know how to frame his emotion; it just sat there within and alongside him.

"There you go, sir," the officer slid the ticket through the window's narrow gap. Gerhard accepted it as though it was something he very much wanted, and didn't mind waiting for. He felt no need to emulate the bravado of the cop and to that end he had opened his window as little as possible. Next to the ticket itself, having a window stuck down in this kind of cold was the least desirable outcome to this encounter.

"Thank you officer," Gerhard said, even though he knew he probably couldn't be heard. How is it we're so polite? he wondered. Of course, some might not be able to resist a soul-cleansing outburst under the circumstances. But the catharsis of an epithet that might be overheard if the policeman happened to be within hearing range would only complicate matters. And a solitary rant seemed undignified at this stage of life. Instead he reminded himself to be careful as he eased back into the line of traffic. Careful and patient.

Now that he was well past his forties, time was unquestionably going faster. When Gerhard worked on a jigsaw puzzle during his solitary evenings, the final pieces would fall soothingly into place exponentially faster as the puzzle neared completion. These later years of life likewise compacted more and more readily, one into the next, without pause or shading to distinguish them. But rather than being a source of peace, this accelerated agenda put him on edge. The minutes of this traffic delay, for example, made him feel the same kind of anxiety that came with any thought of aging, any devaluation of that earthly promise of eternal strength and autonomy he recalled from his early twenties. He had been so sure he had plenty of time this morning, yet as he left the house he noticed that he was already a few minutes behind schedule. How did this happen? What had he done with that block of time since awakening?

Gerhard glanced at himself in the rear view mirror as he waited for the traffic light to go through its cycle again and hopefully allow him to move. He was at least as tall as that police officer, he could have entered that profession himself if he had ever been so inclined. Likewise his shoulder breadth wasn't any less than the officer's. The fine lines around his eyes were no more prominent than last year, and the grey hairs starting to dominate his moustache were a distinguishing feature, they could be signs of wisdom and experience. His eye colour had changed, though. He noticed it not just in his own reflection but in the surreptitious examination of others. They could only be described as a sort of milky hazel-grey, which largely meant no colour at all. And something had happened to his cold tolerance, too, although there was no shame in having one's ear flaps down on such a morning, even if the police officer hadn't. He liked the feel of shearling snug against the sides of his head when the very joints and seams of both his car and his body protested against the arctic air, and the car's interior heater made little headway in the cold. Once upon a time he could spend hours out in the cold, all day even, and from somewhere in his fibrous being there was flame enough to stay warm. Now he relied more and more on layered clothing and heat sources to keep the chill at bay.

*   *   *

As Josie idled and crept forward by centimeters, a little red car behind her used the bus lane to surge around and ahead. She would have tailgated in retaliation, but there was no opportunity in a line-up like this. Besides, she told herself, road rage is going to do nothing to improve your blood pressure. That, too, would surely be on the agenda once she finally made it into the examining room.

She arrived at the clinic parking lot and had to circle it twice before a space freed up. Damned if she was going to park down the road at the coffee shop on a day like this. She'd just have to be later than late. The door to the building resisted opening because of all the snow and ice jammed along the bottom. No sudden exertion, no lifting or carrying, she chanted. The same refrain on all the forms that had passed between her and the insurance companies, brokered by Dr. M.'s nearly inscrutable scrawl, these past few months. Sure, and I'm going to stand here in minus a million waiting for someone to open a door for me. C'mon, heart, you must be good for something. Josie pulled on the handle with both hands and the door opened in grinding protest.

Elevator Out of Service. Taking the stairs slowly wouldn't be too much exertion, would it? She knew she was supposed to wait for the stress test and the cardiology conclusions before she started exercising. Take your time, don't make it a workout, just walk up the stairs, she told herself. Looking down as she ascended she saw the grey-brown discolouration underfoot that told of the tracked in substance attached to people's boots. At one time the snow had fallen as a pristine and gently smothering sheath. Now winter's finest gift had devolved into a gritty mash.

*　　*　　*

Gerhard walked down the corridor to Dr. M.'s office. Ahead of him was a woman in a plum-coloured jacket, going into the same office. She entered without looking to see if anyone was behind her, and he was content to have the door close on his face. Below the plate engraved with his doctor's name — Dr. Roberta Miecznikowski — was a sign taped to the door that reminded him to TURN OFF CELL PHONES PLEASE for the twentieth time. Gerhard did as he was instructed, as he visualized the woman ahead of him making her way past the reception desk then into a chair and a magazine. This way he could make an unobtrusive entrance. He has seen this woman before, wearing the same plum-coloured jacket. He was sure she hadn't noticed him the last time. He had situated himself across from her in the waiting area and spent more time reading her than his magazine. Perhaps he would be able to indulge again. He plunged his hand deep into the pocket of his parka, urgently in need of a tissue for the thawing secretions in his nose — it wouldn't do to be blowing and sniffling around her. When he felt ready, he made himself open the door.

Patti, the receptionist, was standing and leaning forward so that the edge of her desk pressed into her thighs, as though she needed a prop to keep her upright. "Yes, that's right, Dr. M. is sick this morning," she was saying to the woman in the plum jacket. "She called earlier and thought she was only going to be late. But now she said she's not going to be able to make it."

It wasn't the first time this had happened, and yet to Gerhard it was still a surprise and he didn't know if that would ever change. Why is it that one's doctor — who is human, after all — isn't supposed to get sick? This magical thinking persisted even after Dr. M. had taken six months of sick leave last year; rumour was that she'd had cancer but he couldn't be sure. He'd bumped into a parent he knew who was also one of Dr. M.'s patients during the time the clinic office was closed. She was seeking to glean as much information as she could about Dr. M., wondering if she needed to start the tedious search for a new physician. Gerhard had been unable to help, since this was the first he had heard of anything to do with Dr. M.'s life outside the clinic. Until that point he had never even considered she might have one.

"Couldn't you have let us know?" the woman in the plum coat asked. She was a head shorter than him, even on sharply pointed heels and toes. Her hair was glossy and skimmed her shoulders, and in her profile he could see a querulous facial expression that matched her tone. But he also noted a fascination of cheekbone and brow, eye and ear, curved together in sculptural perfection.

Gerhard grasped the situation and said in a tone that he hoped would soothe and not provoke, "C'mon, don't give her a hard time, it's not her fault." He felt justified in taking the high road, having had the same initial thought himself without having said it out loud.

"I'm sorry, but Dr. Miecznikowski just called. Can I give you another slot?" Patti's voice was full and at the same time mechanical, ready to repeat, holding back while at the same time holding forth. Gerhard wondered if she was trying not to cry. He reached his hand across the desk to take hold of Patti's.

"Hey, Patti, how about you call us when you know what's happening," he said. "You have all our cell numbers. We'll just go out for coffee instead, how about that?"

He spoke to Patti but directed his voice in the plum-coated woman's direction. He thought she was probably too absorbed in her anger to notice. But she turned towards him with a mouth that no longer went down in a pout, and if possible looked even more attractive in slightly open-mouthed surprise. She quickly reverted to an aloof expression but like Gerhard maintained eye contact while she spoke to Patti, her voice now a few intervals lower and more closely aligned with a situation of minor inconvenience.

"Sure, okay, give me a call with an appointment as soon as you can Patti."

Patti sighed as Gerhard released his grasp. "My apologies, again," she said. "I'm sure the pharmacist will refill any of your prescriptions."

*   *   *

Josie thought of all the times she'd stormed the office, demanding an earlier, or an extra, appointment. How angry she had been with Dr. M., and especially with Patti. The rage. The need to arrive and rage. The knowledge that she could lose everything if she did it too often. Dr. M. had done so much for her when Josie pitched about in an agony of awareness that she didn't matter to anyone, when she needed to matter at least as someone's patient. They had an agreement, Josie and Dr. M.: she was to see no other doctors, she could have a maximum of two appointments per month, no phone calls except to book her appointments. Josie knew of ways to wheedle her way around the limits, and made the most of them when her empty intensity swelled to the point of immolation. But Dr. M. and Patti had both made it clear: push those rules too far, and Josie would be set adrift, referred to another clinic — if anyone would take her.

It happened that this very morning, as she prepared to leave the house, she had been questioning the usefulness of the entire profession of medicine, and in particular how the field of psychiatry had failed to relieve her of her suffering. She thought back to the first time Dr. M. had sent her to a psychiatrist ten or more years ago. And how that psychiatrist had told her that the reason for her breakdowns, her lack of success, why Josie found it impossible to be close to anyone while at the same time desperately in need of someone — was all because she had borderline personality disorder. She had told him to fuck off and walked out of his office. She took a seat in his waiting room and, considering the force of her exit, thought it took an inordinate amount of time for him to come looking for her.

Standing in front of Patti in the clinic, Josie sensed more than saw the tall man behind her. He was made larger by his outerwear and more awkward by being male, in this realm that was mostly made up of, and for, women. For every five or six women in the waiting room, there was never more than one man. Often there were none. When she was in the hospital last week for her scan, Josie thought she might glimpse some attractive specialist — a resident or even a medical student would do, just to pass the time. But again there were several women to every man, and the few males she saw were either pushing patients or equipment. Clearly not a worthwhile place for surveying prospects. Even the cardiologist who did her echo was female.

Now her calculated departure from the clinic was thwarted not only by that bulk between her and the door, which shifted with surprising grace for so little room and so much tension in order to link hands with Patti, but also by his disarming way of taking the focus away from her rejection. His gesture seemed to release a ligature that would have otherwise allowed Josie to generate the pressure she needed to explode. Instead, the ever-present casement eased open a bit and her breath went out with an unintended sigh. Her gloves were no longer clenched in her right hand, and she could relax one hip to stand at ease. Suddenly she was just another patient who wasn't going to have an appointment that day. There was nothing to be done about it, and there was an unexpected relief in that knowledge. She remembered the words from a group program Dr. M. had sent her to years ago: "Don't escalate, instead equilibrate". At the time she had scoffed at such platitudes, but now she could appreciate how little she knew about staying all in one piece. Dr. M. understood that about her, at least she seemed to. Josie should never have taken her for granted.

"Okay, Patti. You will call me then?" Josie asked.

"Yes, of course, and you know we'll do our best to keep to our schedule, Josie," Patti said, and looked ready to move on to the next patient.

"You remember this appointment was an extra one, so I could get my results?"

"*Yes*, Josie," Patti said as she looked past Josie to a cluster of newly-arrived patients.

"Just making sure," Josie replied, annoyed that she should have to mention it at all, especially with others in hearing range.

By now Josie had heard it, seen it, could recite it all — likely causes, symptoms, prognosis — despite having rejected her diagnosis for years. She had been told that this thing, this so-called personality disorder, would get better in her forties. Well here I am, bring it on, she found herself thinking lately. Though really, it was everyone else who had a problem, much more so than her: if only every single person in her life could have been more steadfast, more loving, more accepting. Starting with all the friends she went through during her university years. She remembered how easily she could relate to them during the early, infatuated stages of even the most platonic friendship. Someone always needed to make a late night confession, would descend in crisis for a weekend, or a week. She gathered them close with her charm and her cooking to offset the threat of empty space or — worse — silence. That way she never had to acknowledge either the needling voice or the fitful pumping from within. She wondered now if that was the first sign of her heart failing her, the miserable organ. It had already failed her metaphorically, unable to maintain the bond she so needed with any of those friends or later with Drew. And now it was failing her literally, when she couldn't even carry her groceries without help.

Back when she was a student, when she could easily carry sacks of groceries up several flights of stairs, Josie loved all the old brick apartment buildings she had lived in. The paint-stuck windows and uneven cabinetry, the winter-contracted hardwood floors that had enough space between the boards for nuggets of food and scurrying silverfish — it all fit with her anti-bourgeois posture. The high ceilings echoed Josie's voice as she held court through half a generation of students from the two nearby campuses, through her undergraduate and then her two masters' degrees. She met Drew one evening when he came up from the apartment immediately below hers. At first he asked if she could turn down the music, then he ended up joining the party and staying the night. With Drew, as with so many others before him, the faint light of the shrouded bedside lamp allowed for another kind of illumination: the pleasurable sighing away of time when even hunger went unnoticed, when she was transiently spellbound, heedless in her abandonment and yet not abandoned. All these memories were so vibrant she had to stage a forced re-entry into the loneliness of her present life whenever they carried her away. And in spite of them she couldn't forget all the slanderous and fork-tongued partings that marked the end of every single one her raptures. Only Drew had lasted, who after a year in the apartment said that it was time for real estate, and real jobs. This year would have been their tenth anniversary.

Standing now in the shabby doctor's office, desperate to know if her heart was about to betray her in a new way, shadowed by a tall but not especially handsome man expressing the usual first glimmers of interest, she could recall that transcendent state of her student years. But she had begun to wonder if she was too old to ever experience it again, if she even wanted to try.

*　　*　　*

"So, want to go for coffee?" Gerhard heard his own voice say.
"Sure."
"Gerhard." He put his hand out.
"Josephine. Call me Josie."

Her cool, noncommittal grasp met his more forthright one, as he reminded himself not to make a show of strength with a woman. They began enclosing themselves again in wool and fleece. Gerhard noted that her tailored plum jacket with its wooden peg fasteners was very flattering, but likely insufficient against the current conditions. He had chosen his bulky tan parka today, reserved for outings in such extreme cold. Once they were outdoors, the sunshine reflected painfully against both snow and reason — how could there could be such a solar presence in the context of such cold? It was a paradox no one even bothered wondering about. They walked, silent and absorbed in the weather's indelible reality.

Trudging, hunched, Gerhard considered which tangent his free-range mind should take once he and this Josie were finally engaged in conversation. Since the factory slow-down last fall he was only being called sporadically for shifts, so he had started roaming amongst as much information as his time and attention allowed. Like the eggs of chickens who get to consume everything that crosses their path, he felt his mind had become much more nourished, and nourishing, since being so widely fed. Finding little pleasure in television, he cancelled his cable and used the savings for a subscription to a daily newspaper. He congratulated himself on his sound fiscal decision-making and read the paper every morning with his coffee at the kitchen table. After that he made sure to do some desultory housekeeping and self-care so he didn't forget about them altogether. Then he was free to indulge his absorption, either sitting at the computer he had set up on a card table in the living room, or spread out in the periodical section of the public library. He explored every possible source of information, from scandal sheets to scientific journals. He avoided discussion forums and blogs in favour of what passed for objectivity; he devoured and digested all manner of topics as they made their rotations through the horrific to the heroic, from acts of mischief to those of bravery. It was quite a satisfactory way to spend his time. Only in moments of suspended animation, when he visualized himself having a lively discussion about what he had just read but there was in fact no one to converse with him, let alone touch him, was there any sense of unhappiness.

Which is why his equilibrium could be so easily upended by a profile such as the one presently alongside. When he had first observed this woman in the waiting room, he sensed her vulnerability from the anxious way she pulled at the fringed scarf around her neck. At the same time she clearly protected herself with a many-pointed kind of defensiveness. What was her story? She was able to put forth an unsmiling face and still be notably beautiful, unusual for someone her age. The corners of her mouth turned down slightly, as though she was prepared to be vexed but didn't know why. Would there be someone to warn her, though, when that singular expression started to etch a more unfortunate imprint on her features? Would anyone dare? How could he possibly have a conversation with anyone about smiling, let alone with a beautiful stranger? He was sure it would never happen.

*   *   *

Josie was glad she didn't have to deal with the demands of the frozen door as they went outside: it was body-checked open for her by Gerhard. There had been a few confused-looking elderly women shuffling ahead of them, slowing her and Gerhard to an awkward proximity in the stairwell. Josie would have passed them brusquely at the first opportunity, but Gerhard stayed at a polite distance and only excused himself to move ahead and hold the door open for everyone; he seemed as concerned for their safe exit as he was for hers. A ragged heap of coarsely chunked snow from the parking lot had been pushed onto the sidewalk; as they skirted it Gerhard put his arm out to prevent Josie from being blindsided by a turning car. Josie also noted approvingly that he kept protectively between her and the traffic on their way to the coffee shop. At the same time she judged his coat, rather worn and drab, as something that could indicate lack of money or taste, more likely both. To be fair, most people kept one extra-warm jacket for exactly this kind of weather. She recalled Drew having one like Gerhard's, its back a large rectangular expanse of tan duffle that made no attempt to be fitted, with an attached hood and rabbit-fur trim, patch pockets for extra-large mittens and mid-thigh length for added protection. It probably resembled some type of trapper's outerwear, men seemed to like that kind of association with any item of clothing large enough to attract attention. And the weather made her acknowledge the limits of her own coat. Though they were only walking a block, the searing cold penetrated the deficiencies of seams and fasteners and found its way in between all the layers of clothing she had applied.

She had no expectations of empathy, and knew from past encounters with middle-aged men that Gerhard might not know anything deeper than the lyrics to American Pie. Still, it was a positive force, somewhat flattened and diminished but not completely deflated, that urged her forward. She knew enough psychology to reject the genetic imperative that would otherwise project hope onto every male expressing the least bit of interest. His kindness to Patti, and to the elderly women at the door, did not bespeak anything about his actual values: in fact it was probably just to make a favourable first impression on her. She could never be so easily won over.

The coffee shop was not yet populated by lunchtime lineups and they chose a table without anyone else nearby. Gerhard offered to take her coat, but she said she expected a chill from the door and declined. They settled in and Josie was careful not to place the suede side of her gloves on the streaks of the table's freshly wiped surface. As soon as Gerhard brought her order she wrapped her hands around the warmth of the ceramic mug. She didn't mind its chunky inelegance if it retained the hot chocolate's heat that much longer.

She surprised herself by asking the first question. "Do you have kids?"

"Yeah, two. Adults now but I guess they're your kids forever," Gerhard replied.

"How are they doing?"

"As in...?" Gerhard raised his eyebrows uncertainly.

"As in, are you on speaking terms? Do they still live at home?"

"...Are they in long-term therapy from the trauma of their parents' bad behaviour? Actually, they're doing pretty well, from what I can see. We had a few rough years, but everyone pulled through. I blame some of it on the schools — they put too much pressure on kids these days. Once I had to tell the principal to stop those lockdown practices. They were giving my daughter pre-traumatic stress disorder. What about you?"

"Never had any," Josie shook her head slightly. "One miscarriage and that was it, I couldn't handle any more. My husband didn't agree, but he didn't have to go through any of it so I really didn't think he had a say."

Gerhard paused. "You women have to take the knocks in that department, for sure," he said eventually.

"As for being a parent, that's a job for someone else I think," Josie's frown went a little deeper.

This time Gerhard spoke more confidently. "Actually, it's not that bad. I took over for a while after we separated, and then again when they were teenagers. You have to be strategic, know where their soft spots are, and not let them get to yours. By the last year of high school the playing field levels right out. They'd threaten to buy me polo shirts for Christmas and make me wear them, I'd threaten to get their school picture on a coffee mug and use it every day at work. What do you see Dr. M. for?"

Josie recoiled from the forthright manner of his questioning, however friendly. If this was a seduction it was the most good-natured one she'd ever experienced. And why would anyone even bother to do it like this anymore, when there were so many easier ways. You could just go online and find someone, and yet here they were, strangers sitting at right angles to each other, speaking above the noise of drive-through orders, fretting about empty spaces in their conversation. It all seemed like a particularly unsophisticated form of torture.

"I have a heart murmur," Josie said. "They're trying to figure out what it's about. I was supposed to get some results today — couldn't sleep last night thinking about it."

"Did you have an echo?" Gerhard asked. To Josie's surprise, he seemed genuinely interested.

"Yes, just last week. How did you know?"

"My boy had a murmur as a baby. They let us watch when he had his echo. Most amazing thing I've ever seen," Gerhard's eyes widened and he leaned forward as though he would like to go on.

"I hated it, creeped me out seeing something inside of me on a screen," Josie interjected. Again she recalled the image of her valve, flipping and flopping like a shirt on a clothesline in a fitful wind. She was almost grateful for Gerhard's next question.

"How long have you been single?" he asked.

"Four years."

"How'd it end?"

"You could say I was outsourced."

"By which you mean...?"

"He had an affair."

"That'll do it," Gerhard nodded.

*   *   *

As soon as he'd asked why she was seeing the doctor Gerhard regretted his question. He had walked himself right into the kind of exchange he would never be able to reciprocate. His mind made a quick scramble: high blood pressure, he could say that. It wasn't a lie, it just wasn't entirely true; a vague untruth was entirely justified given the transience of their encounter. She didn't seem interested in asking him why he was at Dr. M.'s office that day, though. Her disengaged drift made her elusive, and therefore more desirable. Still, she seemed to want to take initiative in their conversation, and he saw that as a good sign.

"You know what my sister says about breakups?" Josie asked. She continued to hold the mug with both hands, fingertips flushed with recent cold.

He wasn't sure he wanted to know, but there was no way to avoid it. "What?"

"She says now that we're in our forties, they're not interesting any more. So I should keep them to myself, like she does."

"She single?" Gerhard asked.

"Again."

"What's she look like?" Gerhard thought he would try humour in order to forge a path around the emotion he sensed brewing.

"Ha, ha. Actually, that's not funny. My ex was hot for her for a while. Didn't take him long to move on though."

"So in a way you're glad he left," Gerhard responded. He hoped he sounded empathetic, seeing as humour wasn't the tool he thought it might be.

"I was devastated, but I still wanted him back. I'm sure I could have forgiven him. He was the only one who ever understood me. And the water system on our property. It hasn't worked properly since he's been gone." Josie looked genuinely bereft.

Gerhard leaned on his elbows and made his voice more encouraging. He had always liked being a coach in his children's crises, and he felt surprisingly like that now. "You realize that most people are travelling through life — especially once they hit their forties — just this side of comatose. They think the adventure's over, their routines have become ruts and there's no way out. Shopping at the mall for more stuff and going to the same resort every year is all there is to look forward to. Then something terrible happens, some kind of loss, and it feels like the world's coming to an end. But it's actually a chance to make a break. It's got to hurt, can't be helped. But what's the alternative? There's no other way to enlightenment, not at this stage."

"You sound like you've got it all figured out." Josie's voice took on its petulant tone again and Gerhard did his best be humble in his delivery.

"Well, no. Actually, that's the point. I feel like I'm just starting, or starting over again, only this time I know better. I don't stay in a useless place now. If someone, or something's, not working out, then it's time to move on. Lots of opportunities, you know."

Gerhard discreetly looked at the watch on her wrist. One forty? Was it possible they had been in each other's presence almost two hours? When he was a child time was manufactured in abundance, and one hour was a lot of it. But he could do nothing to revive that perception. What had changed?

"I have to go," Josie said. Abruptly she stood up and began the winding and muffling of head and face and hands. "Thanks for the hot chocolate."

Had he offended her? Did his ideas and advice sound like someone passing judgment, over-simplifying? Was his glance at her watch too obvious?

He fumbled in his wallet and found a business card. He'd spent a whole day learning to make them and was modestly proud of his accomplishment. He held one towards her and it fluttered at the tip of his tremor.

"Here's my number. Call me, if you like," he said as she took it from him. It got away from him before he could snatch it back again. Hadn't he learned? What if she texted him two hundred times like the last one he gave it to on the first date? Then he'd have to get his cell number changed all over again. He knew he couldn't ask for her number — the disparity in their looks alone was too obvious, he knew it was a privilege just to be in her company. But the longing was too sweet for him to completely give up.

*   *   *

Josie could predict how every encounter with a man would turn out with a kind of step-by-step clairvoyance. Like the one she met today, Gerhard, who only made the slightest impression with his final comments about starting afresh now that they were middle-aged. His idea of philosophy, no doubt. And through it all, she was made ever more sharply aware of the hurtful pressure coming from her inarticulate and unattached core. She wondered if she had betrayed Drew today. Technically, they were still married, and she thought of him often. But it was four years now since they had separated, and this wasn't the first time she had been sought after.

She let herself into the house, appreciating its warmth and stillness after the cold and disruptive way her day had unfolded. The entranceway welcomed her with a brief flare of late-afternoon sun through a westerly window. She took off her scarf and unbuttoned her coat, glad to be doing this for the last time today. She considered filling the quiet house with her howls. She'd done that before, and it afforded a certain release. But it was considerably less satisfying when there was no one at home to react. Maybe she'd put on some music and dance herself into a dervish. Drew couldn't stand any of those things — noise or dancing or tears. She could indulge in all of them tonight if she wanted. And she must get back to painting, every year she said that. When she could determine what it was inside her that needed to come out.

*   *   *

For Gerhard, the day ended alone and with the knowledge that there had been another inevitable bit of physical contraction: a few muscle fibers lost here, a slight sag there, another neuron laid to rest. By increments the aging process was painless and very nearly unnoticed. But he had watched his own parents deteriorate at close range and he knew that at some point, like a pinched toe in a poorly-fitting shoe, the downhill side would pass the threshold of tolerance and became debilitating. He should get on the exercise machine and ward off the day's impact. Tomorrow — he didn't feel up to it tonight.

Bedtime had always been his jurisdiction when his kids were young, and to this day he missed it. The whole routine went according to his rules but he made it special and fun, blowing bubbles in the bathtub and making their towels into animals before they got out to dry themselves. While he made them a snack he would anticipate their bedtime story by talking in the voices he had made up for it, then sing a silly song for the allotted two minutes of tooth-brushing. The image of small, clean, flannel-clad people, half-avoiding their bedtime while fully embracing the lead-up, often populated his now-silent glen of late-day thoughts.

Lying in bed was when he most noticed the empty embrace, just before the transition into the vault of unconsciousness. But that too was something he could improve upon: Gerhard made sure his dreams at least started in a partly-lucid state, with a measure of voluntary control. That way he saw the latter part of his day the way he wished it could be, before he fell utterly asleep.

SILENCE & SETTLED DUST

When Nettie stopped talking, at first I didn't think I was going to mind. For many of our thirty-some, going on forty, years of marriage, there'd been a great deal of comfort in the times when I was not obliged to say anything. What further strengthens the appeal of silence, I admit, is the feeling in recent years of being overwhelmed. I insist it has nothing to do with my age. There's just too much change and I can't possibly keep up with it all. Every day I am confronted with a new directive, another initiative or a draft for review, from someone well-intentioned but completely unlike me in thought and action. These missives arrive in quantity as faxes and memos that further fatten my already bulging file folders; my receptionist prints out all the emails because my eyes can't stand any more time staring at a screen than they already do. Meanwhile, I've noticed how infrequently anyone sits down to talk the way we used to, the way I still need to but cannot because of the constraint of confidentiality. In the little windowless room that used to be called the doctors' lounge, we could chat about cases, new research, gossip, whatever came up, over coffee before clinic started. Now that room houses a snarl of wires and thrumming black and silver devices all meant for our greater good. Ready or not, here they come. Don't complain or hesitate, just be glad of the opportunities they present.

Of course, the newer, younger partners at work have no difficulty. They've been inducted into this mantra of passwords and alerts, instant messages and sidebars as though they were born into a cult. Every part of them has been amplified and — what is it they say? — hardwired for such a high degree of integration and receptiveness. Probably their neurons were shaped by all those double-clicks and dropdowns during the critical early years of infancy and childhood. I notice, though, that they have learned to protect themselves from excess input. They often establish a boundary for their hearing, one that goes no farther than those little pastilles worn in the outer ear canal. Apparently, the devices they carry about on themselves convey music in a sort of direct feed, from the high-speed and wireless signal to the auditory and associative cortex. It seems to me that the brain could be described for millennia as high speed and wireless. But to say so now, or to suggest one use the brain as a primary means of processing and recall, would be embarrassingly passé. Even I know that.

It was just yesterday that I wondered why he was being so rude, the tall thoughtful one, Evan. He so utterly ignored me when I spoke to him. Before I realized it was the pastilles in his ears. What is curious is the simultaneous loss of peripheral vision, for I stood there beside him unnoticed, not just my voice but my entire self. It seems that only central vision is important now.

And despite all these advances and the tyranny of change, I find that medicine still has its mysteries and insights. For example, ever since I first went into practice forty-two years ago, I have arbitrarily attached a certain significance to patients who are my age. When I see that matching year of birth on a chart next to the patient's name, my mind immediately begins its comparisons. Is their blood pressure higher or lower than mine? Do they look older or younger? Should I compare and contrast our cholesterol levels? Who's got the better body mass index? And so on. Now I find myself thinking even more critically: whose mortality is more obvious? If you were to place a bet, which of us would you favour? And what odds would you give?

Those were my thoughts when I first saw Cecil Martin, or MARTIN, Cecil, DOB 18 August 1944, as per his paper chart, during an afternoon clinic some months ago. His old manila folder was placed in my slot, pulled that day because this was his first visit since we've gone digital, as they say. Often the contents of the old files go back many years, seeing as we aren't terribly pressed for shelf space in our small rural facility. Perhaps we're just sloppy, not bothering to cull the charts, but every now and then a bit of information can be extracted from the clutter of ancient microbiology results all crusty around the edges and yellowing operating room reports that describe procedures no longer performed. Sometimes you even come across a birth report from back when we did deliveries here. All of it of little or no interest to anyone but us equally crusty and archaic practitioners.

As it happened, the last note in Cecil's chart was inscribed more than ten years ago in quite a handsome script, with what looked like fountain pen ink. Typical male patient, no use for a doctor unless one of his fingers is actually hanging off, and all he wants is a quick patch-up in the emergency room, a tetanus shot and then I'll be on my way, doc, sorry to have bothered you. I'm not so different. It's only because I'm here in the clinic every day that I ever get any of my own routine maintenance done.

Cecil took off his baseball cap and put out a hand in greeting as he came into my examining room. A handshake isn't such a universal gesture in this setting, but reasonable given the equality of our life stage and the absence of dangling digits on his part.

205

"Pleased to meet you, Dr. Bradeau," he said amiably. "People always speak highly of you."

Except the ones who don't, I thought, but I know about those and it's all been dealt with.

We sat down and I began to poke at the keyboard. "What can I do for you?" I asked, more of the screen than him.

"Can't sleep, doc. Can you give me something for it?"

A common request, easily fulfilled if one has no regard for the long-term. We've had a few of those physicians in our group, ones who give out addictive drugs like there's no tomorrow. Leaving the rest of us to bite our tongues or ask for trouble when that first prescriber isn't around. Luckily we've mostly shepherded their kind out of here, and are vigilant when anyone new comes on board. I have to admit, these youngsters handle that kind of situation among colleagues much better than anyone of my generation ever did.

"What's making it hard to sleep?" I inquired. He may not have come to talk about himself and what's troubling him, but I can usually tease something out of even the most reluctant speaker.

"Well, you get to a certain age and a lot of things don't happen as easy," Cecil admitted. "Then last year the wife passed away. That didn't help." Even though I was wrestling with the functions I wanted the computer to perform for me, I noticed he had leaned forward to rest his forearms on his knees and was rotating the cap in his hands.

"What was your wife's name?" I asked.

"Elvira. Elvira Martin. She died here, in palliative," he offered.

A vague swatch of memory made me look away from the screen and directly at Cecil. "Congestive heart failure? Bad valve?"

He nodded.

"I remember," I said, nodding slightly myself. "That was a long hard slog for her at the end. I looked in a few times when I was on call. You and I must have crossed paths then."

"It's all a blur now, doctor. There's a lot I can't remember, just what comes back to me when it's three a.m."

"Right. Tough year for you." I sat back and stopped trying to type, granting Cecil permission to go on however he chose.

"We'd just moved into town here after we sold the farm. It was a big change but Elvira kept us going pretty steady, what with church and Women's Auxiliary and all. She always had a little job for me around the house or the yard. Now I don't know what to do with myself. I don't even have a shop to work in, sold all my tools. Wish I hadn't done that." Cecil took turns looking at the brim of his hat and at me as he said this. I wondered how long it had been since he put so many words together.

I took him through the usual questions for detecting depression, including the inevitable ones about suicide. I know the statistics, I've been to the lectures. I do my job however uncomfortable it makes an old fellow feel, myself included. Turned out he was just sad, and anxious, and lonely, and sleepless. Not really diagnosable, and not very treatable, not by any of my magic.

"Well, we both know pills aren't going to bring back what you've lost," I summed up by stating the obvious. "But if I prescribe you a few of these, and you only take one occasionally, you won't get hooked and you'll get caught up on the sleep you've missed every so often."

"Thanks, doc," he said. He appeared grateful for both the service rendered and for the end of scrutiny.

The ritual of paper to patient is interrupted these days by me hunting and pecking at the keyboard as I try to complete my note. But with Cecil I managed to remember myself, and the way I used to practice. "If you ever need to just talk about it some more, c'mon back," I said as he opened the door for himself.

"You bet. Thanks again," he said.

He put his cap back on and was away, with me still fussing with the digital record of my impressions. One of the younger partners says she can appreciate how good a physician I am now that she's able to read my notes.

*   *   *

After clinic, on beautiful summer evenings, I sit outside in my bit of backyard paradise. It's unfenced at the far end, and therefore contiguous with the surrounding Crown land. Which is to say, my backyard is one with the nearly endless boreal forest: trees and rocks, lakes and that form of matter that is neither solid nor liquid but bog. From that enormity of space and life there drifts onto my property, like tourists into shops in a pedestrian mall, a variety of wildlife: chipmunks, bats, chickadees, deer, jays (both blue and grey), skunks and raccoons, moths, blackflies and mosquitoes, along with the smell of juniper and spruce. Every now and then, especially early and late in the summer, a great blunderbuss of a bear comes wallowing in. Who would be utterly charming except that the last thing anyone wants is a habituated bear in their backyard, defending its food source. So I carefully hoard and hide my garbage so as not to provide a lure. If one does happen to show up I ring the triangle that never actually got used to summon anyone to mealtime, but serves this purpose quite well. Bears seem to greatly dislike the pitch of the metal's jangle, and after a momentary scan with the nostrils and ears, they invariably amble away.

Along the north border of the yard there is a vegetable garden. Its flora is tamed but transient in our hectically short summer, partially protected from ravaging deer by an electric tape I keep forgetting to activate. Tonight, in among the zucchini blossoms, I watch two butterflies cavort. Whether they are acting out aggression or flirtation I can't tell, insect behaviour is too obscure to distinguish. Not that the social stances of humans are all that much easier to interpret. Of all nature's creatures I find that birds are the most captivating to observe. Their conduct is complex enough to be interesting, but at the same time relatively straightforward and mostly free of troublesome psychology. The birdbath becomes a focal point during these dry August days, even more so than the feeder. Goldfinches come to bow and drink at precisely six o'clock in the evening every day. I watch them and wonder: how is life contained in such a tiny exquisite package? Why bother to create it, in its black and yellow perfection, when it is only meant to die? The robins have bathed and drunk earlier, they retire in the hot part of the day. The heat has removed to the other side of the house so that by suppertime I can sit on the back porch in peace. Often the wind calms by now, and then the nuisance of biting insects begins. But for the last two nights the breeze keeps coming along in pert little gusts, casting the trees and their branches into moveable shapes, making the clouds and the untrimmed grasses sway and show me their undersides in the most graceful way. I often sit here for a long time after I finish eating.

Sitting outside makes me think of Nettie, how she and I spent many an evening here, especially after the twins and their phobia of bugs had grown up and moved away. Those quiet times were exactly what I needed after a long day of continuous interaction at work. What they were for Nettie, now I can only wonder. Were the silent hours we spent together the still spirits of our small accomplishments, or the wraiths of what we avoided discussing? Typically I would come home and she would talk about this and that for a while. I admit I often didn't register except that she was vocalizing. A certain pause informed me that a reply was expected, and I would come up with something generic. If her tone was in any way accusatory, or judgmental, because of the inadequacy of my response I would withdraw further, and that would usually conclude the verbal portion of the evening.

I enjoy a few of the Goodland apples from my neighbour's little tree after supper this evening. It bears so abundantly that I think each year will surely be its last. Like a person who gives, literally or metaphorically, until they can finally give no more, I often wonder how the tree's generosity doesn't exceed its capacity. I know some doctors who are like that, reduced to uncaring shells after too much sacrifice. I always made sure to keep some of myself for myself, and the apple tree must do the same. Aside from the odd non-bearing year — I never know if weather conditions, a pollinator strike, or some sort of arboreal sabbatical is the greatest contributor — I can look forward to these late summer treats quite reliably. More and more I covet such pleasures. Though I try not to dwell, a small but distinct voice asks: what if I knew this was to be the last time I would enjoy these delicacies?

I haven't suffered in my eating since Nettie went away, though many in town wondered at first if I did and apparently continue to do so. The occasional foil-clad casserole still shows up, which I appreciate but do not find necessary. If there is an additional intent, a hidden agenda, on the part of these women who are concerned about my nourishment, I maintain a willful ignorance and offer nothing more than a polite nod and word of thanks in return. I am only interested in simplifying my life at this point. And now I can engage in my own culinary adventures for the first time. Through a process of recall and experiential learning I have become reasonably proficient. To start with I delved into some of Nettie's cookbooks. After all, what is cooking but chemistry, and for that matter what is medicine but following a recipe, or for the more adventurous, making up one's own? Doctors are highly over-rated, just as leftovers are greatly under-rated. My supper this evening, for example, consisted of leftover curried chicken. Its flavours had melded into a much more nuanced delivery than when it was first prepared and served straight out of the pan last night. I will enjoy it even more the next time I have it. Invoking tincture of time, as I have so often done in practice, is a skill worth cultivating in the kitchen, too: the art of not meddling in a way that could make things worse, the discipline of being patient.

The thing I was unprepared for in my life without Nettie was the cleaning. I know this makes me sound like a hopeless excuse of a husband, but I never realized that everything gets dirty. Everything. As soon as you finish cleaning something, it starts getting dirty again. Never mind, while you are cleaning one thing, something else is quietly getting dirtier. How does this happen? Where does dirt come from? Back in the days when the twins were small there were always spills and piles of outdoor footwear and other forms of untidiness. It was understandable that the house would need to be regularly cleaned, though even that phase had its limits. I remember when the twins were about nine and briefly took horseback riding lessons. The displaced hair, the ammoniac odour, the pieces of turf falling from boots, one day a bridle in the living room which they were assigned to disassemble, clean and reassemble. There were cogent arguments to be made in favour of learning responsibility and the development of spatial and physical skills, all of which Nettie and the girls put forth. But this was my home, and a level of sanctity was being trespassed. I cancelled the remainder of the riding lessons. With the household reduced to Nettie and myself, and now just me, and no one trailing around leaving dirty socks and used dishware in their wake, one would think there would be no need to clean more than quarterly. But it does need doing more often, and the only thing I dislike more than housecleaning is the intrusiveness of someone coming in to do it for me. So I grumble and put it off as long as I can.

I still go to visit Nettie in the facility she was assigned after her stroke, regardless of all that has transpired. I try to make it once a week, sometimes it doesn't happen. I was surprised at the intensity of my emotion when she went in, and I was surprised at how quickly it subsided. The twins came for the move-in day, I believe that is the only time the four of us have been together in the past two years. Never ones to be outwardly demonstrative, the girls hugged me stiffly each in turn once we settled Nettie into the care home. Then they clasped an arm each about the other, shoulder and waist, and walked that way across the parking lot toward their rental vehicle. I saw that they were still in their car as I backed out and drove away. They looked like they were talking. I resisted the urge to reverse the direction of our separating selves; I tend to favour each of us finding our own way through. The girls, being of one mind and soul, likely found a mutual path to consolation. Even if not, at least they had each other. I've often thought that having a twin might be better than having a spouse.

*   *   *

It is a Wednesday afternoon and I am attending a house call. Everyone else in the clinic has booked the afternoon off, one of the old customs all are still happy to adhere to. By now they are likely gearing up for golf, or heading to the city for shopping and maybe a supper out. I agreed to do the house call now, and without resentment as it doesn't seem like work. When the request comes directly from the home care coordinator, as this one did, and involves an old farmer, as this one does, I know it's not a question of convenience or entitlement. I look forward to the slightly voyeuristic view into my patient's lives through their possessions and their surroundings; sometimes I can better understand a patient's condition via their household than through the formalities of physical examination. This time it is my year-sake, Cecil Martin, that I need to visit. He was rushed through our emergency department and into the city last week vomiting quantities of blood, never a good thing and particularly ominous at his — our — age. The urgent gastroscopy confirmed a diagnosis of esophageal cancer. Inoperable, all treatment options strictly palliative. This is a good news-bad news scenario: it means he gets to avoid the side effects of surgery, likewise chemo and radiation if he chooses, but it is also a confirmation of death's approach.

He wants to stay at home as long as possible, the home care coordinator tells me. As does everyone, I think. As will I. The question is, what about when it's not possible? Have you thought about that?

There are only sporadic street signs in this older area of town. Even fewer house numbers. Luckily the receptionist was able to provide me with directions, landmarks included, in remarkable detail. All downloaded from that great cache of information that flows everywhere and invisibly. I find it hard to believe that our bit of agriculture and small industrial development, pinched from the wilds of the Canadian Shield, the smallest bit of nothing on the edge of nowhere, is now part of a worldwide knowledge base. But apparently it is so because I hold the computer printout in my hand and like a treasure hunt at a child's party it leads me to Cecil's home. The lanky poplars that line the street are prematurely shedding their glossy yellow leaves. Their branches have been artificially splayed apart in the upper reaches as nature is trimmed back to allow the safe passage of all the wires and conduits that connect us. I shuffle through the leaves, not crunchy like the later fall ones. Cecil's walk hasn't been swept clear of them, and the longish grass is lax and falling softly along all the edges and cracks of the paving stones. Unlike the pristine front lawns of most retirees, this one speaks of the disarray that encroaches as soon as illness takes hold and energy flags.

I knock on the door but I don't bother waiting for it to be answered. I know he's too weak to come down, and as expected the door isn't locked. Still, he's trying to get up with his walker when I enter the living room, and I hastily assure him he can sit back down. The plaid recliner has become his nest, with a pile of magazines, crosswords and assorted papers on the left, the newspaper in a disorderly pile on the floor, while the side table on the right has his personal pharmacopeia along with a water bottle, denture cup, some mouthwash. Around the room are the usual trappings of a life compressed towards its narrowing end: framed photos of arrivals and ancestors on the walls, his own youth enshrined in a wedding portrait on the coffee table. Situated beside it a porcelain bell announcing Saskatchewan Homecoming '71 in gold script. Handmade doilies are neatly arranged on all the tables and couch backs.

"Hello there, doc. Thanks so much for coming. Didn't know if you bothered doing house calls any more," Cecil says. Talking makes him realize he hasn't got his teeth in, and he fumbles with the plastic grin at his side.

"Nice to get out of the office, actually. How are you feeling now?" My hand automatically goes to his wrist, ostensibly for a pulse check but also a gesture that allows a melding of the clinical and the compassionate. I look at his face. The forehead is ridged deeply and his eyes are guarded by cataracts, I don't even need my ophthalmoscope to see them. His mouth was caved-in before the insertion of his teeth, and the sagging of his mottled facial skin forms a downward fleshy trend that only improves somewhat with his dentition in place.

"I'm getting my wish, doc," Cecil says after I complete the check of heart, lungs, abdomen and extremities. I sit down on a chair I've drawn over from the dining room set.

"What's that, Cecil?"

"I wanted to join her," he replies with a nod towards the wedding photo a few feet away.

To this I have nothing to add, so I just nod in reply. As always, I wonder — is there really a joining up in the afterlife, or is it merely a void?

"Do you have any pain?" I gently redirect the conversation to the linear and the logical, where I can be the most help.

"These pills are doing the trick." He holds up a bottle that has large black handwriting on it — FOR PAIN TAKE TWICE A DAY.

"I see someone's helping you with your medications. That's good," I say.

"Yes, my daughter came over and sorted them all out after I got back from the city. She didn't want me to mix anything up."

"She's right about that," I affirm. We talk doses and side effects and comfortably solid facts for a while. He confirms my initial impression: he now does all his sleeping and eating in the easy chair. It's a small but solid place of security. Can he make it last just a little longer, is what he wants to know.

"There's a nephew I'd like to see," Cecil frames the question as a statement. "He comes off an oil rig, week after next. He'll be here by Sunday the 28th." He picks up a calendar from the table on the left, and gestures to the end of the month.

It's easy to recognize this conversation as the bargaining phase of dying, and times like this I become a stand-in for the one who can really parlay with fate, assuming any such negotiations exist. Except that I'm without any real sphere of influence in this stage of life as it progresses towards death. But I don't say so for fear of destroying hope.

"You should be able to see him, yes. Have you thought about anything beyond that?" I take advantage of this opening to broach the main reason for my visit. I recall, but don't mention, his recent birthday. Its relevance is lost in the current circumstances.

"We signed all those papers here in town, before we sold the farm, and we did the will and everything. Then I had to do some more after Elvira died so I think I've got most everything in order. And we did our medical forms together, meaning no jump-starting the heart or any of that. She made sure I did it with her when she was in the hospital. She knew I wouldn't do it on my own. I said whatever was good enough for her was good enough for me. Sort of brings it all home, doesn't it? I wonder if she knew something was going to happen to me, even then," his eyes return to the wedding photo.

As he says this I am suddenly accosted with a memory: I have met Cecil before, outside of the doctor-patient realm. When I saw him in the clinic that time I was too preoccupied with electronic fiddling to remember. It was a midsummer day last year, much like today, and we were both picking Saskatoons in the hot, quiet air near the little roadside campground just outside of town. I had pedaled my bike out there for a bit of an outing, and I noticed a truck in the parking lot. We met in the bush where the Saskatoon trees were laden with dark clusters of berries. He looked good at that point; a weathered but not beaten look had hardened into his features, along with the smile lines. His gallon ice cream pail dangled at thigh-height. It was held up by means of its handle being looped through the belt of his jeans, whereas I was merely eating as I picked. Since he seemed to be going ahead with more purpose, I offered to help him fill his bucket.

Mosquitoes hummed in our ears but only occasionally landed to sting. From time to time a slight breeze lifted the leaves and cooled where the sweat trickled. We picked in silence, pulling down the gently-yielding branches one at a time, checking underfoot for the drooping leaves of poison ivy before moving ahead. He began to speak when the bucket was half full.

"Like to come out here when the berries are good. You can see what a difference a little rain makes. Over near Arden they never got any, and their bushes haven't more'n a few shriveled up berries on 'em."

"Do you farm around here?" I asked.

"Used to. Used to have a big place over west of here. Sold it all, coupl'a three years ago. Guess I was lucky to sell. Still, it's something of a crime the price I got. Don't know what the fellow who bought it is making anything. He's talking 'bout selling to one of those big corporations, what takes over and runs a bunch of farms at once. Maybe it's the only way to keep the grain coming," he shrugged.

"So you live in town now?" I reached towards him and dumped a sizeable handful of Saskatoons into the bucket.

"Yep. Moved with the wife just after selling the farm. 'Till she died — passed away in June, she did. Now I don't know what I'll do with all these berries. She's the one what always had to do with 'em..."

He tried to laugh, but nothing came of it. Instead, he just shook his head and waved an arm in my direction. He turned his face away, but not before I saw what was there: the sadness, mixed with shame at being caught.

We went on picking in silence again for a while after that. Both of us swatted at bugs, once or twice he wiped his face. The bucket filled, he turned around and thanked me for my help.

"I'd invite you over for some supper, but the place is in kind of a mess and I'm not much of one to cook anyway, still haven't got the hang of it..." he gestured vaguely with his free arm.

I assured him there was no obligation, we thanked each other and waved good bye. I shaded my eyes against the now lowering sun and watched him go. Stooped a little, he walked as though he might always be on the verge of catching himself from falling forward. He seemed small once he was seated behind the wheel of his big old Ford. The engine roared the way elderly diesels do, and the truck rattled hard against the washboard of the gravel road.

The chalky dust took a long time drifting to where I stood. I tasted the few tart berries in my hand, now mixed with the dryness of the road. I thought about the old farmer, his berries forgotten and rotting on the porch, calls from the kids on Sundays, cribbage and beer at the Legion, the quiet house and empty bed. Him falling asleep on the couch again.

I see and hear all this as we finalize the details of my house call. I make my notes for the home care communication and give him written instructions about symptom control. There is no need to speak of our previous encounter now. We have both been moved to another plane of existence since then, and those kind of shared memories have lost so much ground they are now merest atoms among the infinite details of eternity, whatever and wherever that is.

I note the crumbs of a tea and toast meal, not even what would I might recommend as low fat or no cholesterol in a different setting — just subsistence. He assures me he's able to eat, and I suppose he does manage to swallow something in between the cough, the momentary choke and gasp, in spite of the ache that can't be rubbed away even if there was someone here to do it.

After I finish the house call I find myself still recalling that elevation of land where the scrubby forest is edged with Saskatoon bushes, where I'd first encountered Cecil. So I follow the highway out of town to the same place. I am unsuitably dressed, and my shoes may be the worse for it after I walk about here, but only a bit because the summer has been so dry. The recent lack of precipitation has meant a deficit of bugs, something that pleases everyone but the odd fly-catching bird, so I won't be troubled that way. I can recognize the exact curve of the path and the place that lets one in deeper to find the slim, usually well-laden, Saskatoon bushes in a small clearing. But they are not as bountiful this year. This is a less desirable result of the season's dryness: too little moisture to plump up the berries. There also seems to be a disease that has withered and decayed the few that managed to mature. I feel a slight disappointment, though without a pail, and now, like Cecil, lacking an adept hand to put the harvest to its best use, I wonder why I came here with any expectation at all.

Afterwards, I drive a long circuit home by way of the country roads. In the delicate infusion of early evening light, I can see to the east there's a machine shed aglow with all the cast-off light the sun can throw. Northwards, grey threads of rain fall in slender curves from a solitary blackening cloud. On my left is the new wind farm. There's a kind of cruel but sensuous grace to each slowly rotating triad of blades. They look like something just a bit too sharp, something that could draw blood without intending to.

I wish I could do more for Cecil. I know his path is as inevitable as it is unenviable. Medicine, if it actually is an art, has to be the lowest of them all, scrabbling about amongst the vagaries of barely-regulated chemical reactions, chromosomal damage and chaos. Indeed, how can it be an art when it is a slave to science, lacking a muse to guide the hapless practitioner through the clamorous needs of the injured, the ill, the imperfect. Healing may be more closely aligned with the ways of magic or even religion, though many doctors would sooner strangle themselves on their stethoscopes than agree. More than once I have observed an inexplicable improvement or decay in a patient. Inexplicable, until one considers how some have a tough inner tendril that clings to life, on the one hand, while others succumb to the forced retirement, the recent bereavement, the festering alienation that finally comes, physiologically, home to roost, on the other. It all counts, we just can't tell how.

And if anyone should be having these illuminating thoughts all, or most, of the time, shouldn't it be me? I'm at the far end of the arc; I've seen the full spectrum of fire to ice, earth to earth, the mirrored reality of my own mortality. But instead of profound and revealing insights, what do I find myself thinking about? The words to a theme song for a long — and just as well — forgotten TV show, or wondering if I left the garage door up, or even recalling the shape and satisfaction of my morning bowel movement. It is complete and utter absurdity for me to be the carrier of this mass of accumulated knowledge and experience, over such a long period of time, and for all of it to be rendered inconsequential, eclipsed by the trite.

*   *   *

Once home I make a salad out of mostly carrots and beets, as it is their prime season. In a quaintly regressive way there is a tiny farmer's market that sets up in the strip mall parking lot on Saturdays mornings the past few years, and I can buy my vegetables fresh and local. I consider it a step backwards because, truly, in this country and in this age, no one wants to grub in the earth and make a living from it. It's impossible anyway if you want to have household electronics and an education for your offspring. There's a reason why there were serfs and slaves, now replaced by machinery or workers imported just for their backs, who get the job done on minimal upkeep. Still, I'm ready to support the faithful vendors at the weekend market who do it for pin money. If nothing else it gets them up off the couch.

To make my salad I use the gadget I bought the last time I was in the city visiting Nettie. It has a series of serrations on a blade that swivels slightly, allowing it to follow the contours of the root and produce an abundance of fine tendrils. It fills the bowl with a beautiful tangle of orange and cerise. Drizzled with a vinaigrette that I make using fresh dill and thyme from the garden, topped with a sprinkling of toasted almonds, it makes quite a satisfactory meal.

While she was still here and in her kitchen domain, I would watch Nettie's ingredients and methods closely on days when I felt I could be interactive. Sometimes I was granted a role approximating a line cook. I would gather the spume about the perimeter of a pot of kidney beans boiling in anticipation of the minestrone soup they were soon to join, or glean the brightest and best of the cherry tomatoes she'd brought in from the garden for our salad. I did a good bit of chopping. I knew my place, and in the kitchen I was a subaltern to her authority. In all matters of decision-making, there needs to be a final authority. She made her decisions, I, mine. Now that I am the cook, I like to stray from the recipe. I think of it more as a guideline, like the ones we're always receiving at the clinic: applicable to some, but not all, situations, meant to be malleable the way life is. I doubt Nettie so much as used the other side of the grater. It was a trifle tedious, that degree of competence without creativity — I would have tried alluring garnishes and provocative new spices, but she made the same thing over and over. And everything was delicious, without a doubt, but as predictable as a Hollywood movie, which she also preferred to the more enigmatic films I liked.

"But that never really ended, Paul," was one of Nettie's typical protests after the closing frame of a movie I'd chosen.

"What is an ending? We know everything goes on, after the last scene, the departure, the funeral. Why not acknowledge it?" I would counter.

"I want a conclusion, some kind of satisfaction. Something to make me happy," she continued with her own line of reasoning, not wanting to engage with mine.

"Are you not already happy?" I asked even if I didn't want an answer.

That would be the start of one of those silences. A scene of our own without end, panning forward into the bedroom and bathroom where doors were closed before the shoulders were bared. A poor scriptwriter, an even more worthless editor, made a mess of our dialogue for at least the last ten years of our marriage. She stopped talking altogether the week before she left. I would try and make a few observations to engage her again, about my day's work, the weather, minor plans. She remained steadfastly mute, beyond reach of reason and attempts at distraction. She'd used up all her words, I believe was the last thing she said to me before she started her vow of silence. It was a comment that proved almost forensic in its prescience, as if such a consequence could be arranged by uttering it then its will would be done. Less than a month after her she left me, she was silenced permanently. It wasn't a large stroke, but the lacuna was strategically placed to ensure no further output. So it is in clinical neurology as it is in real estate: location, location, location. She damaged that one little piece of cerebral territory for which there is no substitute. At least it happened — I am rationalizing, I know, as a form of self-consolation — at a juncture when I knew she didn't care to hear any of my anecdotes, observations or opinions. Imagine the torture of her in that bodily prison, visit after visit, being forced to listen to me, who would just as soon not say much of anything. So I don't bother. I bring along a book or a newspaper and I read aloud to her when I go to visit. I admit it's of my own choosing, but aside from the formula of greeting and parting, I limit my words to someone else's.

And if anyone in town here knows the reality of our situation, they aren't saying. There may well have been speculation during those first weeks, when it was apparent that Nettie was not at home. People in small towns pay attention to details, such as the absence of her car and her daily walk, and gossip can quickly escalate. But that curiosity was just as quickly replaced by solicitude when news of her stroke got around, then surprise at how quickly I returned to work. How many of the dots the twins have connected, I don't know, and I don't inquire. There was always a pact of closeness between those three, mother and twin daughters. The loner male was an easy role for me to assume, once we were established as a nuclear family. I let them have the after-supper conversations, do the planning, welcome the guests. I always felt I was justified in my reserve after a day in practice. Now I hope that my conjugal faithfulness and the maintenance of the trappings of marriage — not the façade, for it is a real representation — can make amends for what the girls probably see as my deficiencies.

I am once again seated at the outdoor table and chairs on the back porch. I have finished my colourful and sculptural salad. The evening stays comfortably warm. From the glow all about I sense somewhere nearby there is one of those long and many-shaded prairie sunsets, in the wide-open panoply that some describe as flat but is in fact so much more dimensional than that. Hereabouts the land is not as redolent as that lying further south and west, where the glaciers deposited their bounty in the form of rich topsoil. We got the rocks. Beautiful rocks, they can be landmarks and historians and almost friends in their silent permanence, but rocks nonetheless. The fields are hard-won, extracted from forests and regressing in low places to their watery past. The soil is infused with acidity that better suits the growing needs of blueberries and black spruce, but these men are hardy, and they are farmers, and there is no denying an acre of land that a disc and harrow might be able to turn. When the frost comes early and the markets show no mercy, there's always next year.

I know these men, how their countenances sag and their defenses protrude when their doctor suggests they take time off work, or, worse, need to stop working. They don't say anything, but they don't need to, I can read it in their faces: the prospect of being unable to roll along a field of wheat or rye and count its progress as a reflection of one's own merit, far beyond its dollar value, is devastating. They often don't heed their doctor's advice anyway; they'd rather have their next heart attack in the cab of their combine than anywhere else. I have great respect for them, and their long-suffering wives, and I have often considered how badly suited I would be to such a life. If my well-being and that of my family depended on such vagaries as germination rates and weather and commodity market prices I could not remain sane. And yet how many of them have said to me "I wouldn't do what you're doing, doc" and they are probably right. So right, that like them I will never be able to do anything else: not retire, not change, not be disabled or senescent, heaven forbid. The worst patients are the physicians.

TRY NOT TO CARE SO MUCH

> "Then the enchantress allowed her anger to be softened and said... 'I will allow you to take away with you as much rampion as you will, only I make one condition, you must give me the child which your wife will bring into the world; it shall be well treated, and I will care for it like a mother.'"
>
> *Rapunzel*, Grimm's Fairy Tales

Iris had been running late all morning the day her doctor died. Before hearing the news she had stopped in at the conservatory, desperate for a reprieve from the arctic air, so dry and bitter, that had descended on the city in recent weeks. Although the region's residents were reminded of their northern latitude the early months of every year, it still came as a shock when it happened. Iris turned into the conservatory parking lot, took note of its surface — an impenetrable fondant of smoothly packed snow — and reminded herself not to hurry. Even so, it took a number of sliding stops before she could get her car immobilized. She forced herself to walk slowly after the first step nearly sent her tumbling. When she finally reached the conservatory's front doors, mental stopwatch ticking, she questioned her judgment.

The pressure of the morning's collapsing time-frame was undeniable, and she briefly considered turning around and going back
to her car. But as soon as her skin encountered the soft, humid
surroundings of the greenhouse it felt less like medium-grade
sandpaper, and further inside she could hear the soothing patter
of water.

Iris nodded to the volunteers at the entrance as she headed
towards the palm room. Being here reminded Iris of her mother,
Astrid. They used to come when Iris was a child to visit all of
Astrid's favourite plants. Astrid would recite the botanical
names as if they were incantations, possibly inventing the ones
she didn't know. Sometimes they would wander the brick paths
for what seemed like hours. Iris couldn't ever recall her mother
worrying about time or being late; Astrid simply expected people
to be pleased about her arrival when it happened. She loved all
things green and growing, and often judged them more worthy
than humans. At the conservatory she would luxuriate in the
glorious outcomes of someone else's labour, perhaps because
in her own garden she was a pragmatist and appreciated ample
reward for her work. Seeing calla lilies in the conservatory, Iris
remembered how she once gave her mother one for a birthday
present, thinking it the most beautiful and elegant flower ever.
When it shriveled after a chilly late-spring night in the garden,
her mother promptly dug it up and replaced it with a tough-
rooted tiger lily.

Iris hadn't been to the conservatory since before Astrid died
two years ago. The image of her mother the gardener, nurturing
and knowledgeable, came with the sweet rejoinder of nostalgia.
At the same time she was aware of other memories that stood
like effigies made for some dark art and needed to be kept at
a distance.

Iris perched on a wrought-iron bench and noticed a delicate
sweetness in the air. She twisted her neck until she located
the source — clusters of waxy pale pink flowers dangling from

a nearby vine that was growing up the bulging trunk of a date tree. Iris reminded herself why she had booked this day off from her own clinic: to be occasionally stilled in the course of her busy life, and to avoid the neglect of her own viscera the way so many doctors did. The way she used to do. It didn't seem to matter where she went, though, or what she did, the needs of her profession followed her like ducklings behind their mother. Just as she was becoming settled among the palm room's quiet arrangement leaves and fronds, she remembered she needed to review the two patients she admitted yesterday with the charge nurse. She located her phone in her coat pocket and called the hospital.

"Hi Rona, I'm calling to check on those admissions," Iris said to the answering voice.

"Good morning, doctor. Hold on, let me pull the charts." They spent the next few minutes reviewing medications and test results.

"Can you reduce that IV rate please, Rona? If she does well with a clear fluid diet we can discontinue it later today. I think that pretty well covers everything."

"Yes, doctor. I suppose you've already heard — Dr. Miecznikowski died this morning," Rona said.

"Oh no, Rona, that can't be — I'm just on my way to see her," Iris said, aware of the illogic of her statement even as she uttered it.

"So you didn't know? I'm so sorry, I was sure someone would have called you already. I shouldn't have just come right out and told you," Rona sounded truly apologetic about her offhand disclosure.

"It's not your fault, Rona. But what happened?" Iris asked.

"All I heard is that she collapsed in her clinic. By the time the ambulance got there she was pulseless, no respirations. Maybe a pulmonary embolus, they're saying. I'm sorry."

After the call, Iris cradled the phone in both hands and gazed into its blankly reflective surface. A tear distorted what she could see of herself: a round face with neatly pulled-back, if greying, hair, eyes with a trail of darkness underneath them even before the flow of dissolving mascara, the slight pursing of her lips. Superstitious thought pushed its way through the detachment of her shock. Was it because she'd decided to call the hospital, when she was supposed to be finding some kind of peace here in the conservatory, that Dr. M. had died? Was it because she was doing something she wasn't meant to be doing — stopping at the conservatory when punctuality was already a stretch — that the news came to her at all? Then, as if to further rebuff all of her accumulated knowledge and training and professionalism, it was the hardest thing possible not to say the word "no" out loud to the device that lay quiet before her.

Instead of the surrounding flora Iris now saw Dr. M.'s focused expression and unveiled intensity, bent over the latest test results. Dr. M.'s eyes, recently enlarged by reading glasses, would make brief contact with Iris's and convey the ratio of empathy to objectivity that the results deserved before return-ing to numbers and normal ranges. If there were stigmata and auguries heralding this abrupt departure, Iris had either missed them, or saw them only in hindsight. All the appointments Dr. M. had cancelled: Iris would need to repent for the annoyance felt and expletives uttered at the time. She remembered the way Dr. M.'s lab coat hung more loosely on her form after she came back from her sick leave. The herringbone pattern of her tights and beautifully variegated patent leather pumps she often wore denied anything the least bit deteriorated about her appearance. Her hair had maintained its strength and demure styling. But her face had aged out of proportion with the amount of time she had been away. Iris had wanted to ask about her doctor's health during appointments, but hadn't. It seemed like it would disrupt the flow of their transaction. Already it was difficult to distinguish between when Iris was a colleague, and when she was the besieged.

Iris thought of all that was unique, and possibly irreplaceable, between them. No one else knew about the shame Iris had felt a year ago when she had to call her clinic to say she wouldn't be at work that week, and not for the next indefinite number of weeks. The way her mother's death and apparent resurrection through dreams and flashbacks had triggered a paralyzing aversion to any reminder of her childhood, had sent her into territory that required medication and painful regression before she could tunnel her way back. It was a dark place that they had been together, Iris and her doctor. Though Iris had seen it many times from the other side of the desk, that role was no comparison to being the subject and the object of such a depleted state.

Glancing down at her phone again, this time registering the time while no longer being propelled by it, she noticed she had dripped coffee on the front of her cream blouse. She wished mistakes like that didn't bother her. Last night she had underslept, awakening off and on even after she finally fell asleep around midnight. Towards four a.m. she descended into her best sleep until being startled awake by the voice on the clock radio. She had to will herself out of bed, uncoordinated before and shaky after her morning coffee. That was probably where the stain came from. Iris forced her awareness away from her own flaws and gazed through the strata of life around her. There was something remarkable about the existence of these plants, fragile and yet flourishing in this haven. The brutish weather on the other side of the domed glass roof would kill everything here within minutes. A hungry wind made the flailing, barren tree branches outside mock every living thing from temperate to tropical. But here in the conservatory orchids bloomed, dignified and languorously beautiful, drawing sustenance from the enriched air exactly as her face was doing. She switched off the power on her phone and leaned back as much as the hard bench would allow.

*   *   *

Iris could recall her mother being as intense and conflicted as only a writer or an evangelist could be. Astrid managed to be both in the last few years of their small town life, before it was swallowed by the nearby urban whole and the uniqueness of their community was diluted beyond recognition. A receiver and maker of confessions, her words were occasionally made public in the local paper, or heard, to Iris's chagrin, over a megaphone at rallies and demonstrations. Whatever the setting, Astrid managed to bind together a sacred expression of small truths and transgressions with a secular exuberance of language. People in hard-worn and mismatched clothing clustered around her and Astrid tolerated them as long as she could; despite her pessimism about humanity she thrived on its attention. When she was sixteen Iris stopped attending events with her mother and took to reading her journals while she was out.

On days when the house was inert, without the vibrato of her mother's presence, Iris would enter the washed-out and dusky aesthetics of Astrid's bedroom and head for the shelf with all the journals. They were haphazardly arranged and intermingled with excerpted recipes, newspaper articles of unconnected significance, novels in smallish font on yellowing pages. Iris thought of the shelf as an archaeologist's dig, where everything she unearthed had a meaning. The challenge was to determine what that significance was, in relation to everything else. The daily entries themselves were like fables and fairy tales, entertaining to read but every line and indentation possibly weighted with another, darker significance. Although there were dates, and the writing was mostly in first person, there was no way to distinguish tortured fact from fictional sketch. Iris recognized Astrid's imprint, ever triangulating towards some center of rage or passion, often naming a conflict without feeling the need to resolve it. Few corrections, many omissions, numerous smudges

— whether from haste or tears Iris couldn't tell. Sometimes Iris could connect the written content with an actual event, other times the mismatch between description and reality was obvious. Like the entry that described a gallery outing with an unnamed daughter, on a date when Iris knew her mother had been a speaker at a conference. Some of the lists were so mundane she wondered why her mother bothered ("The contents of my pocket", "Name all feelings today"). Occasionally a phrase stood alone at the top of a page: "If only I could achieve the right amount of rest, I would think the most excellent thoughts and that would change everything." Or, "A history of shared trauma could be the strongest bond." She noticed, with repeated visits, how such a sentence could remain unconnected, as though the initial foray went into territory not yet ready for exploration.

All else became transient and insignificant as she worked to decipher and absorb the script on the lined pages. Her mother's bed was sway-backed along its edge and Iris would sit slouched in the middle of its depression until there was a sound at the front door. When she heard the signal she would replace the journal in its memorized spot and ease herself back towards the small desk in her own room. She made sure to assume an absorbed flex of her head over her homework before her mother came upstairs.

*   *   *

"Do you want an adult? I can hear you scream but I am so sleepy I can't tell what it means. The shards of those waking dreams are still unpolished: they press into the raw and fleshy wound. The one that is already having a hard time healing. So can you take it all back? Not just the words, but entire stanzas; the way your hand brushed mine, even."

*   *   *

In the morning the kitchen would be silent except for the gurgle of tea as it was poured from the pot; Iris's task was to assemble a breakfast tray and leave it outside her mother's room just before she left for school. That and preserve the family vow of silence at breakfast, to help shelter Astrid's hearing from acoustic intrusions until mid-morning. By then she seemed to become less sensitive, able to assume the pitch and drive that propelled her for the rest of the day. Iris would remove two plates and cups for her herself and her mother, taking them out of the dishwasher carefully so as not to make them clatter. She would make two servings of toast and marmalade, with warm milk and honey in her own mug on cold mornings. If the newspaper arrived on time she fetched it from the step, keeping her footfalls tender on the linoleum. Even the door handle, with just the right grip, could be made to hold its tongue. Not just anyone could make it slide without a click; Iris came to appreciate that maintaining the household code gave her a kind of power, almost like being invisible. She read the paper while she ate her breakfast alone, checking the weather forecast. If it was meant to be cloudy she would pull the blinds halfway up. The low midwinter sun, its rays amplified by snow, was an especial affront to Astrid's eyes when she came downstairs. On those days the blinds were to be left fully drawn. Iris knew her mother didn't linger in bed very long after she left for school: Astrid liked her tea hot and it was steaming when Iris placed the tray outside the bedroom door. In the afternoon when she came home from school she would often find her mother singing along with the radio or talking on the phone if she hadn't already departed on a mission.

Through the long winter evenings, November to March, Astrid would again become less tolerant of her own senses. She would light candles and trade illumination for ambience, making it a strain for Iris to read a recipe that had been saved from a package or written in the spiral-bound notebook. Marcus, her oldest brother, sometimes dropped in for supper. He was the only force that could reverse Astrid's painful hyperacuity. Arriving on a gust of machine oil, sweat stains and diesel residue, not bothering to remove his shoes, he hugged Astrid and called her mammy while he pulled at her apron strings and made her giggle. They would uncork a bottle of wine and toast themselves. Iris would station herself at the opposite end of the counter to chop vegetables, and she would pour her own drink from a can of warm pop laced with ice cubes that tasted of freezer burn. She kept her focus on making perfect discs of the radishes she was slicing. Astrid wanted radishes in everything, from stir-fry to salad to stew. She scoured the supermarkets to find them in the dead of winter, a departure from her usual frugal shopping habits. Iris stood her ground but remained aware of Marcus' every move, the way a dancer is aware of a partner, prepared to respond to that presence and to the least bit of pressure.

"So, you have a boyfriend yet?" Marcus would ask. Iris remained silent while Astrid answered for her.

"She's always studying, or reading, or at the pool training. She might be sixteen but she's above all that, right Iris?" Astrid momentarily looked away from Marcus to glance at Iris.

Marcus's face made a leer. "I dunno. She's going to be away again, lifeguarding at that camp half the summer. We won't know what's going on there, will we?"

Iris kept to her paring and cutting, contained and unresponsive, going on to cucumbers and peppers, leaving the onions to last the way she'd been taught so as not to mar the flavours of all the other ingredients. Marcus and her mother went on to discuss the twin middle siblings, Blake and Josie. He offered to teach them some manners if they weren't being respectful, as if they were still malleable children. Iris tried not to listen, but sometimes their comments made it past her barriers. Like rogue molecules through a cell membrane as it was illustrated in her biology book, their words slipped into passages that should have distinguished between nourishment to be absorbed and toxins to be excluded. Words carved into imperatives by Marcus' deepening voice, and reflected by her mother's animated self as the bottle of wine emptied. Astrid's upper registers were nearly flirtatious, and always deferential towards her older son.

One evening he directed his comments to Astrid but kept Iris in his sightline as she moved about making supper. "Just look at her, will you? Filling right out, looking so gorgeous. How do the guys stand it? She must be fighting them off tooth and nail."

"Takes after her mama, don't you think?" Astrid swung her hips and Iris angled her gaze so that she couldn't see.

Suddenly it was his hand, his hand on her hair, in a moment of unawareness. Reaching for dishes on a shelf, still partly blinded by onion miasma, she didn't blink fast enough to see him coming. Her fault, she had been too absorbed in her task and had turned her back. The roots of her hair interpreted his touch's intent. His hand made a sliding motion, naturally, for her hair was so straight and fine and blonde it seemed to invite the light passage of fingertips.

"Don't!" she yelled. Her own hand likewise asserted itself as she swung about and hit Marcus in the shoulder. With that gesture she dropped the mug in her other hand onto the countertop. Its sharp fragments mixed with the larger ones of the platter it landed on.

"Idiot! How can you be so clumsy?" Astrid shouted. It was the serving dish she had made in her pottery phase, specially glazed with the imprint of leaves from the oaks out back.

"I'm so sorry," Iris whispered. She tried to fit the shards and triangles back together knowing it was hopeless, now unable to see clearly because of the tears.

"You can't possibly be sorry, you're too stupid. Get out." Astrid gained inches in her indignation, making it difficult for Iris to get past.

"Hey, it was just a mistake. I startled her." Marcus managed to sound genuinely contrite. "I wanted to ask if she'll think about me when she goes away this summer."

"Get out," Astrid repeated her command. "We'll call you down when you can eat."

Iris' legs were of half-set gelatin as she climbed the stairs. The pause at the top landing confirmed that no one was coming after her. It would be possible to slip in and take a journal from the shelf. She wiped her eyes and selected a spiral-bound, plastic covered one that was padded with additional sheets of loose leaf, as though the original journal-maker had forgotten to put in enough pages.

*   *   *

There will be a few weeks of opportunity, maybe only one or two. The deal closes, the cleaners and renovators come (but surely only during weekday, and daylight, hours). Then a moving van shows up and the occupying forces arrive. For all I know they hate gardening, have arthritis, ascribe only to annuals, go away to the lake all summer. I can take what I like, for it has no actual value. If they were around to know what I'm about to do, Miranda and Sue would be glad to have their little perennial patch live on. We always shared everything, I am beholden to no one. There was that time about the baby, but that's all behind us. Good thing, too: there's no reconciling from the place they've gone. None of us saw this coming, the least I can do is help them have a legacy.

*   *   *

Somewhere among the canopy of palm-fronds, banana trees and fig leaves there were birds as small as their chirp who also lived in the shelter of the conservatory. Iris trained her eye to see not their outline, but their movement. She let her central gaze dissolve so as to maximize peripheral acuity. Anthony had taught her to do this the summer she was seventeen and had worked at that camp. When they went into the woods together, he adjusted his field glasses to her dimensions, and when her arms grew tired of holding them he made her use his back for support. The imminence of his voice's deepening range transmitted his lore through her elbows and forearms. She offered her back to him one day when it was a mass of blonde almost to her waist, and she pretended not to notice at first. They let the field glasses remain suspended between them, for a while acting like a sincere but ineffective chaperone, doing its best until they were dropped on the ground.

A week after she got home from camp, Anthony still hadn't called and Iris realized he wasn't ever going to. Tomorrow she would be leaving for university, and she needed to ritualize the rejection, to sever the one expendable part of the whole that he had briefly possessed. Astrid was out in the garden and Iris was glad to have the house to herself. But without her mother's help it took a while to find scissors that were sharp enough. Most were so dull she knew they would not overcome her hair's thickness, and she wanted to be cleansed of her selfishness and remorse as quickly as possible. Eventually she found a pair in her mother's sewing corner, still unopened and in their original package.

She had trimmed her own hair before, convenience and economy coming ahead of vanity. But this time she wanted to be shorn, and the first cut would have to be sufficiently dire or she might be tempted to call it off. She decided to begin at the front, where the change would be more obvious. At first she was alarmed to see so many strands of hair falling in tangled, useless, random crosshatches and intersections all over the bathroom floor. A few swatches were a noticeably lighter burnish from when the sun had flattered her in recent weeks,

ANN E. LOEWEN

and were therefore especially hateful. Once Iris had completed her task, all the scattered indicators of indolence were saluted, swept up, and left to consider their idle wanderings in the plastic trash can. Now that autumn and seriousness were approaching, both the days and hope had shortened and darker growth would prevail. It was time to put her mind to new tasks. She would not be diverted again.

She found her mother digging up tubers and uprooting annuals in the flower garden. It was only a few days into September but fall had arrived and settled its debt with summer early. Now the frost could collect its bounty: a rigor mortis of blackened stems, tarnished leaves and writhing flowerets caught in mid-bloom and filling the wheelbarrow.

"Seems like such a waste of effort, a year like this when the season is so short. All that work just to be thrown away." Astrid knew Iris was there behind her, but she kept at her work.

"But you love your flowers," Iris said against her own will. She had wanted to be neutral, if possible silent, without an idea or opinion for the rest of the day as part of her pact with her new self.

Astrid paused and rotated towards Iris while still squatting. "What have you done? You look beastly!"

"I am beastly," Iris said.

"But your hair. It was so long, so beautiful and blonde. It was the one..." Astrid stopped.

"Go ahead, say it. It was the one nice thing about me. But you couldn't say it while I had it," Iris accused, glad to have broken her own vow.

"I didn't need to. You don't care about those things. You care about other things."

"See? Then it doesn't matter." Iris shrugged.

"But something should matter. Or you'll go about looking like someone who hates themselves," Astrid was almost pleading.

"Couldn't I just hate my hair? Do I have to hate every single bit of myself?"

"Don't twist it all around. I could have taken you somewhere and had it done nice, if I couldn't talk you out of it. I never knew you cared." Astrid rotated back towards her previous task and the expression of empathy was over. "Give me a hand with the tomatoes and zucchinis over in the vegetable patch, will you. The frost got all of them too. Then get me a few buckets of compost. I have to finish dividing up the perennials."

Iris found the gloves she knew fit best and started to work. When she had finished untwining plant remnants from the tomato cages she nested their awkward legs and waists together in a stack and placed them behind the garden shed. Tall weeds had invaded that space and for a while she worked at pulling them out, finding a certain release in seeing the lanky invaders conquered and the small domain cleared. She found a burlap bag in the shed and began stuffing it with dead plants. The frost-decayed zucchini vines retained a rope-like strength; they had to be dragged intact from the ground and then cut into segments with shears to fit in the bag.

Farther back in the yard, one of the piles of compost smelled like the sweetness of next year's growth and Iris shoveled two pails full. She delivered them to the places Astrid wanted and went back for a second load. After the last trip she started to rake a pile of fresh-fallen leaves. But a little caprice of wind quickly came along and untidied her work. Astrid waved her off the task.

"You can do that when more leaves have fallen. Come and help me divide up the bulbs and tubers instead." Iris set the rake aside and joined Astrid on the stone pathway beside the flower bed. Dozens of rough brown root structures were scattered about next to where they had been unearthed.

By then Iris couldn't put off asking any longer. "Why did you call me that?"

"What? Beastly?"

"No. Iris."

"I thought I'd name you exactly what I wanted you to be: a beautiful, tough, highly evolved life form. How much more could a person want, starting out in this awful world?" Astrid didn't look up from her task as she spoke. Instead she beckoned for Iris to kneel down with her so she could show her how to count segments on the rhizomes and then break them to maximize blooms next season. Iris knew that once Astrid had planted her own garden she would put the rest of the root sections in her favourite willow trug and take them to her next meeting. When she was younger Iris used to go along and bear witness to Astrid's generosity as she distributed her garden's bounty to the faithful and the friendless, basking in the praise she felt she deserved for her generosity.

"It also means rainbow." Astrid kept her eyes lowered and spoke to her task.

"What?" Iris asked.

"Iris. It means rainbow. Remember how you used to love rainbows? You'd recite the colours — redorangeyellowgreenblueindigoviolet — when you saw a picture of one. You were incensed if anyone got it wrong. In the summer you would go through the garden, trying to find a flower in each colour of the rainbow. I've always thought of you as an iris, in so many ways."

"Did you take them from someone?"

"What?" Astrid looked up.

"The irises, the ones growing in your garden."

"Why would you ask that?" Astrid said sharply, and Iris noted the slightly startled expression on her face.

"No reason," Iris replied. "Just thought I'd heard something about that one time."

"I don't know where you would have heard it. But yes, actually, they're from a friend's garden. Two women who used to live next door, they were a couple actually." Astrid gestured to the yard beside theirs. "They drowned together in a boating accident."

"How did it happen?"

"They were visiting a friend's cottage and it was early in the season. They didn't expect the wind to come up while they were crossing the lake and when it tipped them over the water was so cold they couldn't survive. I wanted something to remember them by."

"So you stole some flowers from their garden." Iris found that saying it brought less satisfaction than she had expected.

"It's not really stealing. They're plants, not possessions. In fact they were just coming out of their dormant stage so it wasn't like I was taking a living thing. How do you know about it?" Astrid looked genuinely puzzled.

"I don't know. I think someone just said so, once."

"Maybe me."

"Maybe."

Astrid had stopped sorting the tubers and gazed in the direction of her dead friends' property. Seeing her mother's flushed and stained face, a bruise of dirt on the forehead over the left eye, Iris remembered the passage she'd read just yesterday:

Today I looked in the mirror, and was surprised to see my lips so unusually red. Then I remembered: they had been kissed.

The date was correct, August 30, and the entry followed the one Iris had read a few days before that. Since she'd returned home from camp their nights had mostly been as solitary as ever, as far as Iris could tell the fitful light of the television in the dark living room was her mother's only companion. And she had seen Astrid falling asleep in the arms of no one but her favourite chair. Does she go somewhere after I fall asleep? Iris wondered. Does someone come over when I'm away? Are her journals full of what she wishes would happen? Iris recalled that Marcus had been over two nights in a row this past week. Iris was accustomed to the nocturnal comings and goings of her siblings Josie and Blake, and often didn't hear the door when they arrived. But it was different when Marcus came by to collapse on the couch and recover. His footsteps triggered an alert that would bring her to consciousness until she could sense his location and judge the safety of his distance. On those nights she remained spring-loaded, aware of every sigh and shuffle in the house in case it was him. Even after she locked her door she remained uneasy.

Iris wanted to talk about that, and about the times when she was young and Astrid would be out late, supporting a cause, with Marcus left in charge while the twins snuck out. The times when there weren't any sleepovers and she had nowhere to go. She would hear him climbing the stairs to her room, then a word, or a knock at her bedroom door, and she knew Marcus wanted more of something he'd already taken.

Iris had found Astrid surprisingly easy to convince that she was suddenly afraid of some unnamed threat at night even though she was twelve, and that being able to lock her bedroom door would help. Iris was accustomed to her needs being deferred for weeks, even months. This time, though, a man from down the street was called and a new door handle that locked from inside her room was installed within a week. Not long after that Marcus moved out, and Iris was left in charge whenever Astrid was away.

Now, seeing Astrid in her usual garden squat stance, wearing a plaid shirt over a shapeless sweater, in dirty gardening trousers and trailing hair that had lost all natural colour and shine, Iris knew she hadn't been kissed. Not last night. Not ever, in the childish subversion of the imagined parent. Not the way she, Iris, had been kissed by Anthony, so light and slight a sensation that it was conducted over her body's entire surface. That touch now as dead as the nasturtiums she had helped to gather, but the memory like the shriveled flowers still pungent and peppery.

"Do you have to go?" Astrid straightened herself to standing with a grimace.

"Where?" Iris looked up from where she still knelt on the path.

"Away, Iris. To that college." Astrid made a vague gesture to the east.

"University," Iris said. She stood so that she could meet her mother's gaze.

"That one," Astrid nodded.

"I've got a scholarship, you know that."

"There's a university right here. You could go to it and still live at home."

"You have Josie and Blake."

"They're not the same."

Astrid squatted down again on her haunches, the balance and strength of her thighs still apparent through the loose clothing. She rubbed her forehead with the back of her right wrist. She tried to use the clean patch of skin just beyond her soil-laden glove, but she still managed to add to the facial smudging. Iris' shirt was a faded flannel taken from the holdings in the front closet. It might have been Marcus', or even one of her father's before he died. The long loose shirt-tail was the only clean thing between them, so Iris used one section of it to wipe some of the dirt from her mother's face, and another for the tear sitting in the dark furrow beneath her eye. Astrid didn't flinch.

"They wanted you, Miranda and Sue did," she said.

"Me?" Iris halted, the shirt-end still in her hand.

"I was showing pretty big and your dad wasn't long dead. Marcus was non-stop, in trouble all the time. The twins were still small. They wanted a kid, they were running out of options. I probably looked like I had too many. I guess they thought it wouldn't hurt to ask."

"That's terrible, asking someone for their baby." Iris looked down at her mother, saw how her hair thinned at the crown.

"All over the world, women get pregnant when they don't want to be, and other women want to be but aren't or can't.

241

Makes sense for babies to be with people who want them."
Astrid shrugged and sniffled weakly.

"But that's me you're talking about. Didn't you want me?" Iris
felt a pressure in her chest but maintained her tone.

"Well, you were a surprise. My schedule was all fooled up with
the twins still nursing at night. Never even knew I was carrying
you 'till after your dad died, and it wasn't such a happy moment
when I found out, truth be told. I did a lot of thinking."

"But you didn't say yes," Iris needed to hear this conclusion
from her mother, not read a version of it in one of the journals.

"Didn't say yes, didn't say no, then they drowned and their
earthly troubles were over." Astrid was back to surveying her
root stocks, setting aside piles of bulbs and brushing away
clumps of dirt from her work space on the path. "Can you get
me that little stool from the shed? I can't stay crouched like this
much longer."

Iris had wanted to tell her mother about Anthony, how
he loved birds the way Astrid loved plants. She wanted to ask
why something that had felt so good was bad, and whether she
herself was good or bad, and why, if she was good, Anthony
hadn't called like he said he would. Now Iris understood the
burden of truth, that it was better to keep her stories to herself.
She would fabricate, or conceal, as the code decreed for everyone
else in the family, and follow the precedent of their accumulated
secrets. There was no need to confess what had happened during
the summer, much less tell Astrid why she had asked for a lock
on her door when she was twelve. It meant she could never find
out for sure what her father liked for supper, would he have been
good at teaching her to drive if he had lived, did he love Marcus.
Iris tried to sort the tulip bulbs through the blur of her own
tears, but Astrid said just to put them over near the shed, she'd
do it later. Iris could go on now, she'd been a good help.

*   *   *

There were more people in the conservatory now, parents with babies in strollers, a few seniors and people making a brief visit as Iris had intended to do, still dressed against the cold. Noises were made to sound distant by the foliage even when nearby. Aside from a toddler enjoying the chance to run and be free of his snowsuit, the narrow curved paths encouraged visitors to move at a slow and pensive pace.

Sometimes questions and thoughts arose during her regular appointments with Dr. M., the way they had when she used to try and talk to Astrid, ones that Iris would like to have spoken aloud. And now, as with her mother, wouldn't ever have the chance to ask. Iris recalled the signs that they were winding up during her last — and now, last ever — appointment with Dr. M. She appreciated the expenditures that came her way because she was a peer, not just a patient. They would always banter for a while about classmates and clinical practice at the beginning of an appointment. Although it diverted them from the nagging cluster of symptoms Iris wanted to discuss, it established a mutuality that kept the flow going when they eventually turned to the task at hand. Iris kept her own interpretations to a minimum and gave Dr. M. her full due.

"Do you still have trouble sleeping?" Dr. M. asked. The question always marked the transition to their doctor-patient selves.

"That's gotten better," Iris replied. "I do have a lot of vivid dreams." It was easier not to talk about the wakeful hours that occasionally still confounded her nights. And she had just seen Dr. M. discreetly suppress a yawn; she considered it possible that her doctor's needs were greater than her own.

"Ah yes, the serotonin sleep effect. Are you needing h.s. sedation?" Dr. M. asked as she reached for her prescription pad.

"Not at all. I really do sleep like a log. Most of the time," Iris said.

"Good. You mentioned weight gain. Has that stabilized?" Dr. M. asked as she filled in the name and date on the prescription.

"Yes, and I've decided I'll just live with it. Not so bad after everything else."

"Really, the side effects of medications are over-rated, compared to depression itself, don't you think," Dr. M. said and looked at her directly for affirmation.

Iris nodded. "Just frustrating, you know, the anorgasmia."

"You aren't in a relationship now, though, are you?" Dr. M. inquired and tilted her head.

"Do I need to be?"

Dr. M. looked down at the chart as though there must be another result that needed to be reviewed. She continued to make a concerted perusal of the file while Iris sat quietly, appreciating the slight subversion in their usual exchange.

"I think that making it past the anniversary of your mother's death was a big milestone," Dr. M. said as a way to move on to another aspect of her care. "And you did really well at Christmas this year, which is often such a hard time. There is a natural progression to grieving, and you've gone through all the stages. Do you feel ready to get back into practice?"

"As a matter of fact, I called the clinic the other day. I'll be starting next month."

"Good for you. Work's as good as psychotherapy." Dr. M. seemed genuinely relieved.

"I'm just afraid of all the heartache, all the things that haunt me when I finish my day and go home," Iris tried to articulate the vague unease that continued to hover about that decision.

"Like what?" Dr. M. seemed more prepared to accommodate this disclosure than the last one.

"The way people look when they suffer. All the times when I can't help them. The diagnoses I might be missing, that I might have gotten wrong. And the time pressure, I always feel like I'm in a hurry. There's never enough of me to go around."

"When I leave here I'm gone. Never give anyone, or anything, a thought," Dr. M. waved a slender hand for emphasis. "Why don't you just try not to care so much."

The manila folder of her chart closed, pointing to the end of the appointment. Iris had her prescription, and enough equilibrium to simply stand up and leave. Dr. M.'s last comment would have upset her greatly just a few months ago. This time Iris noticed an unfamiliar, but welcome, barrier between that external cue and its ability to make an impact. Could this be how others managed to get by, how Astrid had coped? Channel the difficult feelings into a dead-end corner, then knock them senseless before the slippery things could make their way back and find a place to fester. Care enough, but not too much. It wasn't what she wanted to hear, but now that she'd had a chance to reflect, maybe it was what she needed.

*   *   *

They had sat down to supper together for the last time, Josie, Blake, Astrid and Iris, on a beautiful evening in June two and a half years ago. It had been several months since Iris moved back to the city but they hadn't shared a meal until now. Iris's fortieth birthday seemed to break the inertia. Astrid had called everyone and surprised them with her cognizance, getting the date right and sticking to it.

Iris and Josie spread the table with a snagged synthetic table cloth, the fold lines still impressed on a surface no one had bothered to iron. They searched the unit and managed to find candles, but Astrid couldn't be trusted with matches so they thought they would have to do without. Luckily Blake had a lighter, and even though the sun would last long past supper it was a necessary part of the ritual to bring the candles to life. Several stained placemats, a slightly flayed bread basket and a plastic butter dish clouded from too many cycles in the dishwasher were placed on the table. Iris and Josie had wanted to buy their mother all new kitchen ware when she moved into the residence, but Astrid was adamant about bringing along every item possible.

Still, the setting was festive enough with the tablecloth a vibrant plum and a vase full of oxeyes, bachelor buttons and papery fronds of statice from the common garden. Iris noted that the bouquet might be big enough to interfere with the guests' sightlines, and decided to leave it where it was. She discreetly straightened the cutlery that Astrid had clattered into place, not wanting to offend her. But she noticed her mother could still align the casserole dishes accurately on their cork mats, and that she served herself a generous helping at the same time as directing everyone else to come and get theirs.

Blake indulged Astrid with a walk after supper, his arm a buttress for the side with the bad hip. Josie and Iris worked on the dishes and made their surveillance of Astrid's fridge and cupboard contents while she was outside.

"She still says she hates it here, but I don't believe her," Iris said as she reached into the refrigerator to see what was lurking in the farthest containers.

"When she remembered your birthday and organized all this I thought maybe we'd made a mistake, maybe it wasn't so bad," Josie replied.

"Same. Then I remembered the fire on the stove, and all those times she wandered at night, and I quit having any doubts. The management called me to get permission to plug in the stove today. I hope that doesn't make her want it on all the time." Iris dropped a bag of mold-spotted bread into the garbage can.

"She talked about Marcus for a while when she called me, said she was going to invite him too. That was the only slip I noticed," Josie said.

"Really? I haven't heard her mention him for a long time."

Iris had never made mention of the inside lock on her bedroom door till years later, when Astrid was beyond the reach of reason and Marcus had left to work overseas. She only told Josie, who didn't believe her. She claimed Iris was just looking for the attention she had missed growing up without a father, and maybe a bigger share of the estate. They had never discussed it again.

"Do you suppose we should try and call him tonight?" Josie paused to look at the clock. "What time would it be in the Emirates now?"

"He's on vacation in Thailand."

"Oh. Again. You'd think he'd come here and visit her for once."

"He'll never be able to come back here." Iris kept herself busy but only handled containers that wouldn't break if dropped.

"It's not like that," Josie scoffed.

"Oh yes it is," Iris replied. "No one goes to Thailand over and over again just to see the sights. It'll all be there in his passport. And then he has posts online, you know how he always brags so much. They check up on leads like that in customs, you know. They're not stupid." Iris was shaking as she spoke, but she held onto a liquefying red pepper with both hands till she could deposit it in the compost pail.

"Let's not talk about it, okay, sis?" Josie brushed past her and clattered the dishes loudly as she put them away.

Iris rinsed and dried off her hands, then walked over to the table where she could keep her back to Josie. She looked past the flowers and the remainders of food and dishes on the table to the gardens outside. Along the adjacent path Blake and Astrid had paused. The beds were in full bloom and Iris could imagine Astrid reciting names and life cycles and origins of each.

*   *   *

I got them. Firm, shapeless, they look like bits of ginger root dried beyond use, but in fact they are a preservation of life. It was easy: follow the remnant of a stem down to the rhizome, pry at it with my fingers and break a piece off. It doesn't matter which one they come from, they are all as beautiful as children. They will grow and bloom so well along the west side. By then I will have you in my arms, and I will show you the cascading tongues, the yellow and purple petals, floribundant and licentious expressions of wanton colour. I will name you for them, and they will name you.

*   *   *

There was the sound of a chime, pleasant but insistent. I wonder why they're ringing it, Iris thought. That's the bell for closing.

Her phone vibrated with the impatience of unread messages as soon as she turned it on. Four o'clock. How was that possible? Iris couldn't ever recall losing track of so much time. Outside the day had grown dim, and in the canopy strings of small white lights reflected in the glass roof. There was a general, if reluctant, movement in the direction of the exit.

Iris stretched, and wondered what else she was supposed to have done today. For once it didn't matter. Carrying her coat and hat, she felt a similar reluctance about leaving. She would have to be sure and book off another day to come here.

FLOOD

"People can't die, along the coast,' said Mr. Peggotty, 'except when the tide's pretty nigh out. They can't be born, unless it's pretty nigh in — not properly born, 'till flood. He's a-going out with the tide."

David Copperfield, Charles Dickens

April, 1997

The first night after getting away from the flood, Marlene heard water coming over the dike. Flowing, flowing, flowing, like the rush of a brook. The house is going to get wet, everything will have to be moved, we're not fast enough. Where's the pump? Do we have time to sandbag? She opened her eyes and she could still hear it swishing past, but now she knew it was only the air that got mixed with hot water in the heating pipes. I wish somebody would bleed those she thought. Then they wouldn't make so much noise. Eventually she went back to sleep.

The next night one of the children awoke, distressed. It was her middle child, Jean, two and a half and still not reliably sleeping through the night. Marlene got up and brought the crying child into her bed, with a detached, somnambulist's awareness that she might still be partly asleep herself. Why else would she think the child was crying out of fear the floodwaters were coming too close, while a segment of her consciousness knew it had all been left behind. She crooned gently, stroking her daughter's back, offering assurance that the threat was far away. They went back to sleep curled together.

In the morning, when Marlene was properly awake and the thin tissue of that half lucid state floated back, she knew Jean was much too young to have any understanding of those strange and urgent events back home. It was just another night-time awakening. In her sleep-deprived state Marlene knew she was vulnerable to these hallucinatory dreams, and shouldn't over-interpret them. Still lying in bed, she turned her head to the right to see Perry, her youngest, sitting up beside her and rubbing his eyes with his soft fists. He would be one in another month. He, too, could make himself known at night. Now that she thought about it, she could not recall gathering him up out of the collapsible crib during the night. At least she'd had enough sense to lay him down between herself and the wall so he didn't fall out. She must have done it, because she was sure he started out the night in his crib. Especially here in Newfoundland, among the in-laws, Marlene had learned not to mention her children's restless sleep. It always resulted in an avalanche of unsolicited advice, a wordless disapproval of her habit of sleeping with the children, an opportunity to brag about the solid sleep of their own children. Even when she had lived here and worked as a physician, her own instincts and knowledge base couldn't compare to that of the sister, the neighbour, the friend who had already raised so many children.

Last night, their third night here, she became vaguely aware of rain patter on the windowsill. Oh no, she thought, now the river will crest even higher. She slipped into a motionless sleep, awakening in the same position hours later. Stiffly she raised herself onto her left elbow to look outside. The shroud of morning fog almost obliterated the neighbour's clapboard house. Of course rain falling here wouldn't have any effect on the flood there.

Marlene and the children occupied what had been the girls' room of Nan's house. It was still outfitted with a blue incandescent bulb above the chest of drawers, a double bed with sturdy iron rails at the head and foot, and plywood shelves with a few stacks of Trixie Belden and Nancy Drew books. The bed had been pushed against the wall to keep any little ones from falling out, and a cot was set up in the remaining space for her own girls. They delighted in sleeping foot-to-foot, with a head at each end. Charlene, the oldest of the three children, said that made their cot a double bed too. In the next room, her husband Ian and his brother Kevin slept in their narrow single beds, likely with feet and forearms protruding beyond mattress perimeters. In between awakening from a dream and falling asleep again, Marlene lay among her children and wondered if Ian might also be awake. Her charged body was a separate entity that seemed to live alongside her motherly self. She could see Ian as she heard the shifts through their shared wall: his sprawl and the shape of his shoulders and back, and she tried to go back to sleep without wanting it any of it. Although her mother-in-law had offered the larger room and bed to the married couple, Ian seemed to have made up his mind beforehand and otherwise.

"It was always me and Kevin's room anyway," he had said the night they arrived. He marched past his mother and upstairs. "We'll manage." He launched his duffel bag onto the farthest bed while Kevin started talking about their life as brotherly roommates.

"Some glad when I got out of it," Kevin said. "Never felt so good as the time I first slept in a double bed all by meself when I moved to town." Kevin stretched out on the small bed and made the children laugh as he pretended to repeatedly roll over and nearly tumble out.

They had come all this way at the worst possible time, and at the greatest possible expense, for Ian's father's funeral: Marlene didn't want to think about it. There would be some sort of refund for the outrageous airfare, family here assured them. There was a phrase — travel for compassionate reasons — that was used to describe the process. But what did anyone care, really? Compassion, like hard facts, seemed to come at a premium, if at all. The first two days here no one even knew when the funeral would take place, any more than anyone back in Manitoba could predict how their town would fare in the worst flood in memory, with the water climbing daily, hourly. Finally, yesterday evening Uncle Bill arrived from St. John's just after dinner and announced that the funeral would be in two days, having been delayed for the past three by the need for an autopsy. The body would be back by tomorrow evening for the wake.

Perhaps it was the fatigue, maybe all the chaos and uncertainty. Altogether Marlene felt adrift and unconnected in a place that was ordinarily her second home. And it wasn't just her, because normally she couldn't imagine any of the affable extended-family members complaining, for example, about so much toothpaste being used up in such a short period of time. But today at breakfast her sister-in-law had seemed quite distraught about it. Her own reaction was similarly overdone, except that it seemed necessary to defend Charlene's curiosity, normal for a five year old, and probably healthy in light of all the recent ambiguities the children had come through. She knew she should have just made a joke of it, but it was too late. It would be better when the funeral was over and done with, at least there would be that increment towards peace. She had no idea whether it would help Ian purge or absolve whatever it was that blocked him off so completely, not just now but for the past year. He acted as though his distress was infectious, as if he should

STORIES FOR SHORT ATTENTION SPANS

quarantine himself from the rest of the family to save them from its ravages.

In the midst of their abrupt departures during the past week — from their home because of the flood and from their province because of the death — she and Ian had paused to discuss his father's sudden passage. It was the barest of openings, soon sealed off again.

"Unusual for colon cancer to present as an obstruction these days," Marlene ventured. They had just carried nearly all the contents of their basement upstairs in case of an incursion of water.

"Nowhere else but rural Newfoundland would someone have that much cancer going on inside and un-noticed, these days. Nowhere." Ian picked up the few remaining items of camping equipment from the basement floor and stacked them haphazardly on a shelving unit. Marlene tried to make some order of the last box containing photos and children's creations. They had received their evacuation notice that afternoon, then an hour later the news of Ian's father's death.

"That's why we left, remember? Too many people, too far gone to help. I couldn't keep up with it. Work has been so much more satisfying here. You've said so yourself." Marlene paused and tried to put a hand on Ian's shoulder but it was a trivial gesture in the face of his forceful lifting movements, a nuisance.

"Well, neither one of us can work now with the flood and all. Your clinic and my office are going to be closed for a couple weeks at least. We might as well have a trip out of it," was all he said as he turned and headed upstairs. At least he hadn't said holiday.

She had wanted to get away, to escape from being hemmed in by all that water and anxiety, everyone preoccupied by crest dates and levels. But now that they were four thousand kilometers away, her dreams reeled her back at night, and then clung to her for most of the morning. Rather than a barrage of reports, help lines and rumours, of constant media chirpings about lives, homes, businesses, animals, all in some way affected, now there was nothing except a brief clip on the six and ten o'clock news-casts. She found herself visualizing one possible scenario after another and longing for live reporting. She could call her family in Manitoba, but even that was hard to justify more often than every few days. Surely she would hear soon enough if anything happened that was even more unusual than the already extraor-dinary events. Wait and wonder, wonder and wait.

*   *   *

"They opened him up and they said it'd spread right through," Betty sighed as she and Marlene scrubbed and peeled russets from the pile beside them. "Poor Tom. He's the first of me brothers to go." A favourite aunt of Ian's, Betty had taken Marlene aside after the morning's toothpaste argument and suggested they start preparing for the family supper the next day by peeling potatoes in the cellar. Marlene was thankful for the reprieve from the upstairs tensions, and from the escalat-ing traffic of family and neighbours arriving with casseroles and condolences, inquiries and opinions. With an endless supply of older cousins around to entertain her children, she could briefly relax from that responsibility too.

She and Aunt Betty had hardly settled into their work when the description of her brother's last day spilled out of Betty faster than the skins from her peeler. "Couldn't do nothing for 'im. They just sewed 'im back up again. Doesn't seem right, puttin' him through all that surgery for nothing, should've left him in peace. Then he never even woke up from it. You'd think they could do some kind of scan or something to know before they gots to cut somebody up nowadays."

The vegetables were stored in makeshift pens of scrap lumber, with carrots and turnips piled alongside the potatoes. The squat face of the woodburning furnace produced a radiant heat that was comforting in the otherwise gloomy basement. The only light was from a single dim bulb, and it petered out altogether towards the corners. Probably just as well, Marlene reflected, insects and rodents being distinct possibilities around the dirt and crumbled stone periphery.

Betty sighed and rubbed with vehemence at a particularly knobby specimen. "You know, they's supposed to take these goofy-looking 'taters out of what they delivers to the house and feed 'em to the animals. How's a person to peel such a one?" She threw the lumpy thing in with the peels, making a clucking noise of tongue against teeth. "Or maybe save it for next year's garden, that's all." She selected a sleeker potato to work on.

"Didn't he have a blockage in his bowels?" Marlene ventured, not nearly so focused on whether her potato was gnarly or not, making the best of whatever she pulled from the pile.

"What?" Betty, moving briskly on to the next potato. Stubby hands meet stubby tuber, Marlene thought. The joints in Betty's fingers were misshaped with arthritis, and yet she could peel two and a half, even three potatoes, to every one of Marlene's.

"I thought he had a blockage in his bowels," repeated Marlene. "They had to do emergency surgery. Maybe things have changed, but when I worked here they didn't do scans on the weekend." One potato, two potato, she counted, digging out an eye. Keeping her mind on the task before her.

"Yeah, well, that's true enough. You would know how these things go," Betty muttered. "Pukin' his guts out, he was. First night the doctor here just said 'twas a stomach flu, gave him Gravol and said drink flat ginger ale. Flat ginger ale, sure. His last meal, turns out. Puked it up anyways. Never seen the like of it. Hope I never do again."

Three potato, four.

A swell of nausea passed over Marlene like a cool mist, leaving her slightly shaky and damp. Somehow that sensory memory from pregnancy took a long time to dissipate. She groped for another topic.

"How many people do you think will be over tomorrow?"

"Could be as many as eighty, all told. Now they won't all be expected to stay for supper. That's just for close family. But even that'll probably amount to forty-some."

Five potato, six potato.

"So how many of these do you think we'll need to do?"

"We'll fill this tub. That should do it. Wouldn't want to be short," Betty said briskly. "Mary and I'll boil 'em up tonight so we only has to heat 'em and mash 'em tomorrow.

An infant bathtub, salvaged from a stash of baby things in a corner, held the peeled potatoes. They had to bend over while extracting it as the ceiling was only about five feet high.

They sat on tiny wooden chairs which had also been dragged from the baby pile, with the bathtub of peeled potatoes between them, about two-thirds full. Marlene didn't look forward to how stiff her entire lower body was going to feel by the end of this task. Then they would still have to make a hunched journey up the ladder-like stairs while they held the bathtub between them, keeping it level up through the trap door and into the kitchen of Nan's house. A seeping ache was finding its way into her calves, her hips and her lower back. Despite all that she was glad to be here beside Betty, and to be useful.

Seven potato, more.

"I'm getting some sore," Betty said.

Marlene wondered if she had mentioned her own discomfort. She didn't think so, but lately she had noticed she could say or do one thing while being preoccupied with an unrelated thought. Then she couldn't recall the phrase or gesture she'd just uttered. Charlene found this entertaining and would deliberately ask the same question again and again, goading her mother along in this amusing vulnerability. Marlene's dreams, likewise, disintegrated into shards and fractals that managed to stick despite the daylight. Their intrusions made distinguishing fact from fiction almost embarrassing. It was worse than déjà vu. Daytime and

dreamtime overlapped like a Venn diagram, with her percep-
tions lying in the shady intersection where nothing quite made
sense. Marlene found it best to be passive: allow the talkers to
set the course, speak only when spoken to.

"Better that Ian's back home, now, in spite of it all, isn't it?"
Betty paused in her peeling and looked at Marlene with tilted
head and softened eye.

Again Marlene realigned her awareness. "Well, of course he
has to be here. I don't know if it's better or worse or what." She
hated to sound petulant, even if she felt it. The comparison
between living away, and staying "home", as it forever remained,
had been explored in every sojourn they had made since moving
away from Newfoundland. In the final judgment, it was indis-
putably better here than anywhere else. Just that you couldn't
work, be decently educated, get any support if you were old,
dying, depressed, disabled. Marlene enumerated the frustrations they had felt, herself a newly-graduated family physician,
Ian in his first job as a physiotherapist, both brightly idealistic
until the demands of their work made them hate the sound of
the phone's ring or pager's beep after three years in practice.
Except for all that, it was perfect, sure, it's a wonder everyone
doesn't live here.

"But the way things were, nothing to do but wait and wonder,
and watch and worry, where you was to. Not much of a way to
be, not for a man anyway, is it? Least women have their families
to take care of. That don't go away."

Marlene realized that Betty was talking about getting Ian
away from the flood zone as much as coming here for his father's
funeral, and she regretted the flare of bristly thoughts she had
just experienced. It was true. So much frenetic effort in some
quarters, those places where contractors and machinery were
seconded to toss up dikes and barriers and diversions ahead of
the inexorable flow, making use of everything from hay bales to
old school buses to stave off the water's force. Such amputation

of activity in other places, where the ring dikes were securely in place and there was nothing to do but live with suspended breath and disbelief that such a vast amount of water could actually be approaching, and if it was, that it could possibly be contained. Their town was in a bow of the river's slow curl such that the gradual strangulation of exit routes produced a tension beyond what was already being generated by changing crest dates and the swirl of rumours. Flood of the Century, one newspaper began called it and within a day the phrase was everywhere. Good thing it's nearly the end of the century, Marlene had thought. Shame to be wrong about something like that.

"We were right in the middle of getting ready to evacuate when Kevin called us with the news about Tom's death," Marlene said. "For a while I didn't know what to do."

"Must've been some hard. How'd you know what to bring along?"

"I didn't, I couldn't. It was impossible, deciding. So I didn't."

"Not your baby pictures? Your wedding pictures? And your books, I know how much you loves your books. How many boxes of them you carried with you when you moved out west." Aunt Betty paused in her peeling and looked at Marlene sympathetically.

"I had to leave it all behind, Betty. There was no way to get organized and pack everything up. And then fit it all in the car and find a storage place that wasn't in a flood zone itself before catching our flight. We couldn't do it. We just had to leave."

"I remember when we had that hurricane, only got a bit of warning so we couldn't try and save anything, just ourselves. Even so we lost old Sam up the road," Aunt Betty still hadn't resumed peeling as the memory overtook her thoughts and actions.

"That's it," Marlene replied. It was a relief to talk to someone who really understood. She recalled how Newfoundlanders, the women in particular, had their own complex relationship with water. It gave them their living, and it took their loved ones away. Nothing to do but wait, and wonder, and watch, and worry, while their men were out fishing at sea or working on a rig. Now that there was no longer a fishery, the younger men went even further afield to work in mines and plants, likewise both a blessing and a burden to their families.

Marlene told Betty how a camera crew found and approached her in the last few minutes before she left town. Even though she managed to blurt out something about the evacuation for the lens in her face, immediately after she had no idea what she had said. All she could think about was whether she had counted the socks and underwear before doing up all the zippers on her backpack, and she hoped she hadn't talked about that. Betty laughed so hard that she had to wipe her eyes with the back of her hand and try not to get dirt on her face. Marlene could only smile, because she was already visualizing the next scene: a slow pan of their vehicle, and those of their neighbours and friends, all leaving in a convoy, army vehicles at the head and the rear, water lapping at their tires in the low spots on the highway, spring winds ruffling the surface of a grey lake that should have been a field almost ready for seeding. For Marlene the ratio of relief to regret had been nearly equal in that moment. To be able to walk in a direction that did not lead to an impasse of water, to be no longer physically penned in by the floodwaters, would be such a weight removed from her consciousness. To forcibly part from home, friends, landmarks, life and work, had left her hollow, unable to grasp the size and substance of what she felt.

Better, then, bereavement aside, for all of them to be transplanted to a place that could be considered home. Not as real refugees, and yet a sense of their earthly selves adrift and part of a forced migration. Enough that even squatting in a cellar and peeling potatoes, anything the least bit attached, felt like a welcome place.

*   *   *

"Howya doin'?" A robust voice rang out in the evening stillness as Marlene and the three children crossed the parking lot. It was Len, sweeping the step in front of the hospital doors. Health care center, they called it now.

Marlene walked up the ramp to the landing. Bent forward from his substantial breadth and height, Len leaned on his broom and smiled so broadly that she couldn't help but smile back. She checked over her shoulder to make sure she could still keep an eye on the children, all happily engaged in jumping over, in, or through the many puddles.

"Sorry 'bout your father-in-law. That was some shocking." Len's blue eyes had lost none of their colour or kindness over the years Marlene had known him. "'Spose the funeral's all set to go, soon's the body's back? Heard 'e might be here later this evening."

"Yes, and thanks, Len, for the condolences," Marlene replied. "We're all topsy-turvy, the children haven't even adjusted to the time change yet. But I guess it'll be tomorrow all right. I don't think anyone can wait any longer. They'd be heading into St. John's to have the service in the pathology lab."

"Some sad, when it has to be this way with an autopsy and all. No proper wake, that's the worst of it," Len said it lightly but his expression was concerned. "I expect all hands'll be staying up with him tonight."

"There'll be a few keeping watch, all right," Marlene nodded. "I'll be doing my best to get some sleep with the kids. Wakes aren't something we do, where I'm from, so I don't feel like I'm missing out on something like the others do."

"That's it, b'ye. And Ian, I guess he's not sayin' much these days."

"You're right there. Hardly a syllable today. How'd you know he'd be like that?" Marlene didn't really need to ask, having met

Len's remarkable intuition years ago when she first came to work in the little hospital. More than just a maintenance man, never abashed and yet not overbearing, he had the right tool and insight for any situation. He had predicted her delivery dates with an accuracy not accounted for by chance. Phase of the moon, was how he'd called it. "Never on the decay," he would pronounce, sizing up her mid-section as she neared term. And he had read her need to leave this place before she was able to make the decision herself.

"Them Noseworthy men's all like that," Len said. "Tom himself, God love 'im, he'd go right quiet. So you knew something's up. You gets to know that 'bout a person, after a time."

"Tom was always so friendly with me. Made me feel part of the family, from the day Ian first introduced me. I guess I never saw that side of him."

"They keeps it to themselves, when they can. Just don't go nowhere, don't talk to no one, 'till it passes. Sort of wonder, now, does it all just go inside, people like that. All that feeling what never gets out, it gots to go somewhere. His went to his gut, I'd say."

Marlene didn't smile, but she would have liked to. Len at his metaphysical best, putting mind and body together in a way an academic would have either had trouble grasping, or would have been proud to have thought up themselves. Len was close to the source. He didn't need credentialing, he just knew. Talking to him never failed to make her feel better.

"We sure misses you here," Len said in a level tone, not pleading.

"I know it, Len."

"Maybe a good doctor like yourself could've noticed in time, done something for Tom before it was too late," he mused.

"It's hard when you have doctors who only stay a short time. But you know I couldn't have been his doctor, anyway," Marlene replied. And that's part of the reason why I left, she thought, but I won't say it. She didn't need to.

"'Course you're right there. 'Twas hard on you, being asked for favours by his crowd, and t'others around town, up the shore, all the time. I knows it. Don't have to deal with that where you're at now," he said.

They were quiet for a time, leaning against the cool rail of the hospital landing and watching the children's formless games. Their clothing bright, their faces aglow in the twilight. Charlene, fully responsible for her mismatched outfit, her hair shiny and straight like her mother's — now long enough for ponytails and a fringe that flirted with her eyes — tried to ensure that her followers paid attention to her directives. Jean, however, had an opinion about everything, and was not constrained even by her much-admired older sister. A modest nest of tangles lived at the nape of her neck, untouched by either brush or comb. She wore her splash suit and red rubber boots like a suit of armour out into the world whenever she could, and helped wash the boots off every night so she could bring them to bed. Perry stood up and ran a month ago and hadn't stopped since. There was forever a spot of mud or food on his chin or cheek, and his head was topped by reddish curls that were a throwback to some Irish ancestor whose name Nan was sure she'd someday recall.

Marlene was the first to speak.

"Such a beautiful evening, Len. I forget how peaceful it can be here when the weather's calm." Suddenly she was glad to be here, to smell bog and balsam fir, to hear the lilt of voices in conversation and the faint churn of waves from the cove.

"What dat, Mommy?" Jean, her endlessly curious middle child, ran up the slope towards her. Pulling at Marlene's hand and pointing to the sky.

Marlene looked west, above the trees. A low sliver of a moon, slight but strengthening in the fading light.

"That's a she-moon, my dear," Len pre-empted any other response. They must have looked doubtful and he proceeded to provide an explanation — though for Marlene's benefit only.

"Layin' on her back, see?" His grin was not entirely a leer, but approached it. Now Marlene had to laugh, and then fend off questions from Jean about what was so funny.

She supposed, as she wandered back to the house at toddler's pace behind the children, Len's intuition wouldn't take him so far as to guess that she hadn't lain — on her back or otherwise — with Ian for over a year. Just imagining the possibility that anyone might know brought on a deep shame, though she couldn't tell why.

And now that reality had replaced the bond she and Ian had once shared, the one that had translated their pleasure into this gentle, glancing tableau of the three children before her. Despite their existence as a testament of the love between herself and Ian, she couldn't help seeing past them and into the bloodsplatter of Jean's birth. Into that moment of suspension, when the only thing paler than the delivery room walls was the colour of Ian's face. He stood stranded between his bleeding wife on the delivery bed and a clutch of activity around his newborn infant; he told Marlene later he couldn't tell if the silent baby was newly born or recently dead. She came out on a streak of blood and mucous while Marlene heard the urgent overhead page and wished it would be quiet. She was suddenly free of pain, and even though she could feel the blood's free flow she just wanted to be left in peace. Hours later, when everyone was stabilized, Ian stretched out carefully on the hospital bed beside her. The strength and good sense of his arm beneath her neck made her fall into the deepest sleep. But it was a long time before he lost his look of caution around her and their newborn daughter, as if he had seen the ease of their possible exit from this world and couldn't trust them not to try taking it again.

"Mommy, do you know what they should call this kind of a puddle?" Charlene asked. She stood next to a particularly large one that extended from a low spot in the road well into the adjacent woods.

"What, dear?"

"A muddle, because it's such a muddy puddle!" Charlene laughed and twirled with delight at her own cleverness. The other two began to spin about in solidarity. Predictably, Perry went face-down into the puddle, or muddle, as it were. Unhurt, he lifted his head and released the great bellows of an offended yearling child. Marlene picked him up by his jacket and made a chair for him with her arms. She sat him forward to save having to wash all her own clothing and swung him side-to-side to distract him from his dismay. When she started to sing the chorus of *My Bonnie Lies Over the Ocean* the girls joined in and each grasped a side of her jacket. They arrived in Nan's kitchen red-cheeked and noisy.

*　　*　　*

Smoothly, sweetly, the shearing forces of the waves rolled the stones over and over one another. Their bodies had been worn perfectly smooth, often flat, and symmetric in their axes from millennia of mutual rubbing. Blue Beach, one of Marlene's favourite places on earth. Just being able to come here made up for a lot. The composition of the stones varied only minutely among the thousands that populated the cove's gentle curve, creating a soothing monochrome of blue-grey.

Walking the Blue Beach path from Nan's house would ordinarily be a welcome pilgrimage, but not with three youngsters in tow. Wayne, one of the Noseworthy cousins, offered to drive her and the children to the closest juncture along the old mining road and then make the short hike out to the shore with them.

Together they alternated carrying and holding hands with the children.

The funeral had finally happened that morning. The guests would be filling Nan's house now. But the need for air and space was agreed to be a priority for the children who had been so good during the crowded church service, and Marlene herself was glad to be near the ocean and hear the waves' hiss after the claustrophobia of the mass.

It could not possibly be helped, but this morning her sister Wanda had called with the news: the dike had failed around one of the towns downriver from where Marlene and Ian lived. The entire community was inundated; like a prank pulled by some giant adolescent who wanted to see what would happen if he snuck up from behind, the water came through at a low spot no one had taken into account. The story retold on every news source in the province simultaneously, incessantly. The obsessive way everyone was already perched next to a television or radio now intensified — Wanda said she wished she had some reason to leave the province herself. Wanda was also evacuated, and Marlene did her best to absorb and soothe her sister's dread of a similar fate for her home while she stayed her own anxiety. She didn't know if anyone here in Newfoundland would understand the impact of this news, especially the family in their time of grieving, so Marlene didn't even mention it at breakfast.

She could see it all, as clearly as if she was hypnotized herself by a screen: the dark muddy river water, cold and indifferent, taking possession of all the small neat houses. The faces of her friends who had put up drywall in their basement to make an extra bedroom for their teenager, had installed new flooring themselves to save money, packed away their Christmas decorations and photos in a corner for safe storage. Every one of them betrayed by measurements and forecasts that lacked the cunning of water to find an alternate route into the sanctum. The painful information seemed to be lodged in some unnamed part of her thorax; she could imagine it exactly the size and shape of one of the stones on the beach. By now it had penetrated through to a sensitive spot between her shoulder blades and settled into a constant ache.

"Mommy, keep dis for me, o-tay?" Jean thrust another flattened oval into Marlene's pocket. The laden seams of her jacket might just give way with the weight of the collection. But the perfection of the stones was undeniable. Like children, they could not be graded for superiority, all were worthy. They might end up with the whole beach in their luggage.

"Some glad to get that funeral over with," Wayne said suddenly when the children were beyond voice range.

Marlene was surprised to hear him say anything, assuming the mute archetype. "It seemed like a long wait, though I guess it was only a few days," she replied.

"Yeah, but I gots to get back, home and work. Can't sit around forever like some folk." He looked down as he spoke, as much in thought as to make sure he didn't slide on the rocks.

"True. You came from northern BC, right?"

"Yeah, thirty-two hours travel, door to door. 'Twould have been easier to go to China."

"Your Uncle Tom must be very special, for you to have come all that way," Marlene looked up for a moment at his profile.

"He and Aunt Mary helped raise me and me brothers, when ma was sick and dad was away working. Never thought anything of it at the time, just the way it was done then. But I gots youngsters of me own now, and I can see what a task it would be to take on a few more. I'm grateful, is all." He shrugged. It was a simple equation: you take a hand in bringing me along in the world, I come to pay last respects, no matter how far. It made Marlene take stock of her own misgivings about coming here.

A tender piece of a voice, partly lost to the noise of wind and wave, pushed her qualms aside. Some ways ahead, the slow pitch and rush of foam and water had pushed a long ways beyond the primary line of wet rocks. Perry's boots, bottom ends up, in the commotion. How can they float upside down?

Wayne why do you shout and rush against such resistance of loose round stone? What do Jean and Charlene point to in the waves, when they are all the same? These precious seconds, these messages fore and aft, right brain to left, action finally arriving to Marlene's suddenly slothful limbs. Stretching, plunging into cold, pushing ahead to wade in further, a hand, Wayne's, yes, it's Wayne's, hold on to it for balance and for life. Perry's jacket an air-filled balloon above the water's clutch.

Wayne do you have him? I'm screaming — Wayne, what are you holding is it a 100% polyester shell exclusive of trim or is it my son? Get the jacket off — the one that saved him but it's blocking the view of his chest because I need to know whether he's breathing or is it just a breath of wind that is mocking us.

"Mama?"

Those are your eyes. That is your mouth. Not the voice I know but this is near drowning so who would expect a normal voice and why would anyone care. Now the cough the heave the fresh spit of vomit. She has never been so happy to have a child throw up. Go ahead get rid of all that crap it's your right to fight it to fight it to fight it to fight it.

*   *   *

"'E's not the tide, the spring tide we calls it anyways, what's to blame. That's not till tomorrow or the next, since new moon's tonight." Len leaned against both his broom and the door of the resuscitation room. Movement was once again in real time, voices back to normal range, ice cream cups all around for those who could eat without gagging. Which excluded Marlene, heart and throat still constricted and her whole body unable to stop shaking.

"Not even cold, sure, look at him with the ice cream nearly gone. That's some good now, my son," Joyce said, warm and bustling as ever. She gave Marlene the kind of smile only a mother could read: she'd been here in this room with injured child and shattered conscience herself.

The drive to the hospital had been gaspingly brief. To Marlene's dilated eyes, everything seemed intensified — colours, movement, a partly shredded piece of tarp, pressed by wind into the shape of a figure kneeling over flattened yellow reed grass. She recalled this exact hyper-sensory experience the day she came home after giving birth to Charlene, when the world had seemed made all over again for her. That time she viewed it from the back seat where she sat with her arm around the infant car seat, a new and uneasy mother.

Perry, reborn from the sea, was having nothing to do with bedrest and observation as ordered by the doctor who had checked him over. He risked head injury every time he crawled to the edge of the bed, and beguilingly played for a reaction which Len was happy to provide.

Wayne must have called Ian as soon as they reached the hospital, while Marlene was in with Perry and the doctor. She was surprised to suddenly feel his arms about her waist; she felt him nod as she started to murmur an explanation. "Yes, I know, Wayne just told me," he whispered.

"Talk?" Marlene only had to say into his ear, against the backdrop of toddler laughter. Ian nodded again, then released her to make a quick squeeze of Perry's arm and a backhanded swipe at his own face. He followed Marlene into an adjacent room.

As she closed the examining room door, Marlene didn't know if he was going to speak, let alone touch her, again. What surprised her when it happened was that after so many months of distance, the alignment of their arms and torsos was as natural as it had been when they were students.

"A sneaker wave," he said into her hair.

"A what?"

"Sneaker wave. Remember that guy from the Marine Institute? We had dinner with him over at Donna and Sam's, maybe a year or so before we left. We got talking about different kinds of waves, some of the folklore like every seventh wave and such. He was nice enough about it, not arrogant. Just gave a name to those big waves at the shore that happen every so often. Admitted there's no actual explanation for them."

If she hadn't been pressed so close to him her jaw would have dropped. Just keep talking, she thought. So she could enjoy the resonance of his chest against hers. It was possible that the way their lean bodies fit together was what she missed most.

"You going to be okay?" Ian stroked her hair.

She could be asking that of him. She nodded enough respond, not otherwise moving. "Just a scare, that's all."

"No, I mean going back to work soon and all."

"Well, no worse than the last two times. I should be used to it by now."

"I was afraid you'd say that."

This time she needed to push away and search his face, unfamiliar at this range. "You don't think I can handle being at work with three kids?"

His defensive downward gaze, his hands sliding lower to cup her elbows. They could hear voices in the hall, the children declamatory and excited, Len's rolling drawl managing to contain them for now. With Ian free of his refractory isolation, Marlene braced herself for what he might say next.

"You get so preoccupied, when you have work and family on the go. And I know it's always hard for you to readjust to thinking like a doctor when you go back. You say so yourself. You're already not sleeping much the way kids wake you up. It's worse again when you have to be on call. It's hard to live with you. Sometimes I think we shouldn't have had another," Ian kept his eyes down and sideways, but his voice was steady.

"But you know I love the kids and I love my work and I can't do just one and not the other. I have to keep up or I'll lose all my skills, my license eventually....How would that help?" Marlene wanted to keep her tone level the way Ian did but she felt the rise in her voice.

"I didn't say you couldn't, shouldn't do it. I'm just saying it's hard to be with you. The way you come home all worried about someone who's sick or dying. It makes the rest of us, our problems, not very important, relatively." Ian hadn't stepped away and his arms still encircled her, but Marlene felt less and less enclosed as he spoke. She had nothing to say; her silence acknowledged both a degree of truth in what he said, and her resistance to it.

A screeching objection drew them back into their children's orbit and released them from their embrace. Marlene felt the conversation shoved like too much leftover food into a freezer, certain to tumble out the next time the door was opened, but contained and concealed for now.

*   *   *

The wind pushed solidly from the northwest and they had to brace themselves against it between Nan's house and the rental van, carrying armloads of car seats and suitcases. A multitude of goodbyes rang out in all directions as Nan leaned inside the door for a last kiss with her grandchildren. Perry was already making sustained arguments against restraint, so the girls sang loudly to calm him. We just got used to being here, Marlene thought as she hugged yet another cousin, and now we retrace it all over again. She made herself think about the home they were going back to. The crest had safely passed and the river was slowly receding. Ian had started to speak again, he had even shared the bed last night if not his body. So why did she feel like she could strangle on sorrow if a single word of permission was granted?

Waving, calling out their final farewells and being hailed in return with warnings about fog and moose and other highway hazards, they pulled out of the driveway. Ian drove slowly and cast a lingering gaze at his hometown and the map it traced around his childhood and adolescence. Marlene knew all the landmarks: the dam that still held back a reservoir where his friends Johnny and Tom had drowned. The paths into the woods for picking berries and collecting firewood and having parties. The steps down to the stage, now surrendered to weather and neglect since the end of the fishery. A few kilometers out of town the highway curved and rose to the peninsula barrens.

"Everyone asleep?" Ian glanced in the rear view mirror to check for lolling heads.

Marlene nodded. After the long drive into town today, there would be an overnight stay at Ian's cousin's house and an early morning flight tomorrow. Sometimes it seemed like a giant trick being played — this vast tract they were about to cross merely a backdrop, the way scenery would scroll past a car window in an old film, but better adjusted for credibility.

"So what are we going to do?" Ian kept his eyes on the uneven highway, still settling from the winter's upheaval of freeze and thaw.

Marlene knew which thread she should pick up, as it was still the only one attached to anything of substance between them. She didn't say anything, and her reluctance was a mystery even to her, the communicator. Ever since residency, she had been praised for her verbal skills. This time, though, she would be rated as neither meeting nor exceeding expectations.

In the early twilight there were no shadows, such was the effect of the westerly glow, and there was warmth to the evening vista despite the wind and the barrens' rough texture. Huge erratics stood glazed with lichen, and the ponds were still ringed with haloes of snow and ice. She so loved this landscape, she wished she could just get out of the vehicle and walk and walk and never have to worry. To embrace the simplicity of having her needs met by what she could carry on her back for a few days. The way she had once done, before so many others needed her.

The van's tires crunched to a stop on a small turnout from the highway. "We need to talk some more, I think," Ian said. He peered ahead through the windshield as if he was still driving.

"That's usually my line. So I guess I'm not going to say anything to the contrary," Marlene replied.

He turned with a small but visible effort and looked at her. "Can I tell you how much I still love you — in spite of our not seeming to have a connection lately?"

"If by lately you mean the last year, or more, then I'll put it in that time frame and be glad you've said it. Because I don't know what's important to you any more. Your own father dies and you hardy say a word," Marlene was unprepared for her own anger.

"Because I don't want to be your patient, Marl. I don't want you to diagnose me. I don't want you to give me a list of solutions or resources or whatever you come up with at the end of the fifteen minutes allowed. Or do you book a half hour for difficult cases like me?"

"I've never wanted to be that for you," Marlene frowned. "In fact, maybe you do need a doctor. Who is not your wife."

"Hunh. Yeah. Easily said," he countered. Now the smear of irony was imposing itself, from both sides if she was honest. And why not? They used to be ironic together all the time — eschewed melodrama and made their own rules about romance and roles, made light of tension and never needed to argue.

After a pause Ian took a deep breath and started again. "All it takes is one or two things nagging you from the day, on top of what you haven't resolved from the week before, plus everything going on at home, and there's no fun in...."

Marlene opened her mouth but Ian pushed on.

"Before you get defensive, because I know what you're going to say — you have lots of fun with the kids. That's not what I mean. And you're a great mother, we both know that. But you and I don't, can't, have any kind of fun. We don't laugh together. We don't read aloud together. We don't go out together."

"We don't sleep together." Someone had to say it.

Ian resumed driving position and gaze. The silence absorbed Marlene's sentence.

"I feel nothing that way, Marl," he said finally. "Nothing. No arousal. No desire."

"Is it anything I did?"

"No, no, no. Not you, it's not anything like that. I got kind of scared, this last pregnancy, worried that things might go bad again, after how it was with Jean's delivery. I felt like I shouldn't touch you, like I might do some damage and then I could never live with myself. So I just turned off, mentally, physically, and focused on other things, and before we knew it there was Perry and everything was fine and I don't know why but I never got turned on again."

"Did you think the hemorrhage with Jean was your fault?" Marlene asked.

"Well, I thought about it. Remember I asked you after you'd recovered, what could cause that sort of thing and you said intercourse could sometimes precipitate, oh, I forget now just how and what but there was some kind of implication. Sort of jarred me, like we'd gone right back to thinking of sex as original sin or something. Another place, another time in history, you would've been dead, that's for sure."

"Ian, I had no idea....I didn't mean...what you would think...." She leaned back on her headrest. After a moment she turned towards him and put her hand on the curve of his neck, ran her fingertips up and down the midline furrow, swirled through his hair and then over the bony ridges.

Ian went on. "And since then, since Perry anyway, it all seems so black. I can't find a focus past this sinkhole I find myself in every time I try to get ahead. Nothing turns my crank, nothing.

Now Dad's death, that's just more futility. Never got to talk to him about what it was like to grow up with his weekend binges and then going back to being so respectable on Monday morning. What he put Ma, what he put all of us through. Such a good man, everyone keeps saying, and he was, but there was that other bit too. And not like people didn't know, some of the most respected folk came over and drank with him and saw him sloshed and offensive nearly every weekend. Ended up in the same state themselves. Ma just took it all in. I don't know how she did it. I've got to wonder if she's not rejoicing inside now, except that it would kill her to say so. She'll be doing rosaries for years about it, I expect."

"So you're feeling really down. Have been for a while." Marlene still had to push herself to find the right response. What would someone who wasn't a doctor say?

He relaxed back from the attentive driving position and repositioned to better absorb the trace of Marlene's hand. With an effort she continued. "I guess I knew it, and at the same time I didn't want it to be happening. Wanted to help you but didn't want to interfere."

"I should have said something, Marl. I know it now. I kept thinking it would pass, I'd get better. Then I'd think about you back at work with three youngsters at home, and how that was going to go. I went down even further." He sighed and closed his eyes. Marlene didn't stop her caressing hand until he turned and then leaned towards her over the central console. A stronger gust in the wind, working its way across the barrens, rocked the van. His fingertips on her earlobe, his hand cradling the angle of her jaw. Mandible, she thought, as she opened her lips.

ABOUT THE AUTHOR

Ann Loewen studied biochemistry and medicine at McGill University, and trained in family and emergency medicine at Memorial University of Newfoundland. She has taken courses in creative writing through the University of Regina, Canadian Mennonite University and Humber College. She practices medicine, writes and lives in southern Manitoba. She has two daughters and has previously published the novel *Fast For My Feet*.

Author photography by Nicole Verrier
www.facebook.com/candidclicksphoto